# FRENCH LEAVE

*Recent Titles by Elizabeth Darrell from Severn House*

BEYOND ALL FRONTIERS
SCARLET SHADOWS
FORGET THE GLORY

THE RICE DRAGON
SHADOWS OVER THE SUN

UNSUNG HEROES
FLIGHT TO ANYWHERE


*The Max Rydal Mysteries*

RUSSIAN ROULETTE
CHINESE PUZZLE
CZECH MATE
DUTCH COURAGE
FRENCH LEAVE

# FRENCH LEAVE

## Elizabeth Darrell

This first world edition published 2009
in Great Britain and in the USA by
SEVERN HOUSE PUBLISHERS LTD of
9–15 High Street, Sutton, Surrey, England, SM1 1DF.
Trade paperback edition published
in Great Britain and the USA 2009 by
SEVERN HOUSE PUBLISHERS LTD

British Library Cataloguing in Publication Data

Darrell, Elizabeth.
  French Leave – (A Max Rydal military mystery)
  1. Great Britain. Army. Corps of Royal Military
  Police–Fiction. 2. Rydal, Max (Fictitious
  character)–Fiction. 3. Military bases,
  British–Germany–Fiction. 4. Detective and mystery
  stories.
  I. Title II. Series
  823.9' 14-dc22


  ISBN-13: 978-0-7278-6780-3    (cased)
  ISBN-13: 978-1-84751-146-1    (trade paper)

*All Severn House titles are printed on acid-free paper.*


Typeset by Palimpsest Book Production Ltd.,
Grangemouth, Stirlingshire, Scotland.
Printed and bound in Great Britain by
MPG Books Ltd., Bodmin, Cornwall.

# ACKNOWLEDGEMENTS

My thanks again to Lieutenant Colonel (Retd) John Nelson, Royal Military Police, who always manages to come up with answers to my questions.

Thanks also to the lads of Martinique Company 3rd Battalion Mercian Regiment (Staffords) for telling me about their experiences, and for allowing me to clamber over and inside one of their Warriors.

# ONE

The oppressive heatwave over Germany had been burning up most of Europe for ten days, with no end yet evident to the Met men. Crops and grass had withered, small streams had dried up. The levels of rivers and lakes had lowered drastically. More alarming was the extent of evaporation in reservoirs providing water for people needing more than usual. Restrictions of usage, recently put in force, threatened failure of fruit and grape harvests, which would bring hardship to many peasant families come winter. The death toll of the frail and vulnerable was rising daily.

Private Smith believed he was slowly roasting inside the Warrior advancing over a simulated battleground. His underpants clung soggily to his skin, his feet felt spongy in damp socks, his throat was dry and dust-filled, his vision blurred by sweat running from wet hair beneath his close-fitting helmet.

Enclosed in this armour-plated personnel carrier with six other fully-equipped infantrymen, his latent claustrophobia was getting difficult to control. The high temperature, the overpowering reek of diesel and the stink of sweaty bodies combined to induce the fear of being unable to breathe.

That was not the only fear besetting him as the tracked vehicle bucked and plunged over the undulating, rock-hard earth of the military exercise area. Once they reached their designated objective, Sergeant Miller would order them out to attack and capture some entrenched rocket-launcher, or a small contingent of pseudo-enemies. Seven soldiers would disgorge from each of the four Warriors of 3 Platoon, Purbeck Company, advance in a crouching trot and attempt to overrun the hostiles' position. They would be met with gunfire, and cascades of soil as hard as large pebbles when dummy explosives were activated. This had been the pattern of the last eight days and he was reaching breaking point, both physically and mentally.

The exercise had been set up to prepare men of the 2nd Battalion, The West Wiltshire Regiment, for deployment to Afghanistan in October. Staff Officers were delighted that temperatures hovering around 40° provided the kind of conditions their troops would encounter in the war zone, but *they* were sitting in their offices back at base, not experiencing them themselves.

Thrown violently against his neighbour as the Warrior plunged steeply, he was given a mouthful of abuse and shouldered hard back against the metal rear exit. He always endeavoured to be last in so he would not be squashed against the inner bulkhead, but that meant he was also first out. That did not suit him one bit, so he always paused pretending to adjust his equipment until several were off and running.

They drove on and on. How bloody far were they going today before they reached the grid where the action was to take place? The headache he had awoken with was growing worse. He had always been prone to them and sleeping for nine nights beneath the awning attached to the Warrior, close-packed with six others, had given him little rest in this stifling heat. At night the pong of diesel invaded his lungs with every breath, and he could barely turn over without rolling against one of his companions, who invariably retaliated with force.

He raised little friendship in others. At school he had always been on the periphery of those little gangs of boys who did everything together. He had once tried to find favour with one such group by reporting the transgressions of their arch-rivals to the teacher. To his total mystification, both gangs then ostracized him. He was now twenty and had still not worked out why.

It had been the same at the woodyard where he had first been employed on leaving school, and again at the music store. He had liked that more than stacking wood because girls came there to buy CDs and DVDs. He had gone out with one or two, but it had never progressed beyond one-night stands when they had been drunk enough to have sex with anyone. Silly bitches had little idea what they were doing, or who with. His mum said it was always the boys who got the blame, never the slags, and she was right.

The big plus about working at the store had been the opportunity to augment his own collections. Every Saturday, bunches of kids practically took up residence. He had claimed it was impossible to watch everyone the whole time, and daft Susi had backed him up, never cottoning on to his little scheme. The boss had written off regular amounts each month to shoplifting. Pity it had had to end.

Ten months ago the Army had seemed the ideal solution. Paid employment, free accommodation, working clothes provided, three hearty meals a day, plenty of leisure activities on tap, decent enough pay and the opportunity to *belong*. A squad, a platoon and a company were the military equivalents of schoolboy gangs, but a guy could not be excluded from them. They were closely-knit bands of young men with mutual dependence on the members.

Were they, hell! 3 Platoon had accepted him with bad grace. He had tried to make allowance for the fact that he was the replacement for one of their number killed at Basra – a semi-bloody-hero, to hear them talk – but time had not altered anything. He had decided to force a change in their attitudes. He had certainly done that.

It had been the turning point; the realization that he was trapped in an organization he now loathed. Things had gone downhill from that day.

Glancing up after another sickening plunge into a crater, he met the knowing leers of Chas White and Corky Corkhill and knew they would never let up.

The Warrior halted; it was all systems go. Time to shake the drowsiness from his brain cooked by the heat, force his lethargic body wrapped in wet clothes into action, remember the battle plan, think *aggression*. Practically falling out when the door opened, he followed his usual practice of lingering to adjust the straps of his daysack while the other six leaped out and surged forward with the rest of the platoon, led by Lieutenant Farley.

'*Move yer bloody arse, Smith!*'

Sergeant Miller's stentorian roar caused him to look up to where the NCO surveyed everything from the open hatch, and the expression on the man's face chilled him to the bone. It was brutally sadistic.

'I'm going to sort you out once and for all at close of play tonight, Smith, if you manage to get through today, you spineless *bastard*!'

Fear multiplied as he began to follow men who had no intention of ever counting him one of their number. His legs were shaking; his pulse raced. For eight days they had played at war. In Helmand Province it would be for real; men had lost an arm, a leg, half a face, been paralyzed. It had all gone wrong. Everything! He now knew joining the West Wilts had been a dangerous mistake.

Dan Farley stood with his hands on his knees, body arched. Today had been the most punishing yet and he was bushed. The only bright aspect was that 3 Platoon had succeeded in capturing and holding the objective, despite one Warrior breaking down during the advance. There would be a postmortem on that but not until later, after they had cleaned up and had a short period to cool down.

Dan straightened as he saw Eric Miller, the senior Sergeant, making his way across to him, wearing an expression that was even grimmer than usual. The man was clearly on the warpath. Miller managed to stay just on the borderline of respect, but Dan knew the experienced soldier was not prepared to defer to an officer of twenty-three, straight from Sandhurst, until he had proved his worth. Afghanistan in October should resolve any doubts.

'Problem, Sergeant Miller?' he asked in as bracing a tone as he could summon up.

Miller's face, like everyone's, was caked with dust that had clung to the sweat. His eyes were also red from weariness, yet the man still managed to radiate energy. Dan unconsciously pushed his own shoulders further back and raised his chin.

'Smith's absent, sir.'

'Absent?'

'As in no longer with us.'

Dan did not rise to the bait. 'He's wandered off for a pee,' he said, surveying the troops sprawling on the ground beside the vehicles.

'He never returned in the Warrior.'

'Sure about that? Who saw the men back into the vehicle?'

'Corkhill. Said he thought he'd counted six in. I've just given him a bollocking.'

'Have you checked with the other Warriors?'

Miller nodded. 'Zilch. He's gone. Scarpered during the assault.'

'No way would he go AWOL out here, with limited water and rations.'

'The river's only six Ks distant, and he'd have no trouble selling his weapon and kit for a stack of euros. He's gone, sir.'

Dan met Miller's unwavering stare with one of his own. 'I'm not prepared to accept that until I'm satisfied he's not out there hurt or disorientated, which is the more probable explanation. While I call up a rescue helicopter, start questioning the men to ascertain when and where Smith was last seen.'

Thrusting back his dismay at this delay to getting a meal and some sleep, Dan glanced back across the vast military practice ground, shimmering beneath a brassy sun. This was going to be one long, long day. 'Once we know where he was last seen, we'll take the vehicles back out there and start quartering the area.'

Miller turned on his heel and headed back to men who thought their exhausting endeavours were over. Dan was certain he heard Miller mutter, 'You won't find him.'

26 Section, Special Investigation Branch, was working at half strength. Two men were on UK leave and others were without power for their computers. The telephones were working; the air conditioners were not. It was not only the military base that suffered from the power overload. All over Europe the grids were unable to cope with the demand for electricity. If the heatwave continued much longer many

cities were considering half-day closing of factories and shops.

Max Rydal, Officer Commanding 26 Section, had sent his team home early on three days of the ten, not because they would find relief from the heat away from the office, but because there was little work presently on hand. Heat was traditionally believed to inflame passions, but 40° plus apparently persuaded criminals to put their plans on hold. All 26 Section was presently dealing with was a charge of sexual harassment from a woman who had ditched her boyfriend very humiliatingly in front of his mates, and a case of theft from the Armoury of a rifle and a supply of bullets.

Enquiries into the sexual harassment case had shown it was six of one and half a dozen of the other. SIB had found no case to answer, and the pair were being interviewed by social counsellors. The rifle and bullets were long gone, almost certainly flogged to a German dealer. They had had to be written off and a closer watch kept on the Armoury staff.

So it was with no sense of guilt that Max was playing hookey on this Friday morning to indulge in the sport that was usually his Sunday pleasure. Today, the pleasure was intensified by escaping from the worst of the heat to the cool river that ran between meadows and stands of tall trees. Even so, he rowed the skiff more languorously than usual, breaking the dappled surface with his blades to send ripples out towards the banks, where local Germans were walking dogs or quietly fishing before the relentless sun sent them home. Then, picnic parties would come with excited children to frolic in the water, and the charm of that river solitude would be lost.

This quiet activity allowed Max an hour or so of private thinking time. Becoming a military detective had satisfied his conflicting ambitions for soldiering and police work. Commanding 26 Section fulfilled him professionally. His personal life was more uncertain. Being widowed early in his marriage had left him without a focus. No wife, no children, no home. A room in an Officers' Mess among regimental men and women gave him scant sense of belonging, for Redcaps were not much loved by other soldiers. In consequence, Max welcomed solo moments when he could allow his thoughts to roam.

Relishing this sport that stretched his body after a night of inactivity, Max mentally reviewed last night's telephone conversation with Livya Cordwell, the new woman in his life. They should have met in London this weekend, but she had cancelled on her way to Heathrow with her boss, Max's father. An emergency meeting in Washington with their CIA counterparts.

Maintaining a relationship with a woman holding the same military rank, who worked for a brigadier with the Joint Intelligence Committee, was not easy. Duty frequently prevented one or the other from keeping dates. That she was in England and Max in Germany added complications. He was deeply smitten with the Anglo-Czech Livya, but although she appeared to reciprocate his feelings Max was uncertain where they were headed.

Livya was dedicated to her job and highly ambitious. Max was similarly dedicated, but he was in no hurry to rise up the promotion ladder. Reaching senior rank would mean a desk and paperwork while others did the detecting. Not a prospect he welcomed. He feared that marriage to an unambitious SIB captain, and producing a clutch of children, was not a welcome prospect to Livya. Even should she be willing to make such a commitment, would it work?

These deep thoughts were interrupted by a faint tinkling sound from the towel beneath his seat. His waterproof mobile. Livya missing him already, as they said in the States? Musing on whether it was against the law to use a mobile while rowing, he shipped oars and reached for it. The caller was his 2IC and friend, Sergeant Major Black.

'Morning, Tom, don't tell me the rifle and ammo have been found where they'd fallen behind a cabinet.'

'No such luck. Sorry to spoil your investigation of the river, but I thought you should hear this.'

'Go on.'

'The West Wilts have been on a ten-day exercise in

preparation for Afghanistan. Returned to base last night minus
one man. He went missing after a mock assault on an enemy
stronghold. The Platoon Commander called out a rescue helo
and organized a search of the area where it was believed he
was last seen. No sign, but it's a huge area and the men were
all pretty well spent after a demanding day. Interesting fact
is that the Warrior sergeant who transported him is adamant
the guy took off during the action. Says it would have been
easy enough, with everyone advancing strung out across the
battle area and concentrating on the ground ahead.'

'Only a fool would go AWOL in that situation,' said Max
as his skiff drifted slowly towards a clump of trees overhanging the bank.

'Or a man desperate not to return to base.'

'Suicidally desperate, Tom.'

'Well, he hasn't been found after intensive searching.
George Maddox has set his team alerting ferry ports, border
controls, airports; all the usual getaway routes. They've also
given Interpol a description. It's been slow work. Half the
bloody lines aren't working.'

The small boat bumped lightly against the shallow bank
and settled there in the welcome shade as Max said, 'Come
clean, Tom. A man who absconds during an exercise isn't
serious enough to involve SIB.'

'It could be more serious than a case of French leave.
George Maddox has just been in touch to report an anonymous phone call to his office. Brief but concise. *Don't
bother looking for Smith. Someone's finally done him in.*'

Gazing ruefully at the inviting stretch of water ahead,
Max prepared to turn away from it. 'I'll be there in a couple
of hours, after I've grabbed some breakfast.'

At Section Headquarters Max found Tom, Sergeants Bush,
Johnson and Piercey, and Staff Sergeant Melly, all lolling
at desks with their attention on Sergeant Maddox, the one
person in the office wearing the uniform of the Royal
Military Police. The rest wore either lightweight grey/navy
trousers or skirt, with a crisply starched white shirt. The
accepted hot weather 'uniform' for SIB.

After greeting them, Max said, 'George, could you be attempting to pass the buck on this one?'

Maddox grinned. 'I had to follow it up, sir.'

'A hoaxer?'

'Possibly. We've traced the call to a public phone on the base.'

'Male or female?'

'Definitely a guy. Adopted a heavy baritone, but there was a hint of a Brummie accent.'

'Obvious in such a brief message?' Max questioned. 'Could that have also been adopted?'

Maddox nodded. 'I guess so. It's nothing new. You'd be surprised at how many calls we get from daft buggers aiming to wind up the Redcaps, but how I look at this one is it's too bloody hot for anyone to play tricks just for something to pass the time. The lads are flaked out on their beds in their underpants when they're off-duty. Other thing is there's been no reported sighting of Smith in spite of an extensive search and all-points check.'

'Bearing in mind that police dogs suffer from the heat possibly more than humans,' put in Connie Bush, 'and that the chances of them picking up one scent in a vast area that's been covered by tracked vehicles and several hundred men over the past ten days, it's asking a lot of the animals.'

'The terrain will have been greatly disturbed by explosives,' Phil Piercey pointed out. 'A body could lie out there in a shallow grave for months without being discovered. Wait for the next exercise. It'll be disinterred by a mock explosion.'

Tom, always irritated by Piercey's wild, often humorous, input, snapped, 'There's no evidence yet of unlawful killing.'

'If someone's "finally done him in", there'll be a body,' Piercey argued. 'And don't forget there's a wooded area on that training ground where murder could be committed unseen by guys busy getting to grips with the enemy.'

'*Finally* done him in?' quoted Heather Johnson. 'That suggests Smith has been a thorn in someone's side for a while.'

Max turned to George Maddox. 'Another aspect of this

disappearance is that wherever Smith is, dead or alive, a rifle and other MoD property went with him. If he's gone AWOL, he'll also be charged with theft. If he's been killed, we need to know where that equipment is now. Find that and we might find the killer.' He frowned. 'How long do you intend to continue the search?'

'We're already scaling it down. This is the third day. In these extreme conditions there's only a fifty-fifty chance he'd survive if he's still out there. He could have a civilian contact who's housing him until the fuss dies down. If not, the river's only six Ks from the edge of the combat ground. He could've reached it by nightfall on the first day, so water would be no problem, and it's possible he's getting food and shelter at gunpoint from vulnerable locals. If he *has* been murdered, the urgency to find him is diminished. My men are whacked and need a rest while SIB takes a crack at it.'

'Fair enough,' said Max. 'We'll investigate the kind of man Smith is and how he related to his fellows. Uncover his background, find out who might seize the opportunity to get rid of him. If that call to you was a hoax, we'll attempt to find out why it was made. Our investigation should also point the way to the whereabouts of the rifle and kit belonging to Smith.'

'John Smith,' mused Piercey. 'Are we sure this guy's real with a name like that?'

'You can find out by taking yourself off now and questioning Sergeant Miller, who commands the Warrior that Smith was in,' Tom said promptly. 'Get cracking.'

'Are they on base at present?' Max asked Maddox.

'Off-duty until Monday, but I guess most of them'll be getting some kip ready for the discos tomorrow night.'

'Right, leave it with us on a temporary basis. If you get word of Smith let us know pronto.'

'Course, sir. Thanks.'

Maddox left the building on the heels of Piercey, who looked disgruntled at being excluded from the rest of the briefing. Max then proceeded to delegate tasks.

'Connie and Heather, track down the men who travelled

in the Warrior with Smith. Get their views on him and why he might have decided to skedaddle.' He turned to Melly. 'Staff, find out what you can about the men in Smith's platoon: who are the dodgy ones that have to be kept on a tight rein, who might have a specific grudge against Smith, which of them speaks with a Brummie accent. You'll get most of that from the Colour Sergeant. There's not much that escapes their notice.'

Left with just Tom in the Incident Room, Max said irritably, 'Can't we get one of these bloody computers up and running?'

'No chance. What power there is is monopolized by the various regimental HQs, who have priority usage. I'm fairly well acquainted with Staff Canning of the West Wilts. I'll have him bring up Smith's record on his computer and give me a printout.'

'Good. I'm going to have a word with the Platoon Commander who, according to George, is a new boy fresh from Sandhurst. Must be a worried guy. Losing a man with full equipment during his first command, albeit an exercise.'

'What do you reckon to the notion that we have a murder on our hands?' asked Tom, walking to the door with Max.

'I give it one out of ten. The bastard's probably gone off because he's discovered soldiering is tougher than he expected, and he doesn't fancy the reality of Afghanistan.' Reaching their cars, Max opened all four doors of his to let out some of the heat and looked at Tom across its roof. 'Ever see *The Four Feathers*? Officer's pals and fiancée send him white feathers because he resigns his commission when his regiment is ordered to the Sudan.'

Tom smiled. 'I thought it was World War Two films you knew back to front and sideways. The Sudan was well before then.'

'The sentiment is the same, wherever and whenever. Cowards aren't tolerated by fighting men.'

'So you've just put forward a belief in the premise you gave only one out of ten a moment ago.'

Max grinned. 'It's the heat, Tom. Addles my brain; I think

I'm in a past era. Let's make a few enquiries about the runaway John Smith to show willing, by which time he'll have been apprehended at a ferry port.'

'Or discovered hiding out in some fräulein's squalid bedsit, having sold the rifle and equipment to her pimp.'

Max's grin widened. 'Now who's wandering in the realms of fiction?' he chaffed, as he sank on the driver's seat of an oven on wheels.

Dan Farley occupied a room in a different officers' mess from the one Max was obliged to call home. He tracked the young subaltern down to find him clad just in shorts, lying on his bed reading a science-fiction paperback with his door open. Hastily pulling on a T-shirt after inviting Max in, he offered tea.

'Thanks, but no. I won't interrupt your well-earned rest any longer than necessary,' Max told him, settling on the desk chair and noting a framed photograph of a laughing blonde cuddling a golden retriever with a red rosette attached to its collar. 'Your girlfriend, Dan?'

He coloured. 'Not just at the moment.'

'Ah!' A lovers' quarrel he expected to resolve? 'Nice dog. Best of breed at a show?'

'Yes.'

Touchy subject so move on, Max told himself, trying to assess Farley's character. Not aggressively masculine in build, how did he rate personality-wise? Narrow face with strong bone structure, firm mouth but somewhat dreamy grey eyes. An idealist? Rather too trusting until he discovered his mistake? Afghanistan would test his inner and outer strengths.

Max explained why SIB was taking some interest in what had occurred during the mock assault. 'What's your opinion of the suggestion that Smith was murdered by one of his fellows? Would you rate that a possibility?'

Farley, perched on his bed, looked nonplussed. 'You're not taking the call seriously?'

'Until Smith is traced, or until we discover who made the call and why, we have to. How well do you know the missing man?'

'I only joined the regiment two months ago. I've not had time to familiarize myself with their personalities,' he said somewhat defensively. 'As soldiers they're a decent enough bunch, although it was evident from the start that Smith didn't integrate well.'

'Oh?' said Max encouragingly.

'He was always alone when I saw him walking about the base, and during short breaks in activities he never sat with a group of mates. I mentioned it to Sar'nt Miller during my first weeks with the platoon; said Smith didn't seem a real team player. He promised to have a word with him, but he's been occupied with personal concerns and there's a hell of a lot to do before an exercise: checking equipment, getting vehicles overhauled, lecturing the men on manoeuvres during simulated battle. Things get sidelined until the end of the exercise.'

'So tell me exactly what happened when you became aware that Smith was missing.'

Leaning back against the wall, Farley described how Sergeant Miller had reported the absence of a man, last seen around half an hour into the mock assault. 'The platoon was widely spread out over undulating terrain. Easy for a man to fall from a ledge, or collapse from illness. No live ammo that day so we weren't wearing high visibility vests. I wish to God we had been. Smith would have shown up on the coordinators' screen and we could have pinpointed his position right away. As it was, we assumed Smith was in trouble and instigated an immediate search. I called up a helo and we took the Warriors back out there. We did our best, but we had to give up when it grew dark. The men were dead on their feet. We presently have three men in the sick bay with heat exhaustion. The new MO is apparently on the warpath over it.'

'He's arrived at last, has he?' asked Max with interest, because much of SIB work involved liaison with the Medical Officer.

'*She.* A tough cookie according to my boss, Captain Fanshawe.'

'That'll liven things up a bit,' said Max getting to his feet.

'Thanks for your input. I'll leave you to your futuristic novel.'

'Sorry I couldn't give you a concise summation of Smith's character. As I said, Sar'nt Miller will be more helpful on that score. He seemed quite certain Smith had done a bunk,' he added thoughtfully. 'I can't see it, myself. If the man meant to go AWOL, why attempt it under such difficult conditions? He'd wait until we returned to base and go out in civvies one evening, taking enough cash and his credit card to get him where he planned to go.'

'That's the logical way of thinking, but in my job I've found people can behave in an unbelievably irrational manner. We have three possibilities here. Smith collapsed from heat or other causes and is out there waiting to be discovered, something occurred during the exercise to make him so desperate to get away he had to go immediately, *or* he was killed when the troops were all intent on their individual efforts to capture the objective. The first and third of those possibilities will certainly mean searching for a body. It could also mean the same if Smith simply debunked without prior planning. Whatever we discover to be true, your platoon will be one man short for Afghanistan. Or more, if that phone call was genuine.'

Phil Piercey found Sergeant Miller at home with his wife, and sons aged around eleven and fourteen. The three males wore only brief shorts. Mrs Miller, a short, plump woman with part blonde, part dark hair that she was either allowing to revert to its normal brown shade or badly needed a dyeing session at the base salon, wore a bikini top with her shorts. The patio door was open, although no cooling breeze entered. The interior of the house was stifling. Phil's starched shirt had already grown limp and was sticking to his back. He still felt overdressed.

Eric Miller was mystified by a visit from SIB until Piercey told him of the phone call and suggested they talk in another room. Used to people's reactions to unexpected news, Piercey noted that this sergeant took it in his stride. Away from the rest of his family Miller became completely professional.

'Smith's done a runner. I'm surprised he waited so long to do it.'

'Any ideas on why he chose the worst possible time?'

Miller's mouth twisted. 'Couldn't take any more. Spineless little worm. Saw that right away. Sneaky, snivelling little creep. No guts. Waste of space.'

'You didn't like him?' asked Piercey, tongue-in-cheek.

Miller was too well into his stride to notice the flippancy. 'Just twice in my career there's been a squaddie rotten to the core. First one's still serving time for double rape and GBH. Smith's the second. He'll end up behind bars, take my word.'

'Dead men don't go to jail. Unless he had a civilian contact he might not have survived the extreme heat. How about the suggestion someone in the platoon did for him during the assault?'

Miller shook his head. 'Nah. That little turd isn't worth risking a murder charge, although I'd applaud any man who took it. He's gone, I tell you. Done a runner.'

Back to where they had started. Piercey tried a different tack. 'Know anyone who might have had it in for him?'

'The whole of 3 Platoon, and probably half the other two. More than that, I reckon. Always fiddling around with his daysack until the rest had gone ahead of him. Bloody wimp!'

Piercey realized he was getting nothing useful from this biased man, and the odour of his sweaty body was growing overpowering in that small room. He tried one last question.

'Who were Smith's mates?'

Miller grunted. 'He didn't *have* mates. He tried sucking up when he first joined us, but they don't take to arse-lickers any more than I do. He was on his own from then on.'

'You made no attempt to get to the bottom of his problem?'

The simmering aggression exploded into a verbal attack on Piercey. 'His *problem* was he never should have been born. Yours is you have no idea about soldiering.

Pussyfooting around asking damnfool questions and prying into people's personal lives, that's you lot. If you find the slimy bastard alive you'll no doubt get the social morons to spend time and money trying to understand what makes him so unpopular. The West Wilts is a regiment of tough fighting men. If they have *problems*, they sort 'em out without help.'

'By looking the other way when someone they don't like runs from group persecution to possible slow death? Or by terminating his life themselves?' snapped Piercey.

Miller smirked. 'That's for you fancy-boy plods to find out, isn't it?'

# TWO

'Hi, gorgeous. Pinch me so I'll know I'm not dreaming. Here's my most sensitive spot.' The dirty laugh accompanying these words was clarified by a thumb pointing to the swell in his tartan underpants.

Connie held up her identification, as did Heather. 'Sergeants Bush and Johnson, SIB,' she announced, ignoring the lewd approach often heard from squaddies before they realized who the two young women in civilian clothes were. 'Sorry to interrupt your siesta, but we need to ask you a few questions about the disappearance of Private Smith.'

Heather addressed herself to Charles White, who was sprawling on the adjacent bed where the dividing curtain had been pulled back. 'We were told you are best mates who've been with 3 Platoon the longest. That right?'

White's leer was as lascivious as Corkhill's. 'This is a have-on, in't it? You two are strippers sent by the lads.' He sat up, linking his arms around his spread knees. 'I'd get more excited if you wore a sexy uniform and a copper's helmet.'

'Put some clothes on,' ordered Connie. 'We'll wait for you in the recreation room. Get moving!'

'What?'

She rounded on Corkhill. 'What, *Sergeant*!'

White's jaw dropped. 'Are you two for real?'

'*Very* real,' they said in unison.

Down in the communal recreation room, presently empty, the two women compared notes. Connie, a keep fit addict whose fresh, healthy bloom added to her attractions, raised her eyebrows at her friend.

'The likely lads in person. Why do so many mothers rear male chauvinists?'

'If I have boys they'll be told what's what from the baby stage,' vowed Heather, who followed Connie's addiction to fitness, but was one of those women who remain the same size in defiance of diets and exercise.

'Londoners, those two,' observed Connie. 'Unlikely that they made that call to George Maddox.'

'Unless they're good mimics. They're the sort to think it a real hoot.'

'How about murder?'

Heather pursed her lips. 'I'd say their brand of crime, if they ever strayed in that direction, would be robbing frail old dears of their shopping, and then only in partnership.'

'I agree. More mouth than menace.'

The pair under discussion appeared at that moment wearing shorts, and T-shirts bearing rude logos. They still looked suspicious.

'Why you picking on us?' demanded White. 'We don't know nothing about Smith.'

'We're talking to everyone who was in the Warrior with him on the day he disappeared. Piper and Allen couldn't tell us much.'

'Except that you two were close, and old timers with 3 Platoon,' added Heather.

Corkhill bristled. 'We don't know no more than them. Kept himself to himself, did Smith.'

'By his own choice, or because he was ostracized?'

Some of White's cheekiness returned. 'Big words, Corky. *Siesta* and *ostracized*. Words we squaddies wouldn't understand.'

Heather smiled. 'Perhaps you'd understand them better at Section Headquarters.'

'No way!' cried Corkhill.

'No way, *Sergeant*!'

White turned placatory. 'Look, Sarge, Smith was first out that morning. He farted around with his daysack, as usual, while the rest of us got on with the job. We didn't see him after that. We told Lieutenant Farley that.' Some of his chauvinism returned. 'You wouldn't be familiar with combat, but I promise you we don't faff about smiling and chatting while approaching the enemy.'

Connie had had enough. 'Don't patronize us, sonny! A

member of your platoon came to harm during an assault and possibly died. Our job is to discover what happened that day and attempt to trace his whereabouts. I promise you we don't faff about, either, so unless you stop behaving like ten year olds and answer our questions properly, we'll take you both in.'

Heather turned on Charles White. 'So what happened in the Warrior en route to the objective? You understand that French expression, do you?'

'Nothing happened,' he replied sullenly. 'It was too bloody hot and we was packed in there. You wouldn't know what—' He broke off.

'No, we don't know what it's like,' agreed Heather. 'That's why we're asking you. There wasn't the usual banter? Nothing to upset Smith?'

Len Corkhill took over. 'Seven of us in like sardines. Can't see much except the guy sitting opposite. Stinks of diesel. Noisy? I tell you! Bloody motor's riding the ground like a ship on a stormy ocean. Banter, you say? There's plenty of that at other times. In the back of a Warrior, usual thing is to have a kip. In that heat we bloody near passed out.'

'OK, we get the picture,' said Connie. 'Let's leave that and talk about those other times when banter *is* possible. Did Smith join in?'

'Told you. Kept himself to himself.'

Heather held his stare until he looked away. 'Why would someone like that join an organization that actively promotes team attitudes?'

White answered. 'You'll have to ask Smith when you find him.'

'Did he never make a bid to join in; make friends?'

'Chose the wrong one, didn't he. Jim Garson, killed on patrol in Basra, was Mason's best mate.'

'Lance Corporal Mason?' asked Connie. Getting a nod, she probed further. 'Smith tried to get chummy with him?'

'Had a stripe on his sleeve, didn't he. That little creep always had an eye to the best chance. He didn't know about Jim, of course.'

Seeing emotion now on the faces of these two macho lads, Connie sensed a revelation. '*We* don't know about Jim, so tell us.'

The pair exchanged looks, then Corkhill told the tale. 'Jim was the best. Core player in the footie team, could hit a target dead centre with one eye closed, played a mean guitar. Jokes? Had a never-ending supply. You were on a loser playing snooker with Jim.'

White took over. 'Jim had it all. You know, the birds were all over him. But he never once cheated on Sharon. Not once. Crazy about his two girls.'

'Loved kids,' added Corkhill. 'That's what made it so bleeding obscene.'

'Yes?' urged Connie.

White was visibly moved. 'On patrol through this village some little girl approaches him holding out a toy. Jim stops to look at it. Next minute he's dead. Bullet between the eyes.'

There was a short silence, then Heather said, 'Smith couldn't measure up, of course.'

'No replacement would,' said Connie. 'OK, that's all, lads.'

Letting White and Corkhill return to their beds, the two women lingered where the air conditioning was at least working at half power. 'Four down; two to go,' said Heather with a sigh. 'I think we're on a road to nowhere. Piper and Allen dismissed Smith as a non-person. These two had strong opinions of him, but tried not to air them by baiting us instead. Lance Corporal Mason will be totally biased when we manage to track him down, and Ryan is in the sick bay with the others. Let's take a lunch break.'

Once they were enjoying the cool atmosphere in the NAAFI, Connie said thoughtfully, 'I'm feeling sorry for the mysterious Smith.'

'Why?'

'I don't know. Perhaps because no one else is. None of the four we've interviewed care what happened to him.'

'Well, he had the misfortune to replace one of those men who are at the heart of every regiment. When they're lost in tragic circumstances, they become even more revered.

Tough for anyone to have to fill those shoes. Even so, no man is so unlovable he has no friends at all.'

Spearing some cucumber with her fork, Connie took up that last point. 'None of those four referred to him as Smithy. It's the universal nickname for Smiths. Denying him even that points to real dislike, apart from inability to accept him in place of Jim Garson. He'd been with the West Wilts for eight months. Time enough to overcome resentment over their lost colleague, surely.'

Heather sipped her tea. 'Something *must* have happened that day to make the poor bastard so desperate to leave he was prepared to take such a risk. And *someone* knows what it was. We have to keep digging.'

'I'll tell you one thing, Heather. I wouldn't rate being befriended by those two we've just interviewed as much of a plus for anyone, even the lonely Smith.'

Max returned to his room at lunchtime to shower, change his damp shirt and eat a light snack. The high temperature had reduced his appetite over the past few days.

The dining room was sparsely occupied. It was not uncommon for people to regard Fridays as ending at noon so far as work was concerned. Max had even intended to take the entire day off until Tom had called him in from the river.

George Maddox admitted they received plenty of mischievous calls leading nowhere, and Max believed this must be one of them. Smith was probably now happily ensconced with a fräulein and chuckling over his escape from arduous soldiering. After all, if one of his fellow squaddies had wanted him out of the way, surely he would have knifed him in the guts down some dark alley in town on a Saturday night, making it impossible to trace the perpetrator.

Taking up a cheese salad from the counter, Max headed for a table by the window. He then diverted to another where a woman dressed in a khaki skirt and shirt with neatly rolled-up sleeves sat alone, eating salad too. She looked up as he neared and sent Max's thoughts in a much more pleasant direction.

'I'm sticking my neck out here,' he said with a smile. 'If you'd prefer to eat alone I'll take myself off.'

It seemed very likely that she would tell him to do just that. Her cool optical appraisal practically voiced a rejection, so he hastily explained why he had approached her.

'A Medical Corps captain who's a stranger in the Mess. Our new MO is a woman, I've just been informed. I put those two together and deduced that you are she. I'm Max Rydal, SIB. As we'll liaise now and then I thought we should get to know each other.'

The appraisal continued until she said, 'You don't look too fearsome standing there with a salad in your hand. Why not sit here and eat it?'

He settled, facing her. 'If we're talking *fearsome*, I heard a rumour that you're on the warpath.'

Blue-grey eyes regarded him candidly. 'Word gets around quickly. Yes, I'm on the warpath. That exercise should have been curtailed. Men should not have been put under such duress in these temperatures.'

Taking in her no-nonsense blonde hair, sensible make-up and immaculate shirt (didn't women sweat in the heat?), Max said mildly, 'They're soldiers, ma'am.'

'They're human animals like the rest of us.'

'Ah, but the rest of us don't have to fight in hot countries. The West Wilts are scheduled for Afghanistan in October.'

Her eyes sparkled. 'My views on that war can't be aired on military property.'

Noting the gold band on her left hand, Max asked, 'Does your husband agree with them?'

Again the candid appraisal. 'You're very inquisitive for an encounter of just five minutes' duration. Do you act the detective in every situation?'

'Do you act the military expert when away from your surgery?' he riposted, goaded by her fresh manner.

A faint smile softened her expression. 'Touché. I'm Clare Goodey, by the way. And if you say "oh, goody, goody" our liaison will be a thorny one.'

Max smiled back. 'Suffer from that, do you? The usual

reaction when I tell people I'm a policeman is to send them away post-haste, frantically trying to recall what they might have said that could be incriminating.'

She leaned back in her chair, quite relaxed now. 'Several years ago in Florida I was eating at a roadside restaurant when in came the local sheriff and his *deputee*, both massive men with necks like bulls' and shoulders that could barge down a steel portcullis with one shove. They were each hung around with a truncheon, handcuffs, rubber-coated flashlight and a very business-like gun in a leather holster.'

Her mouth twitched in another smile. 'Gee, I thought, these guys will order the hindquarters of a cow apiece and wash it down with a ten gallon jar of root beer loaded with three dozen ice cubes. Know what they each had? Slice of quiche with salad, and iced tea.' Her smile broadened. 'I've never been in awe of policemen since that evening.'

Max laughed. 'So, I'm already on the bottom rung of your ladder of respect. I should be eating a mammoth steak and a mountain of chips instead of this rabbit food.'

'Don't fret. I'll be living in the Mess until I find more congenial quarters. You'll have chances to redeem yourself.'

They fell to discussing the difficulty of tracking down suitable accommodation. Max assumed her husband would not be sharing with her, but forbore to probe again into that relationship. Clare made no attempt to discover his own marital state, so he thought that subject was best left alone.

They both poured themselves coffee in the ante-room where Clare surprised Max by saying, 'I suppose you're caught up in this awful business of the soldier who went missing during a mock battle.'

'Word gets around quickly,' he replied, using her earlier words.

'I have three participants in my sick bay suffering from heat exhaustion and hypothermia.'

'We'll need to speak to them,' he said over his coffee cup.

'Not yet, you won't.'

Max put his cup and saucer firmly on the low table. 'Let's

sort this from the start. Unless a patient's condition would be endangered by questioning, we have the right to interview him or her if we feel we could gain useful evidence.'

Her eyes narrowed. 'As I'm the only person qualified to judge a patient's condition, you'll have to abide by my rules. Those men are exhausted and semi-delirious. Ask me tomorrow. I may allow questioning then.'

Max's hackles rose. 'You realize the missing man might be lying somewhere on the brink of breathing his last. Your patients could point in the direction to save him.'

'It's too late for that. Anyone lost out there beneath this intense sun for this long without water would be dead by now. That's why I'm on the warpath over this exercise. My job is to keep soldiers fit to do the job they enrolled to do. Any mad macho scheme that endangers their fitness will meet with my fierce opposition.' She got to her feet. 'I'm small, slim and female, but don't let any man on this base underestimate me.'

'Smith, you say? I dessay I can call up his record for you,' Staff Sergeant Canning told Tom. 'As for a printout –' He hissed through his teeth – 'Bloody lack of juice has set the printer on the blink. How are we expected to run an army on half power?'

'Same way we're expected to run it on reduced funds and last decade's equipment,' offered Tom, voicing a universal grouch.

'And we always manage it, somehow. Ah, here we are. Smith J.H. Take a look-see.'

Tom studied the screen showing a somewhat faint image of Smith's personal details and a rundown of his service with the West Wilts. The date of birth showed him to be just twenty. Place of birth given as Bournemouth. Nationality, British. Next of kin: Edward Frederick Smith (father), with a Bournemouth address.

A lad who had lived all his short life in his home town? mused Tom. Recruits who had never left home before were the ones who found it most difficult to settle on joining. Not unnaturally, they could not take the taunts of others who had had more experience of life, and they had a rough ride for a while. However, Smith had been approaching the first anniversary of signing on, so he should have found his feet by now and sorted out how to integrate.

Smith's educational standard just met the minimum requirement, and he apparently had no technical or manual skills. The grade he was given after basic training showed he was an average recruit, no more. During eight months' service with the battalion he had received no disciplinary charges or warnings. Reasonably well behaved, then.

Tom glanced up at Harry Canning. 'Nothing here to suggest he'd do a runner, as Sar'nt Miller claims.'

Canning grinned. 'Read on screen the records of half the regiment and you wouldn't recognize the men you meet. Seem like model soldiers according to what's on there,' he added, pointing at the pale image. 'That simply classifies them, but they're all individuals, aren't they? So Private Bloggs has a low educational standard. Does that make him thick as a plank? You'd be surprised how many Bloggses make first-rate soldiers. Brains that might not absorb academic subjects can be right sharp on tactics.' He grinned again. 'More use to us than guys who can quote Shakespeare as they panic under fire.'

Tom straightened from studying the screen. 'And Smith was a sharp tactician?'

'He was sharp. That's as far as I'll go.'

'Oh?'

'Nothing specific. Just things I heard,' Canning said hastily. 'Anything going, Smith was first in the queue. Unless it involved effort, hard work, or loss of free time. Then he was nowhere to be seen.'

'Not popular, then?'

Canning's eyebrows rose. 'You know what it's like, sir. Every so often you come across a soldier you know right off is a bad 'un.' He waved a hand at the computer. 'Doesn't say so there, but experience tells you.'

Tom knew what the other man was saying. He had come across men who exuded malevolence, although they had already committed a crime when he had encountered them.

'Thanks for that, Staff. I need to take a look at Smith's room. Detail someone to go with me as a witness. You'll get a copy of the inventory.'

Smith's living space was still enclosed by curtains, although the other occupant of that room was lying asleep in full view from the corridor. The NCO with Tom made to rouse the man, but Tom stopped him.

'We'll do this as quietly and swiftly as possible.'

Pushing aside the curtain, he entered to find the bed neatly made, as Smith had left it to go on the exercise. The room told little about its occupant. No photographs of family or friends; no girlie calendar; no posters of pop groups, footballers, racing-car drivers or other enthusiasms. Curious. All young men hung their walls with such things. It was as if Smith had taken away his personality, knowing he would not return. Had he planned to leave the ranks when he set off from here?

Tom nodded at the scratch pad held by the corporal. 'Not much to list so far. Let's open the locker.'

As Tom and his companion stared at the contents, there was a rustle of curtains. They parted and a face appeared.

''Ere, what you two doing in there?' The body attached to the head then came through as the curtain was tugged further open. 'That's Smith's stuff. Who said . . .' The erstwhile sleeping soldier's words tailed off as his puffy eyes took in the sight of stacked DVDs and two boxed players still shrink-wrapped. A smaller box atop those contained a dozen or more iPods in styrofoam packs.

Tom informed Smith's neighbour of his identity and began questioning the bemused lad, who was wearing only jazzy underpants.

'Were you aware of what Smith had in this locker?'

A slow shake of the head.

'What's your name?'

'Spanner, sir,' he said, eyes studying the treasure he had been living next to without knowing. 'Me and Smith don't mix much, like. We're in different platoons, so we weren't mates.'

'Smith kept himself to himself?'

'Yeah. Wouldn't have the curtain back. Not ever.'

'That bother you?'

Another shake of the head. 'Suited me if he preferred to hide himself away.'

Tom pulled the curtain fully back and told Spanner to put on some clothes while he and Corporal Franks listed the contents of the locker. It looked as if Smith had either been stealing from local stores or was acting as a fence for a local dealer. This information would have to be passed to George Maddox to follow up on.

The thought put a faint smile on Tom's face. Tit for tat. SIB could unload this on their uniformed colleagues in return for being landed with Smith's disappearance. Had he been running a lucrative sideline selling stolen goods on the base? This discovery now raised the possibility that he had run from a boss man who supplied the goods: pirated copies of genuine DVDs to sell at a generous discount. The notion that J.H. Smith had fled from barrackroom persecution vanished and was replaced by a feeling that his disappearance had little to do with the Army.

After counting the number of DVDs in the three stacks, Tom left Corporal Franks to list the titles and put a cross against any porn films. Then he focussed on Private Spanner, now sweating in jog pants and a T-shirt, his pale hair standing up in spikes.

'You really didn't know Smith was obtaining this stuff and storing it here?'

'No, sir,' Spanner repeated emphatically. 'I never saw him bring any of it in.'

Tom believed him. 'You're in a different platoon, you said. Why were you two sharing quarters?'

'It's temp'ry, sir. The room I was in got flooded when a pipe fractured. While me and my mate are moved out, they're drying the carpet and mattresses; patching up the walls. Our own stuff's only just getting dry. Some of it's US now. Sar'nt Thurslow said we can claim for damage to personal property.'

'So how long have you been sharing with Smith?'

'Four weeks, but we've been on exercise for ten days. Only just got back.'

'Before that I presume you spent your off-duty time in the next block with your platoon. Smith could have easily carried stuff in without being seen. Did he ever sell any to you?'

Spanner looked alarmed. 'No, sir, never. I'm not part of what he was doing, I swear.'

'I didn't say you were. Was it general knowledge there were cut-price goods to be had on the base?'

For the first time Spanner's eyes avoided Tom's gaze. 'There's always word going around there's someone with a friend of a friend who can get things at a special rate. Nothing illegal,' he added hastily. 'Tickets for footie games, and that.'

Tom followed up on that. 'They do it from the goodness of their hearts, do they? What's the pay-off? MoD property?'

'Don't know nothing about that, sir,' Spanner mumbled. 'I keep my nose clean.'

Tom dropped the subject. He was well aware of low-key wheeler-dealing in the ranks. It was no different from any large establishment employing people prepared to trade the firm's property for something they desperately wanted. No different from MPs who traded honours for lucrative contracts with a family business. It happened.

'In the days running up to departure on exercise did Smith show signs of being nervous or anxious?'

Visibly relieved at the change of subject, Spanner faced Tom frankly. 'Didn't notice anything but, like I said, we didn't have much to do with each other.' He frowned. 'You really asking me if he had a reason to piss off, make himself scarce? If he did, sir, why wait until nearly the end of the exercise? There was the same chances early on.' Looking at the corporal writing a long list of DVD titles, he added, 'Crazy to leave that lot behind.'

Tom drove home to shower, change his shirt and get a sandwich for lunch. Nora was alone, reading a book in the shade of the single tree in the garden of their rented house.

'Hallo,' she greeted warmly. 'Have you finished for the day?'

'I had high hopes until George Maddox landed us with a stonker. Where are the girls?'

She left her chair and crossed to the kitchen door to give him a brief kiss. 'Ugh, you're all damp and sweaty. Our offspring have gone with the Popes for a picnic by the river. They'll swim, of course, like hundreds of others. There'll be so many in the water it'll overrun the banks.'

Taking in her brief shorts and bikini top, Tom said, 'I'm going for a cool shower. I could make room for one more in there.'

'Never pass up an opportunity, do you? It's too hot.'

'Not for what I have in mind.' He drew her indoors and began untying the lace holding the cups of her bikini top together.

Her eyes sparkled. 'OK, it's a fair cop. I'll come quietly.'

The shower lasted quite a while. With three daughters of thirteen, eleven and nine running around the house, and the demands of Tom's job making a joke of regular working hours, chances for intimate togetherness were frequently widely spaced. A few months ago Tom had had what psychologists would probably call a mid-life crisis, although he did not believe he was anywhere near his mid-life yet.

A beautiful woman involved in a case SIB was handling had made him aware of how humdrum he had allowed his sex life to become. A romantic five days in Cornwall at Easter, while grandparents entertained and cosseted Maggie, Gina and Beth, had revived both passion and Tom's self-assurance as a lover. This sweltering weather had curbed his exuberance somewhat, but he had come to terms with what he had renamed a marriage crisis and was, consequently, easier to live with.

Wearing just towels, Tom and his wife sat in the kitchen to eat ham-and-tomato sandwiches, and drink tea.

'Pity you have to go back,' Nora said sleepily. 'We could have dozed the afternoon away together. I'll have to do it on my own.'

'I won't have my woman turning into a lazy slut.'

She tweaked the towel at his waist. 'Call Max and say something's come up.'

He laughed. 'Something will if you keep doing that. I'm sorry, love, I have a feeling I might be working over the weekend. A guy's missing and George had a call suggesting murder.'

Nora finished her sandwich and wiped her fingers on a piece of kitchen towel. 'An anonymous call, of course.'

'It has to be investigated.' He nodded at her interrogatory gesture with the teapot and his mug. 'So far, the evidence points to just about everyone he came into contact with being possible suspects.'

'Not popular?' Nora added sugar to his mug, which she had refilled, and leaned back in her chair, causing the towel to fall open and reveal a lot of her legs.

Tom stretched out a hand and began stroking them, saying, 'Impression I got was he's a sharp, self-centred bastard whom no one would mourn if he were torn asunder by ravenous wolves before their eyes.'

'That bad, eh? Why wasn't he posted elsewhere to avert this possibility?'

Tom popped the last piece of his sandwich in his mouth and spoke through it. 'The West Wilts have been in heavy demand over the past eighteen months. Iraq last year, where they lost three men; now they're on standby for Afghanistan in October. This guy vanished during last week's exercise.'

Her eyes widened. 'No wonder. Surrounded by enemies at home, he'd be facing another lot with guns out there. He's run from that prospect, take my word. I might have done the same in his situation.'

Although he held the paperback up at eye level, Dan Farley was not reading the words on the page. Max Rydal's visit had revived his sense of failure. Should he have kept a sharper eye on his men during that assault? The objective had been a former Taliban stronghold bombed into near ruin two years earlier, but recently reoccupied by a sizeable group with two rocket-launchers. Their task had been to capture the shell of the building (in reality a brick structure that changed identity to suit the exercise requirements) with enemies and launchers intact, or to force the hostiles to retreat abandoning their weapons.

He sighed. He had been on a high when the marshals had registered a verdict that Purbeck Company had effectively driven off the enemy in disarray and taken control of the rocket-launchers. He had been on the brink of total exhaustion, but enormous inner satisfaction had compensated. Then Eric Miller had delivered his bombshell. Why had it to be a man from 3 Platoon? The additional couple of hours searching for Smith had damn near finished him as he had struggled to appear in command, while a knot of culpability tightened in his chest.

For the past eighteen hours he had asked himself how he could *lead* men, yet keep an eye on what was going on behind him. Useless to wonder why Sergeant Mimms and Corporal Freeman had not seen Smith drop out during the assault. They had both explained that half the men would have been out of sight at a time, when covering stretches of deeply undulating ground. They said it was impossible to advance on an exposed target and check what every other man was doing. Their job was to direct the advance, not mollycoddle the squaddies.

Dan knew they were really telling him his job, but he still felt unhappy. If Smith was dead, and he might very well be, it would go on record that a soldier under Lieutenant Farley's command was lost, and had died in suspicious circumstances. There would be an official enquiry; questions and accusations. Smith's parents would raise hell; go to the newspapers with their story. Max Rydal had mentioned the possibility of murder. If that proved to be the case, as Platoon Commander, Dan would be asked why he had not been aware of violent feelings against Smith and acted to prevent such a tragedy.

Highly agitated, Dan threw the paperback to the foot of his bed and sat up. His face and body were running with perspiration; his pulse was racing. *Get a grip. Get a grip*, he told himself through gritted teeth. *He'll probably turn up somewhere and be charged with going AWOL. No official enquiry, no sensational accusation by parents in the* Daily Mirror.

Filling his electric kettle, Dan switched it on, then took another shower before returning to pour boiling water on a teabag. His grandfather had been one of the famous Desert Rats and advocated tea as the best drink in hot climates. His father, a tank commander during the drive to expel Iraqis from Kuwait, agreed. What would they say about the Smith affair?

'For God's sake leave the subject alone,' he muttered to himself, and moved to gaze from his window at the exciting view of the Quartermaster's stores. Subalterns were allocated rooms that overlooked such places. More senior officers had views over the playing fields or tennis courts.

He jumped nervously when his phone rang. Too late, he realized he had failed to switch it to voicemail, as he had intended. He had no desire to speak to anyone right now, but he crossed to see who was calling. His heartbeat increased as he recognized the number showing, and he fought an inner battle over whether to pick up or ignore it. His hand apparently moved of its own volition.

'Trish,' he greeted non-commitally.

'Hi, Dan.' It was quiet and experimental, and set his senses tingling. He could visualize those wide blue eyes and silky blonde hair. God, she was beautiful!

'Hi,' he said thickly.

'How are you?'

'Pretty exhausted. Just finished an intensive exercise.'

'Poor you.'

'It's my job.'

She had always accused him of throwing those words at her to end their arguments, leaving her no leg to stand on. It appeared to silence her now. He was afraid she had ended the call, but he was wrong.

'Can we talk?' she asked emotionally.

'Isn't that what we're doing?'

'Don't be a beast! You know what I mean. Can't you come over? You must be able to get leave to sort out your private life.'

'Trish, what's this all about?' he asked warily, unwilling to believe this was happening when he had given up hope.

'You know what it's about. I said we should give ourselves some space to sort out where we're heading.'

'We have. Two months of space.'

'I miss you, darling,' she confessed in a rush of words. 'I don't want us to break up. I couldn't bear it.'

'You were the one who decided I wasn't what you wanted. You knew why I was at Sandhurst when we first met. The Army's my chosen career. It's a family thing. I worked bloody hard to get my commission and there's no way I'll chuck it in. No way. You knew that from the start. Why did you let it go so far before you decided you didn't want a soldier for a lover?'

'Don't, *don't*,' she pleaded. 'Let's talk about it.'

He sank on his bed, running an unsteady hand through his hair. 'You'll only say the same things. You don't want a boyfriend who can be sent away at a moment's notice. You don't want a lover who has to obey orders and put his job before anything else. You don't want a partner who might have to fight. Nothing's changed, Trish.'

'*I* have, darling. Please come over. I'll meet you anywhere. Even at Heathrow. I've been utterly miserable since you went to Germany. I *want* you, Dan. I want you so much it hurts.'

His resistance was fast ebbing, and when she began to speak softly of what she wanted to do with him again, exciting him with erotic memories of their passionate love-making, Dan became putty in her hands and agreed to cross to the UK as soon as he could arrange extended weekend leave.

They talked for almost an hour, compensating for more than eight weeks' silence. Eventually, Dan unburdened himself and told her about Smith and how he felt culpable. He failed to notice that her voice had cooled a little when she told him not to be silly.

'They can't expect you to watch over them as if they're kids, Dan. If you were with a civilian company the boss wouldn't hold you responsible for what other employees did, would he?'

'That's no comparison,' he told her with gentle tolerance. 'We were heavily engaged in combat in preparation for our tour of Afghanistan, starting in October. Out there, the fighting will be for real.' Into the silence he said, 'Trish, are you still there?'

'*You'll* be going to Afghanistan?'

'Not until October, darling. I'll get over to see you before then and we'll make up for lost time. That's a promise.'

'Look, I've got to go. I've overstayed my lunch break and I've two manicures and a facial booked in for this afternoon.'

'Can't wait to see you, Trish,' he said with feeling. 'I was so worried before you called.'

'About the soldier who ran off? Surely it's obvious why he went. If you've got any sense, you'll do the same.'

The line went dead.

# THREE

By the end of that Friday afternoon the SIB team had interviewed most of 3 Platoon, and the few men in 1 and 2 whom Melly had been told spoke with a Brummie accent. The Staff Sergeant was the first to outline his day's work as soon as they had all gathered.

'We can discount the men from 1 and 2 Platoons as possible killers of Smith because they held the centre and right flank positions during the assault. They wouldn't have been near enough to attack him. The assault was mounted over a broad front and in two waves, which meant the troops were never closely bunched. If anyone did for Smith it would have to have been a person advancing close to him.

'However, I spoke to the three men with natural Brummie accents who could have made the phone call. Their knowledge of Smith was negligible, their concern for his welfare non-existent. Instinct told me they had played no part in whatever happened. Clues will only be found within 3 Platoon.'

Tom nodded. 'It's not unusual for the men in a company to know and pal up with others in their own platoon, having little to do socially with the rest unless they're members of a team activity – sports, pub quiz, camera club, go-karts.' He glanced around at the team, who had all made the effort to look professional by wearing fresh shirts. 'Any input on that?'

The two women sergeants offered up what they had found by speaking to Smith's companions inside the Warrior. 'The usual mix,' said Connie, 'although our impression of two likely lads named White and Corkhill is that their strong dislike of Smith is largely based on the fact that he replaced an all-round good guy killed in Basra. Smith's subsequent attempt to make his mark with the dead man's best mate put him beyond the pale.'

Heather said, 'We didn't manage to track down Lance
Corporal Mason, but he's certain to be totally biased against
Smith for that reason. We attempted to speak to Private
Ryan in the sick bay, but were denied access to him by the
MO.'

'An MO-ess,' volunteered Piercey. 'The lads'll be
queueing to show her anything from a splinter in their finger
to a blister on their heel.'

Connie wagged her head. 'No, Phil, sick parades will
suddenly fizzle out, the lads preferring to suffer rather than
risk the lady producing a hypodermic syringe, or asking
them to drop their underpants.'

'She won't *ask* – she'll *order* them to,' put in Max with
a hint of amusement. 'I met Captain Goodey at lunch. Not
a lady to be trifled with. By *anyone*.'

Heather had more to say. 'Although we read signs of
overwhelming general dislike of Smith, we feel that eight
months should have been long enough for initial resentment over a poor replacement for a platoon hero to merge
into acceptance. Squaddies are fairly resilient, gregarious
creatures who almost always unite in a common cause,
knowing they all depend on each other in this demanding
job that they do. We believe the answer lies in something
that happened just before the action took place, or at some
point during it. It's the only explanation for why Smith
vanished on that particular day.'

'I agree,' said Max. 'I didn't need Lieutenant Farley
pointing out that any man planning to go AWOL would
never choose to do it when Smith did. If the man went by
his own design, it must be because he felt he had no choice.'

Tom then revealed the interesting fruits of his own labours,
adding that he had decided not to pass the info to George
Maddox.

'It struck me that if Smith had been dealing with an
outside supplier, he could be using that connection to lie
low until the heat is off.'

'Not if the German dealer's putting the frights on him,'
Piercey reasoned. 'I wager that's the explanation. Jerry came
on heavy about money owing, goods not shifting fast

enough. Threatened to send a "persuader" unless Smith toed the line.'

Always scathing about Piercey's lurid hypotheses, Heather said, 'How did the German issue the threat in the middle of a military exercise?'

Piercey was ready with an answer. 'Smith had it on the eve of departure. Knew he would be safely out of reach for at least ten days, then he eventually realized he daren't return to base, and skedaddled.'

For once, Tom saw a thread of sense in Piercey's suggestion, and elaborated on it. 'His room-mate asked why Smith would wait so long to run off when he had equal opportunities to go earlier in the exercise. A build-up of dread could be an explanation.'

Connie said thoughtfully, 'He could have hung on, hoping the weather would break. A decision that worked against him. By the time he had no choice but to go, he must have been a great deal more exhausted.'

'I've had Smith's personal possessions, along with the booty, impounded until we have a clearer idea of where Smith is,' Tom continued. 'Under one of the stacks of DVDs we found a key of the type used to open small safes or individual lockers. Spanner told me he had no knowledge of Smith belonging to any sports clubs, the usual reason for a locker key, so it could be for a bank safety deposit box, in view of his lucrative sideline. No chance of following that up until Monday. If we draw a blank there, the item will prove a time-waster unless we come across something the key fits.'

'It could be for a container in his room at home,' suggested Melly. 'Do we know if he still lives with his parents?'

Max nodded. 'His given home address matches that of his father in Bournemouth.'

Piercey had been loath to give his report on the interview with Sergeant Miller, but Tom then asked for it and he bluffed his way through an encounter he had not enjoyed.

'If anyone did for Smith I'd say Miller's the clear suspect. Hates the man's guts with an excess of vitriol. A bully of the first order who'd enjoy tormenting little runts persecuted by the entire platoon. He's the type who's never got over a boyhood glee at putting firecrackers up a cat's arse, or cutting off a dog's tail.'

'Which did he do to you, Phil?' asked Heather slyly.

Piercey cast her a malevolent glare. 'Miller needs talking to again. Here at Headquarters. Make it more official. He knows something. Why else would he be so certain Smith had absconded?'

'I'll pull him in tomorrow,' Tom said, 'and you can busy yourself checking all the stores in town selling DVDs. Find out if any have stuff going missing on a regular basis. Smith's hoard could have come from one of them.'

Max then told them that the scaled-down search for Smith was continuing. 'George is personally hoping for reports of sightings by any one of the usual sources so he can call his men in. Until we have proof that Smith is alive some-where, they have to keep looking for a body.' He turned his attention to Connie and Heather, who were seated together. 'In the morning, check with the several stores in the area that sell guns and military-style gear for enthusiasts. Push them hard. Find out if they've been offered a rifle or any genuine equipment during the past three days. If they deny it, get the details of their suppliers from them. Threaten to call in the *Polizei* to make an in-depth investigation into their business activities, if they turn nasty.

'I'll attempt to locate Lance Corporal Mason. He could have a hang-up over the death of his friend, which created in him an unhealthy resentment of his replacement. I'll also have a word with the Company Commander about Sergeant Miller and the other NCOs. You stated that Miller was vitri-olic about Smith,' he said, giving Piercey a faint smile. 'Well, even taking account of the well-known myth that sergeants occasionally eat squaddies as a mere snack, there has to be a reason for such hatred of that particular one. I'll dig out what's behind it from men who know more about Miller than he'll ever volunteer to us.' He stood. 'Get what rest you can over the weekend. We'll meet at eight thirty on Monday. With luck, the heatwave will be over.'

\*     \*     \*

On his way to his room, Max passed Clare Goodey in the vestibule. She was studying a large envelope she had presumably taken from her pigeon hole. It bore a UK stamp, and an official-type address on the left-hand corner. Making no attempt to open it, she appeared deep in thought. Not the right time for small talk or a request to interview her West Wilts patients, Max decided.

After showering and dressing in chinos and a pale green shirt he went down to the dining room, feeling his appetite was now sharp enough for a decent hot meal. He sat in solitary state at the end of one long table, unwilling to join a small group of regimental men and women gathered at the second table. They made no effort to encourage him.

He had given himself tasks for the next morning, but the remainder of the weekend was set to be lonely. He should now have been in Livya's flat preparing to leave for dinner and the theatre. It was too early to call her. In Washington it was still the middle of their working day. When she was on duty with Brigadier Andrew Rydal it was wisest to leave her to make contact. Her call often came around midnight. He had no idea when she would come through tonight, but he hoped she would. Her message from Heathrow had necessarily been brief.

Munching his way through chicken pie with an assortment of vegetables his spirits suddenly dropped. How could they conduct a realistic relationship situated as they were? Love at long distance was all very well when there was a home, maybe a child: roots to bind two people together, a dwelling that belonged to them both. He was presently eating alone in a communal dining room; sleeping alone in a single bed, maintaining monk-like celibacy.

Livya, on the other hand, was at the Pentagon with an acknowledged charmer (Max still had a flutter of suspicion about the true relationship between his father and his ADC), and she was most probably being chatted up by flamboyant, extrovert CIA braggarts. She certainly would not be dining alone and, from what he knew of American bedrooms, Livya would spend her nights in a bed vast enough to hold an entire baseball team. He hoped she would be the only sleeper in it.

Why was he *hoping*? he asked himself. Why have doubts? When they were together he had none. Once more he wondered if he should request a transfer to the UK. He could be lucky enough to be posted in the South, which would make it possible for them to be together every weekend. Dropping his knife and fork on the plate in frustration, he faced the holes in that flimsy plan.

He would still live in a small room in a military mess all week, then become a weekend lodger in Livya's London apartment. What would he do on occasions like this present one, when the charismatic Brigadier demanded her presence? Would she want him there in her absence? Would he want to be there on his own? If they shared a house it would be different. If they shared a house he would want them to marry and make it their home.

His spirits dropped further. Until Livya was ready to make that commitment the situation would continue as it was now. He pushed his plate away moodily, appetite gone.

'And there was I thinking you had climbed a rung by tackling a chunk of pie. You'll slip down again if you don't finish it.'

Clare Goodey held a plate bearing a small helping of vegetables and a minute lamb chop. 'May I join you?'

Max half stood, coming back from his gloomy thoughts. 'Please do.' He resumed his seat once she was settled. 'Sorry to disappoint you over the pie.'

Her smile seemed a little strained. 'A bottom-rung companion is a better prospect than that jolly crowd of khaki-clad extreme youth on the other table.'

He looked across at them. 'I suppose we must have been like that five years ago. How soon that phase passes.'

Her smile faded. 'Oh God, a maudlin policeman. Maybe I should have fraternized with merry youth after all.'

'Prescribe a tonic, ma'am, and you'll mark the difference.' Even as he said it, Max recognized the boost to his mood she had made just by sitting opposite him. Her hair was fluffy from the shower, which softened her finely-moulded features, and she looked attractively fresh in a white linen tunic with a V-neck and pale blue stitching that matched her skirt.

'The only tonic I can prescribe out of surgery hours is to be found on a bar stool.'

He watched her carefully separate the meat from the bone. Surely no more than a mouthful. 'Sometimes you can grow even more maudlin on a bar stool.'

Her blue gaze rose to meet his. 'Not if you're with a compatible companion.'

'No, not then,' he said, wondering where this conversation was heading.

She set down her cutlery. 'How d'you feel about testing that theory?' When he glanced towards the bar, she said swiftly, 'Not in there. Don't you know somewhere in town that would answer the purpose?' Pushing away her plate, she got to her feet. 'Let's get shot of this place hung with paintings of men in scarlet uniforms killing and being killed, and mix with the living. What d'you say?'

With surprise, he realized he was being chatted up by this decisive woman. 'Fine with me. I'll fetch my car keys.'

'I'll fetch mine. It needs a decent run. Outside the side entrance in five.'

She was off before Max could say anything more, but he went upstairs to collect his wallet, feeling brighter than he had all day since receiving Tom's call on the river. He knew just the place for a quiet, reflective drink.

The heat assaulted Max when he left the Mess by the door nearest to the car park, and it dawned on him that the riverside inn he had in mind would be full to capacity on a night like this. So would every other outdoor drinking place. And it would be hot, hot, hot. Maybe the mess bar was the best option.

Clare appeared in an open two-seater that was clearly a classic. She noticed Max's slight hesitation after her invitation to hop in. 'Don't say it,' she warned. 'Don't even think it.'

He did not say it, but he could not help thinking it as he stepped over the door and arranged his six feet three inches in the available space with the caution of a man about to dice with death. That notion was soon knocked on the head. Clare was a skilled and very careful driver, and the pleasure of open-air propulsion after the stifling interior of his own car completed Max's sense of well-being.

Once on the autobahn, he said, 'Congratulations. You handle this beauty like a pro.'

She turned briefly to smile at him. 'I've done some amateur track racing. Not in this.' She turned back to the road ahead. 'My father was a triple champion one year. He taught me. I loved it, but I could never push myself beyond the risk barrier the way he could.'

'Medical knowledge of what injuries a crash can inflict keeping you on the side of caution?'

She laughed. 'No, just not enough bottle.'

He thought briefly how much he would like to demonstrate his own bottle on a Harley Davidson – an impulse that had sent him on an unannounced visit to Livya's parents' home last Christmas – but he said nothing to his present companion about his boyhood urge to emulate Steve McQueen's famous motorcycle escapade in *The Great Escape*. Livya teasingly called him Steve when she called him late at night in a particularly loving mood, and he was secretly delighted.

He was so lost in these thoughts he almost missed the turning that would take them to the riverside inn, but Clare was quick off the mark and swung on to it very smoothly. When they arrived, Max was dismayed. The eating place that looked so attractive and peaceful on Sunday mornings was now swarming with people.

'God, it's a bloody circus!'

Turning off the ignition, Clare prepared to get out. 'Just the remedy we need. Come on!'

Edging carefully into a position where he could throw his leg over the low door, Max surveyed the boisterous crowd with continuing reluctance. As a young, single subaltern he had thrown himself into occasions like this with several friends, and had enjoyed every rowdy moment. Marriage to Susan had brought an end to that kind of youthful roistering. Her death had led him to avoid any kind of mass jollity.

The inn was a three-storey chalet laden with scarlet

geraniums in boxes and baskets. Max was familiar with the interior pine booths, which had rustic designs carved in the backs of the seats, and cushions covered in folk-lore-woven cloth. It would be easy to gain intimate privacy in there, for it seemed all the patrons had chosen open air above cosiness.

Before he could suggest they take advantage of the deserted restaurant, Clare had caught the attention of a brawny, silver-haired man in lederhosen who smiled, shuffled along the bench seat, and patted the space he had vacated. Grabbing Max's arm, Clare headed for the offered seat and gave smiling thanks in good German. Before he knew it, two plump, elderly women in dirndls and embroidered white blouses who were sitting opposite the man and his male companion, also in lederhosen, shuffled along their bench and invited him to perch at the end of it beside them.

By now well aware that Clare was controlling this evening jaunt, Max was swept up in the kind of merry-making he had shunned for four years. With nothing about their appearance to betray their military status, they were taken for tourists by these locals who were eager to show friendship. Clare's German was better than Max's, but he was able to follow most of what was said.

Their companions were eight couples in national dress who were celebrating the sixtieth birthday and the fortieth wedding anniversary of various members of the party, and were well into the jollity of the occasion.

Brushing away their protests, the Germans called for steins for their instant friends. For a brief moment Max came into his own when the waitress recognized him and greeted him with considerable warmth, asking with a laugh where he had tied up his boat. This obliged him to explain that he regularly rowed along this river and breakfasted here.

'I've never taken to boating,' Clare confessed.

'Too slow for a brrum-brrum woman?'

'Is that how you see me, Max?'

'I haven't had time yet to get the full picture.'

'You don't need to,' she replied enigmatically.

The evening continued in a fashion Max had no control over.

Wisely limiting his alcohol intake by making the huge stein last a very long time, he was unable to escape the traditional beer garden singing and swaying with linked arms to the rhythm. Clare threw herself into it. Egged on by the birthday girl, whose plump attributes pressed hard against him when swaying, Max soon found himself enjoying the convivial celebration.

When dusk arrived the coloured lights strung around the large garden came on, reflecting shimmeringly in the water lapping the parched grass on the bank. Before long, the river became too great a temptation to a youthful group, whose heedless imbibing had removed any sense of restraint from them. One after the other they left their table to run and jump into the water. This brought the team of waiters from the inn to remonstrate and order them out. They were having too much fun, however, and their defiant frolicking grew ever wilder.

Max watched in some concern, knowing there was a strong current along this stretch. With the water level presently so low it was probably more sluggish, but the fully-clad bathers were too drunk to control their actions, which were irresponsible, if not actually risky.

While some customers found the incident amusing, the older clientele were mostly disapproving and several had mobile phones to their ears. Max guessed they were calling the *Polizei* but, knowing the demands on them over any weekend were as heavy as those on George Maddox's team, he did not believe they would attend an incident like this.

Herr Blomfeld, the inn's manager, strode down to the water's edge to order the three men and girls out and off his premises. They were having too much fun to heed him. Short of wading in and physically removing them, there was nothing he could do.

Then it happened. One of the lads stripped off his T-shirt and began swinging it wildly round and round above his head, chanting football slogans. The other two men followed suit, but one of them was too close to the girls and his sodden garment hit one of them in the face with such force it knocked her off her feet.

Mere seconds passed before Max jumped up from the bench and began to run forward. The girl had not surfaced, but her friends were too helpless with laughter to notice. He heard shouts of alarm all around him as he reached the shallow bank and plunged into water rippling with rainbow colours reflected from the fairy lights.

It was well past midnight when Max let himself into his room and stripped off his damp clothes. The housekeeper at the inn had done her best to iron his trousers dry enough to travel in Clare's car, but they stank of the river, like his shirt and underpants. As he stood beneath the warm shower and washed that smell from his body and hair, he knew he would not row that river in future without remembering this evening.

Clare had ruined her immaculate tunic and skirt by kneeling on the wet bank to resuscitate the unconscious girl, and she had insisted on calling an ambulance. Max could still picture her standing in muddy, crumpled clothes as she berated the youngsters for drinking to excess in such high temperatures. She had not minced words to explain in medical terms the reactions of brain and body to such stupidity.

They had not said much during the drive back to base. It had seemed unnecessary. Walking together from the car park to their rooms, Clare had said quietly, 'We can't escape from what we are, can we?'

'Do you want to?' he had asked curiously.

'I suppose not. Not deep inside.' At her door, she had bade him goodnight, then added, 'You've definitely gone up a rung or two, Max.'

Clad in loose boxer shorts, Max lay on his bed gazing at the hazy full moon outside his window. It had been quite a day, yet the events of the evening had driven from his thoughts the problem of Private John Smith. And those of his relationship with Livya Cordwell.

Tom's morning began badly. It was not unusual for two of his daughters to quarrel with each other. When all three

spat and clawed it was difficult to restore order. The trouble
began at breakfast when Tom announced that they would
not be setting out for the hills until around eleven thirty
because he had to conduct an interview.

Beth looked up from her bowl of cereal in protest. 'You're
always doing this. It's Saturday. Everyone has *Saturday* off.
Why can't you?'

'Because I'm not everyone. We'll only set out an hour
or so later than planned.'

'The *plan* was to go at nine thirty. We'll be going *two
hours* later,' Gina pointed out moodily.

Striving to keep the situation light, Tom said, 'Haven't
you three yet worked out that Mum suggests a departure
time at least fifty minutes early, knowing you won't be
ready until half an hour after that?'

Maggie, thirteen and vastly smitten with a German boy
who lived opposite their rented house, aired a view she
expressed almost every day. 'If we had *two* bathrooms we'd
all be ready in time.'

'You'd hog one of them trying to make yourself beautiful for Hans, so it wouldn't make any difference,' snapped
Gina, at eleven fast reaching the age to hog a bathroom
herself.

'Damn bathrooms,' cried Beth. 'I want to go to the hills
right after breakfast like we planned.'

'Watch that language,' warned Nora. 'We are going, but
later.'

'I don't want to go at all,' sighed Maggie. 'I hate it up
there. There are snakes all over the place.'

'Don't exaggerate,' said Gina scathingly. 'You just don't
want to trek. It would get rid of your rolls of fat quicker
than that stupid diet.'

'Fat! Have you looked at yourself lately?'

Beth shoved her half-full cereal bowl across the table.
'All you two think about is how you look. I can tell you.
*Hags*, both of you!'

Usually a controlled peacemaker, Nora lost her temper and
told them that if they did not shut up they'd stay at home
tidying and cleaning their rooms. Coping with three bright,

sparky girls was a job and a half at the best of times, but Nora was feeling the heat during these school holidays. She probably also missed having wedding or evening dresses to make – her enjoyable hobby that alleviated the demands of motherhood and brought in money for extras.

Tom felt a pang of guilt over leaving her to deal with their offspring, but it did not last long. He found young girls incomprehensible at times. It had been better when they were cute toddlers. Even Beth, nearly ten, no longer believed her father was a totally unblemished hero. Boys would have been easier. He would understand them.

Sergeant Eric Miller was brought in by Staff Sergeant Melly, and was volubly angry at this treatment. Tom had approached the interview with professional calm, but Miller's aggression aroused his own.

A sandy-haired man of average height, with well-developed muscles, Miller's entire mien was belligerent. It was apparent before he said a word. When he did speak, it was in a torrent of them.

'This is bloody persecution. I told your sergeant all I knew about that bastard Smith. What right d'you have to bring me in like a frigging criminal? What authority?'

'The authority of military law,' snapped Tom. 'I don't believe you told Sergeant Piercey everything when questioned at home. Away from family distractions you're likely to remember much more about the day Private Smith disappeared.'

'Bring in the thumbscrews, do you?' Miller sneered. 'Or is it an injection of something that makes men say what you want?'

'We're not the KGB.' Tom pretended to read Piercey's report although he knew it almost word for word. 'You gave my sergeant a scathing opinion of the missing man. Even by platoon sergeants' standards it was excessive. I want to know what Smith had done to prompt such violent reactions in you. I want to know why you were so certain, even on first discovering Smith's absence, that he had gone AWOL.' He glanced at the report again. 'When Sergeant

Piercey asked what you meant by stating that men of the West Wilts sorted out their problems without help, you replied, "That's for you fancy-boy plods to find out".'

Tom stared him straight in the eyes. 'This fancy-boy plod is going to find out before you leave this room. You can be here for an hour or an entire day. We have facilities for an overnight stay too, so it's entirely up to you.'

Miller moved uneasily in his chair. 'Look, he came to my house unannounced, asking questions. My wife was upset; the kids thought I'd done something bad. It riled me.'

'The way Private Smith did?'

'I didn't say that.'

Tom glanced again at the report. 'You called him a spineless little worm, a sneaky, snivelling little creep, a waste of space, rotten to the core, a turd and an arse-licker. I'd say he riled you in the extreme.'

Knowing he was backed into a corner, Miller said, 'You've met 'em, sir. Know from the start they're going to be bloody useless. Smith never fitted in, became one of the team. OK, so there's some who keep themselves to themselves off-duty. Reading or doing crosswords; listening to music. We've one who even listens to people reading books. But they're still part of the platoon; have one or two mates.'

'Go on.'

'Smith was the opposite. Off-duty he tried to latch on to groups, butted in where he wasn't wanted, and made himself a bloody nuisance. Couldn't do anything on his own; always trying to muscle in on what was going down. Even tried to *buy* a place with some of them,' he added in disgust. 'Yet, when they all acted as a platoon, Smith wasn't bloody having any of it. Made sure the rest did the donkey work. Crafty sod always hung back, fiddling with his sack or rifle. I saw it time and time again. He'd be useless in a war situation.' He faced Tom defiantly. 'The West Wilts are better off without him, sir, take my word.'

'So did you make certain of that by killing him during that assault?'

Miller visibly relaxed. 'No chance. I was with the Warrior

the whole time. Any case, he wasn't worth risking a murder charge. He did a runner. It's obvious.'

Tom changed direction. 'Lieutenant Farley said he'd had a word with you about Smith's isolation from the rest of the platoon, and you'd promised to do something about it. Did you?'

'Like I said, there wasn't anything anyone could do. Smith was a bad 'un through and through.' He drew in breath and exhaled gustily. 'Lieutenant Farley's new to the regiment. He hasn't had any experience of squaddies yet. Doesn't understand them.'

'But you do, Sergeant, and I deplore your lack of command in letting the situation reach such a dangerous stage. You should have negotiated Smith's transfer to another platoon. Better still, to another company. I suspect your overt hatred of him encouraged the men to treat him likewise.'

Tom allowed a silence to extend long enough to make Miller uneasy once more. 'Yes, some men are so inefficient, such obvious misfits, so completely averse to team activity as soldiers, it makes you wonder how they ever passed their basic training. Why they would have enlisted. What do you do about it? You do your utmost to help turn them into useful members of your platoon and, when that doesn't work, you move them on in the hope that they'll settle down elsewhere. You do not hang on to them harbouring such violent feelings as you have about Smith. There has to be a hidden agenda here, Sergeant Miller, and I need to know what that is before we can both go off and enjoy the weekend.'

Max found Lance Corporal Mason in the NAAFI reading motorcycle magazines. He was alone. Introducing himself, Max sat at the small table and commented on the super machine pictured on the cover of one of the thick, glossy editions. Mason seemed unsurprised by Max's arrival, but he was unprepared for this SIB captain's knowledge of motorbikes and entered into a discussion almost warily, as if he suspected some kind of trap. His enthusiasm for the subject soon overcame suspicion, however, and he slowly relaxed.

It was a little cooler in the NAAFI than it was outside, but the air conditioning was not working at full power. A few men and women had sought relief from the heat there, amusing themselves with cards or other games while consuming cold drinks, but Max guessed most of the personnel had gone to the open air beer gardens or to the river.

The base swimming pool was closed. It had become dangerously overcrowded and, therefore, highly unhygienic. A notice on the door informed prospective swimmers that for the duration of the heatwave the pool could not be used, by order of the Medical Officer.

Seeing the notice en route to the NAAFI Max applauded Clare Goodey's decision, but he feared there could be repetitions of last night's incident along stretches of the river. The *Polizei* would be kept busy this weekend ... and George Maddox's team, if soldiers were involved.

The motorcycle theme had run its course, so Max got down to business. 'You'll be aware that SIB is looking into Private Smith's disappearance during the recent exercise?'

Mason nodded. 'Aye, but there's nowt I can tell you about it.'

The round, freckled face and steady clear eyes suggested a solid, down-to-earth personality to this detective experienced in summing up people's honesty. Max gave a faint smile.

'We haven't found anyone who can, so far. Nor have we talked to anyone who had a good word to say about Smith. I understand he replaced Jim Garson, who was killed in Basra.'

Mason again nodded and those clear eyes clouded. 'My best mate from schooldays. We joined the West Wilts together. Jim was the best. It shouldn't have happened. Never.' He appealed to Max. 'Why is it them that go early?'

This lad of twenty-two had clearly not yet recovered from the loss of someone who had been akin to a brother. 'The person who has the answer to that universal question doesn't exist, I'm afraid,' said the man who had asked it so many times following Susan's death. 'So you would have found it difficult to accept the man who took Jim's place? Any man, in fact.'

'No, that's not right, sir. We have to mix in or the platoon isn't effective.'

'But it wasn't possible to get along with Smith?'

After a moment's consideration, Mason said heavily, 'He knew about Jim, how it was with him and me, but he never let me alone. Sidling up when I needed to be on my tod; making comments on what I was doing or reading. Trying to be part of my private time.'

'Trying to take over where Jim left off?' suggested Max.

Mason's eyes immediately sparkled with anger. 'That's it. Exactly it, sir. He'd somehow found out a lot about Jim. He'd talk about jaunts we'd done together and about how much he liked all the things Jim liked. It was as if he was climbing into Jim's skin.' His voice grew husky with emotion. 'It was *sick*. When I told him to bugger off, he came back with a handful of DVDs. Said they were a gift to cheer me up, help me forget.' He found it difficult to say the next words. 'It was the last straw. As if a few DVDs could wipe out the loss of the best mate I ever had.'

Max understood his outrage. 'How did you react to that?'

Suddenly recalling who Max was, Mason said sharply, 'I never laid a finger on him. I chucked his *gifts* on the floor and stamped on them, told him never to come near me again.' He took a deep breath. 'All right, I grabbed him by his T-shirt and slammed him against the wall while I told him. That's *all*.'

'Did he get the message then?'

Mason nodded. 'He tried it on with others after that. Giving them stuff; hanging around listening to private conversations, then passing on what he heard to others. He was a real creepy bastard.'

'Disliked by everyone in the platoon?'

'Just about.'

'No one was upset by his disappearance, then?'

'I guess not.'

'So no one looked too hard for him when Lieutenant Farley mounted a search.'

Recognizing the trap at the last minute, Mason said, 'The Redcaps haven't found him, even with dogs. He wasn't out there, sir. He'd legged it at the start of the assault. None of us had any doubts.'

Dan Farley had fully equipped himself for the job. Loose, light-coloured clothes, plenty of bottled water, fleshy fruit and energy bars, a compass, a map, his state-of-the-art mobile phone and a survival pack. Finally, not least in importance, a sun hat. Now he was actively doing something he felt much better.

Trish's call yesterday had boosted his confidence; restored his natural ability to be decisive, take action, seek a resolution. She had abruptly ended the conversation on hearing about Afghanistan, but when they met he would banish her fears. She wanted him enough to make the call and plead for a resumption of their heady affair. Making up would be stimulating and memorable, he knew, and it would happen as soon as he could organize leave. First, he must satisfy himself that he had done all he could to find John Smith.

The man who'd brought the quad bike on a trailer had been waiting for him, and had agreed to Dan's request that he return for it on receiving a phone call from him. Having driven these vehicles over wild ground for fun with friends, Dan was familiar with what they could do and set off as soon as he had secured his equipment to it.

It was now five hours into the search and the heat was getting to him. Not bothering to cover the ground over which the last assault had been made, Dan had marked his map of the entire military exercise ground into six squares and began tackling each in turn. His watch, in addition to the position of the sun, told him it was noon. The hottest time of the day. He had only covered two of the squares so far, but he knew he must take another break. The ground appeared to be moving as in a mirage, and his command over the vehicle was growing erratic.

Beneath his small, three-cornered tent he drank water, then poured some slowly over his head. Then he ate several energy bars, some dates and two oranges. With another slurp of water he swallowed salt tablets. He then set the alarm on his watch for an hour hence, lay back, and closed his eyes. *Rest during the height of the day; move when it's cooler.* Both his father and grandfather had instilled that piece of wisdom in him from boyhood. An hour's rest now would be worth two of activity later in the day. He dozed.

There was a deafening crash; the earth shook. Dan shot upright, pulse racing. His first thought was that night had fallen. His second that he was liable to lose his small shelter, which was flapping wildly and tugging at the pegs he had only pushed by hand into the dry, dusty earth. It took just seconds to identify a major storm, and act.

Scrambling from the tent he swiftly pushed everything beneath it, then took a mallet from his pack and hammered at the tent pegs. It was a race against time, because the wind was growing more and more ferocious and the gusts carried the smell of rain. Knowing the dry earth offered little anchorage, Dan faced the possibility of losing what shelter he could produce unless he could secure it more surely against the storm winds.

Fighting a powerful surge of air, shivering in the sudden cold blasts, Dan started the quad bike's engine and manoeuvred it carefully so that the fat wheels rested on the guy ropes. It did not matter that the pegs broke under the pressure. One side of the canvas was now firmly grounded, and the vehicle itself provided a barrier against the gale.

Another great thunder clap shook the ground. It was followed by another and another, until it was as if the earth would split open. Lightning flashed into the semi-darkness like an alternating neon sign. Then the deluge began, hammering at the canvas above Dan's head and blotting out all sight of anything beyond his frail haven.

An hour passed. The storm appeared to be centred directly above the exercise ground, for the thunder and lightning continued unabated while torrential rain fell like a solid curtain. Dan thought he might as well be sitting in the open. He was wet through, along with everything under canvas that had pulled free from one corner. It was now flapping so forcefully that it threatened to dislodge the corner not held fast by the quad bike.

Soil that had been baked dry was unable to absorb the amount of rain falling, so it was rushing into mini rivers from any rise in the ground. These were meeting and forming great surges of water seeking an outlet. One of these mini rivers overwhelmed the man huddled beneath inadequate shelter, engulfing him up to his waist and threatening to sweep all before it. Dan had already stowed his gear and supplies in his backpack, and he slipped it on, ready to make a dash for greater cover during a lull in the storm.

There was no lull, but he moved fast when the water surged over him. The seat on the quad bike provided the only higher perch available to him, but full exposure to the elements was preferable to being swept away.

During the next half hour the storm moved away, but rain continued lashing down relentlessly. The area around Dan had become a flood plain. Knowing it would be next to impossible to read the map or compass in the heavy downpour, Dan decided to drive to a distant wooded rise, which would be safe to enter now the lightning had ceased.

The tough vehicle fired up at the second urging. Dan set it in motion with hands that shook with the cold. The quad bike battled powerfully against the impeding flood, but Dan had to constantly wipe his goggles to keep the trees in his sight. It took a good ten minutes to reach the edge of the wood, where he drove through, on to a fire break running straight as far as he could see.

It was still wet in there, the leafy cover not being dense enough to keep out such heavy rain. Water also lay in this area, but shallower and more static. When Dan left his seat, only his feet were covered. Shrugging off his backpack, he unstrapped it and pulled out his map.

His attention was otherwise caught, however, when he shifted slightly and his boots encountered something solid. He glanced down and experienced a jolt of excitement. Caught up by the bracken at the foot of a tree was a helmet bearing the badge of the West Wiltshire Regiment. Beside it was an SA80: the rifle used during the recent exercise.

# FOUR

William Fanshawe was a genial, relaxed, modern type of infantry officer, who would surely earn respect and regard from the members of the company he led, Max thought. Dressed in shorts and a white polo shirt on this hot Saturday morning, Fanshawe greeted him without a hint of the reserve Max often encountered in his fellow officers.

'You're following up this business of Smith, I imagine. I doubt I can offer anything useful, but come on in.'

Max followed the sturdy, dark-haired captain who, rumour went, had turned down the chance to play professional cricket for Sussex and instead joined the West Wiltshire Regiment. He still wielded a bat with great panache in inter-services matches, his personality reflecting his sporting gusto.

The garden of this married quarter resembled the kind of entry frequently seen at the Chelsea Flower Show. Fanshawe led Max to a corner arbour shaded by a rose-covered trellis, where wrought iron chairs stood around a matching table. There was an ornamental pond where the dolphin fountain was presently not playing due to restricted power, and this was surrounded by a mass of pink and white flowers. The lawn was burned brown by the heat, but Max guessed it would normally look as perfect as a bowling green.

So what does all this tell you, Watson? thought Max with an inner smile. Well, Holmes, the Fanshawes have no young children. And? Mrs Fanshawe does not have a career, because she spends her days tending this garden. How do you know it is she who tends it? That's easy, Holmes. This lusty man would never plant *pink and white* flowers. Well done, Watson!

Mrs Fanshawe appeared, as if by telepathy, with a tray

bearing glasses of lime juice chilled by ice cubes. Max got to his feet and shook her hand, wondering as he often did how such a pair ever got together. Chalk and cheese personified, yet when she smiled her plain face came alive and her soft Irish brogue was immensely attractive. Max then had his answer. The pair were clearly devoted. Was this wonderful garden an outlet for the childless woman's maternal instinct?

Will Fanshawe broached the reason for Max's visit as his wife left them with their cold drinks. 'Never pleasant when one of your men simply disappears, but this business of Smith is unsettling in the extreme. If some kind of accident occurred during the assault we would surely have found the man by now. I know that's a huge area, and some sections of it are rarely used, but if Smith had come to harm his body would be somewhere within the parameters of the exercise. We searched, and then your lads took over with dog handlers. The other option makes little sense.'

'What option is that?' Max asked, sipping his lime juice.

'Taking French leave. I mean, in the middle of an exercise, and in weather like this? No man in his right mind . . .'

'So we have to consider the possibility that Smith was not. We deal with quite a few cases arising from temporary loss of control; a rush of irrational fear, dread or hatred. If Smith took off three days ago the odds are that something happened that morning to set him running from it.'

Fanshawe's boyish face creased in doubt. 'Even so . . .'

'Panic overrides reason, Will. Why do people climb higher and higher to escape danger when they know once they reach the top they'll be trapped with only one way down?'

'You're saying Smith preferred the risk he was taking to facing something worse by staying?'

'That's one theory. We've had a call suggesting Smith was murdered during the assault.'

'*What*?'

'A probable hoax, but we have to include it in our investigation until Smith is traced.' Max set his empty glass on the tray, noting its design of pink and white flowers. 'As you said, no sign of him has been discovered to prove accidental injury or death on site. If we don't soon receive intelligence that he has been sighted somewhere, a search for a possible shallow grave will have to be undertaken.'

'God, what a mess!' Fanshawe sighed. 'I pride myself I run an effective company. They're a competent, enthusiastic band of men, on the whole. We have our pranksters like every unit – guys who push things as far as they can, and one or two barrack-room lawyers – but I had no suspicion of really deep undercurrents in Purbeck Company. My NCOs are first class. I'd expect them to have informed me of a dangerous situation in the ranks, and I'd have sorted it pronto.'

Knowing his next words would not be well received, Max put a theory to Fanshawe. 'Sergeant Miller is somewhat less than first class. The Platoon Commander was aware of the concerted dislike of Smith and asked Miller to get to the bottom of it. Not only did Miller ignore this directive, he appears to be at the heart of the campaign of loathing. Miller told us, with very colourful adjectives, how he viewed John Smith. He has to be regarded as a front runner in a possible murder case.'

Fanshawe frowned. 'Ah, I can be of some help there. Miller is under a great deal of stress right now, following an accident when his daughter fell from that bridge over the river in the park near the town centre. Hit her head on the way down and subsequently almost drowned, despite being a capable swimmer. She's in the local hospital under observation while they assess the extent of any lasting brain damage.'

'Should Miller have been on the job under those circumstances?'

Fanshawe showed resentment now. 'I know my own men, Max. After the first couple of days he needed to work.'

'I understand that, but I should have thought a spell on admin would have been preferable to the demands of an exhausting exercise requiring swift decisions and swift reactions.'

The resentment doubled. 'Mmm, the thinking of a policeman, not of a fighting soldier.' Fanshawe got to his feet in very obvious dismissal. 'If I learn anything I believe would be relevant, I'll be in touch.' He began walking back to the house.

Max followed him. 'One more thing. Jim Garson: most popular man in Purbeck Company. Star quality. His death hit everyone hard, and Smith had the misfortune to replace him.'

Fanshawe halted and faced Max, now looking faintly belligerent. 'I'm not familiar with how SIB commanders deal with their subordinates, but we regimental men don't baby ours. We expect them, as fully-trained combat troops, to handle whatever comes their way. *Including* stepping into dead men's shoes.'

'Something Smith apparently failed to do, and subsequently paid the penalty,' Max replied smoothly. 'When we policemen discover the extent of that penalty, we'll be in touch.'

Emerging from the house with the show garden, Max looked hopefully at the deep purple sky to the west. A decent storm might bring the heatwave to an end and make life more bearable. He checked the time and decided to take a shower, then go in search of a light lunch before planning how to fill the rest of his day. By that time the storm would have come and passed, giving him more choices.

Stepping from the shower, Max wrapped a towel around his waist and contemplated the telephone on the desk. Livya should be on the verge of waking. Should he call her or wait for her to call him? If she had a heavy schedule yesterday she would probably need to sleep in, and would not be thrilled by her lover disturbing her at the crack of dawn. Better wait.

The dining room was empty. Accepting from the service bar two fat, brown, shiny sausages, one spoonful of savoury mash, another of peas and one of carrots, Max took his meal to a table and began to eat while reviewing his sessions with Lance Corporal Mason and Will Fanshawe. He had almost finished the meal when it occurred to him that he had failed to pick up on something Fanshawe had told him; failed to recognize what the man had *not* said.

Miller's daughter was in hospital in a serious condition after a fall from a bridge, putting her father under great stress. The emphasis during that conversation had been on Miller's attitude towards Smith, so Max had not delved into the details of the tragedy. They were not obviously relevant to the case SIB was investigating, yet Max now realized Fanshawe had been very economical with facts.

His mouth twisted in a wry smile. The thinking of a policeman, not a fighting soldier? So do some more police thinking! Why had the girl fallen? Had she been pushed during some larking that went wrong? Had she been with her father, her family? Somebody must have pulled her from the river and called for medical help, as he and Clare had done last night. Was a sense of guilt over the tragedy making Miller unstable enough to kill someone who was a persistent goad? Had Smith learned the truth of what had happened and confronted Miller with it?

His train of thought was broken by the rumble of distant thunder, and flashes of lightning across the dark rain clouds. The storm was approaching fast. Through the window, Max saw the branches of trees beginning to thrash around in the rising wind. Not the time to consider outdoor activity. Wait a while. Returning to his room, Max nevertheless knew the weather was not the reason for delay. He had to satisfy his curiosity.

Stripping back to just a towel around his waist, Max then punched out a number he was very familiar with, and hoped Klaus Krenkel would answer. He did. Max greeted him, and they exchanged the usual pleasantries until they reached the point when he had to give the reason for his call to the *Polizei* area commander, with whom the Redcaps often had to liaise.

'I've heard the daughter of one of our sergeants fell from that bridge in the park and sustained a serious head injury. What can you tell me about the incident, Klaus?'

'Did you not receive a report copy, Max?'

'It would have gone to the father's regimental commander as we were not involved. No crime was committed, was it?'

'That is correct. One of my mens took a statement from

an adult man who pulled the girl from the water and called the medical wagon. It was Saturday evening. There was much drinking and silliness with young persons, as is Saturdays. This girl is but sixteen with the looks of eighteen. She has had the drink and will walk with balance on the top of the wall. And so she is falling in the river.'

'A German resident rescued the girl?'

'That is correct.'

'What time did this occur?'

'It had been dark for some time.'

'And the girl was alone?' Max asked in surprise. 'Surely she was with a group.'

'The witness says there was a man, but he went away at the run when she fell. The English saying, "He took up his heels," yes?'

'He left her to her fate?'

'It seems that is so, Max. A bad person, I think.'

Deeply intrigued, Max probed further. 'Any evidence the runaway man *pushed* the girl from the bridge?'

'I will just recall . . . no, if there had been saying of that we would start the investigation of attempt to kill. If you will wait for moments I will see the report and tell you of it.'

Max heard the sound of a drawer being opened, followed by the crackle of paper. Then Klaus said, 'Here it is that Sharon Miller is pushing away the man who is trying to keep her from climbing the wall of the bridge. He is then watching. There is no account of attempt to kill. The witness is saying his attention is on Miller until she falls. The man is then running away, so Herr Braun is having to enter in the river to bring her to safety.' There was a short pause. 'Is it that there is now a problem?'

'No. We have been questioning Sergeant Miller as a witness in a different case altogether. I just wanted a few facts about the accident involving his daughter. You've been a great help, Klaus. Many thanks.'

'If there is to be more of this case of the girl you will be informing of us?'

'Of course. Mutual cooperation, as always.'

\*     \*     \*

Cutting the connection, Max waited only a few moments before calling Tom's mobile number. When his friend answered it was to a background of female voices in loud disagreement.

'Problems, Tom?'

'Multiply by ten, then divide by three, and you'll be getting somewhere near an answer.'

'It's the heat. It makes people bad-tempered.'

'I can't get through to them that it's equally hot for me. We're en route to the hills for some fresher air. You're not still on the job, are you?'

'Interesting angle I'm checking out. Piercey's interview with Miller mentioned he had a wife and two boys. There's also a girl.'

'In hospital with head injuries.'

'He told you that?'

'Only after water torture and the removal of his fingernails.'

'And?'

'Offered stress over his daughter's situation as the basis of his loathing of Smith. Said he couldn't come to terms with the destruction of a young girl with brains, beauty and a lot of talent, while a pathetic, useless apology for a human being freeloaded his way through life unharmed.' The connection crackled making Tom's voice come and go, until Max heard him say, 'As the father of daughters I understand his anguish over the fate of his girl. Not having met Smith, I reserve judgement over Miller's use of the man as a whipping boy.'

Max held the receiver from his ear as more violent crackling came through. When it subsided, he asked, 'Could it have driven him to harm Smith?'

There was no reply. The line went dead as the storm arrived overhead. Day became night under a sky slashed by forked and sheet lightning. Soon, rain thundered against the window, obliterating any view from it. Clap after clap of thunder rattled the glass in its frame and shook the building's foundations.

There was nothing for it but to ride the tumult out, so Max stretched out on his bed, thinking about those old

World War Two films he owned on video and watched frequently enough to know some of the dialogue by heart. Closing his eyes against the vivid flashes, he thought of those forties soldiers waging desert warfare against Rommel's army; battling through Sicily and Italy; landing on Normandy's beaches; defending the bridges at Arnhem; desperately trying to hold on to Singapore; all the while deafened by a bombardment ten times more menacing than this storm. How had they withstood it?

Unbidden came an imagined vision of John Smith. Apology for a human being? Certainly an apology for a soldier, if the collective descriptions were true. Was that a basis for murder? Would those old-time warriors have rid themselves of a John Smith by quietly killing him under cover of a battle? Given enough provocation, maybe. And the West Wilts were on the brink of departure to a war zone.

An hour later there was a lull in the maelstrom outside. It was already considerably cooler, so Max dressed in cotton slacks and polo shirt, then drove across to the Medical Centre to speak to the men suffering from exhaustion. His landline telephone was still dead, and his mobile had failed to connect with Washington. Craving action, yet knowing it to be folly to attempt a recreational journey just now, the chance to hear further views on John Smith was a safer option.

The three patients were listless and disinclined to talk to a detective officer about the exercise that had put them out of action. Two of them hardly knew Smith, being in different platoons; Joe Ryan reiterated what others had said, offering no new lead.

Further frustrated by the resurgence of elemental violence after the lull, Max reluctantly headed back to the Mess, knowing it would be silly to venture further until the storm had blown itself out or moved on. He guessed Tom was having to hole up somewhere en route to the hills. That would not improve family tempers, or his.

Driving around the perimeter road, Max once more debated whether his own solitary life was preferable to

Tom's with its frequent family chaos. He supposed he would one day have children of his own. With Livya? Unlikely in the present state of their relationship. Should he make a move to facilitate their meetings? Apply for a UK posting? Would she welcome that?

Lost in these thoughts, he did not see the tree crashing down until it was two feet from his windscreen and still falling.

When the storm broke, the Black family were halfway to the hills. The large picnic basket was full, and copious amounts of bottled water filled the stowage area. Sudden torrential rain made driving hazardous, however, so Tom pulled in to a lay-by where others had sought refuge, and they ate in the car the food put up by Nora and three grumbling girls.

Conditions worsened and remained that way for an hour or more, scaring Maggie, Gina and Beth into silence. Recognizing that the outing would have to be abandoned, Tom elected to make a dash for home during a lull that appeared to be the eye of the storm. Water was already lying on the road and would surely increase in depth as the day wore on. The 4 x 4 was useful for surging through water, but it was still a journey made uncomfortable by the tempestuous wind that buffeted the vehicle and drove rain against the windscreen in defiance of wildly oscillating wipers.

On reaching home, their sense of relief was modified by the sight of the large magnolia tree in the front garden, split open by lightning, half the burnt trunk across the driveway blocking access to the garage. Comforting young girls further awed by this Tom and Nora led them indoors, privately thankful the 4 x 4 had not been standing where the tree had fallen, and praying lightning would not strike twice.

Some minutes passed before Max was able to attempt movement. Blood was running freely down his face over his right eye and, from the amount of pain in the area where a sturdy bough had smashed through the windscreen to pin him against his seat, he guessed he must have a couple of broken ribs.

There was no way he could thrust back the solid branch. It was attached to the tree, and the tree was embedded in the crushed bonnet. Only a crane would lift it free. Very gingerly he reached down to the seat adjustment lever, praying that lying flatter would not mean the bough followed him down.

Lowering the back rest to its fullest extent thankfully gave Max the opportunity to inch towards the door, only to find it would open no more than a few inches before hitting more branches. The pain in his chest area worsened with every movement, but he knew there was a way to end his predicament, and fumbled in his trouser pocket for his mobile phone. If that was out of action he would have to wait until the storm lessened enough to tempt someone out along the road. At the rate he was presently losing blood it was a daunting prospect.

Knowing the emergency numbers, he keyed in the one he needed and held his breath. He let it out in relief when the base Fire Officer answered the call. Then Max simply had to wait for rescue. The business took longer than he imagined, and he was in a distinctly light-headed state by the time firemen had cut him free and paramedics had settled him in the ambulance, all of them by then soaked to the skin. Max managed to voice a few words of thanks, getting a nod in reply and the comment that he had had a lucky escape.

At the Medical Centre they stitched the cuts in his head and temple, which stopped the bleeding, then examined his torso, which was already turning purple with bruising. An X-ray proved Max's suspicions. Two broken ribs. While the male nurse was strapping these up, Clare Goodey arrived in the treatment room.

'Not another river rescue!' she exclaimed in joking tones. 'What were you up to this time?'

'What are you doing here?' Max asked muzzily.

'I'm the Medical Officer. This is my domain.' Turning aside to listen to a brief update from one of the orderlies, she then instructed him to prepare a bed for Captain Rydal in the small side ward.

'There's no need for that,' Max protested. 'It's only a couple of busted ribs.'

'And a nasty head wound,' she responded crisply. 'You need to be under observation for at least twenty-four hours. Whatever arrangements you've made for the weekend will have to be cancelled, I'm afraid. I'll call in at regular intervals to keep an eye on you. All you have to do is enjoy a good rest.'

To his surprise Max found he welcomed the starched sheets and clinical coolness of that small ward, where he had once or twice questioned injured or sick patients involved in a case. He dozed off and on while the tempest continued outside his window. At some time during that limbo period he remembered Livya. His phone lay on the locker beside his bed, but she would be back at work now. In any case, the elements would probably still prevent a link-up with Washington. Talk to her tomorrow.

Piercey was having a crazy kind of morning. He was not in the least averse to spending his Saturday haunting stores selling videos, DVDs and CDs. Several of them had taken his money in exchange for the latest film or pop album. He had started with the better class shops, then had progressed to the cut-price ones, the exchange marts and, lastly, the sex shops, although none of the stuff hidden in Smith's locker had been pornographic.

The crazy aspect of this lengthy search was that, with the exception of the sex shops, Smith had been recognized in each one he visited. Always the same story. *He is here every weekend. Searching along the shelves and making notes, but never buying.*

One store manager told Piercey, 'I send someone to ask if he needs assistance. Every time I do this. He says the denial. We see he is making the list, but why? We say to him that if he wants what is not there, we will make the order for him. But he says he is not deciding what he wants. Never does he know what it is he searches for, and still he makes the lists.'

'Do you ask him to leave?'

'There is no cause. He is quiet. He behave himself. He is polite. Yet never does he buy.'

'Have you ever seen him take anything, hide it in his pocket?'

'No. We watch very close. He just makes titles on paper and goes.'

Deciding to take a break, Piercey was eating a large steak with fries and a pile of mushrooms when the storm arrived. While attempting to make sense of Smith's behaviour he had been eyeing a girl at the next table who was alone and looking upset. Around seventeen, he guessed, with long hair an impossible shade of cerise, large amber eyes, luscious lips set in a pout and full breasts almost falling from a low-cut vest top. Nice, for a weekend diversion.

After a period of distant rumbling, the thunder announced itself with a deafening crash directly overhead. The girl squealed and cast Piercey a look of such appeal that he responded by moving to sit at her table.

'Thunder's just a loud noise. It can't hurt you,' he said, noting how she trembled.

'I thought the place was falling down.' She bit her lip. 'I'm scared.'

Ah, not a fräulein, as he had imagined. A rather posh accent, too. 'How about another coke?'

'Not right now. Stop and talk?'

'Sure.' He smiled. 'Not thinking of going anywhere until this passes. What's your name?'

'Zoe. What's yours?'

'Phil.' Unable to ignore the lure of her breasts, just a few feet away across the table, he set about securing a satisfying outcome to this chance encounter. She was giving him the come-on, and he was no man to turn away from offered treats.

'Couldn't help noticing you as soon as I came in. Had to beat a couple of local guys heading for the table next to yours,' he lied. 'Told myself I was out of luck when I saw how sad you looked. Sad and lonely. Put two and two together and decided the boyfriend had failed to show up. He must be totally brainless.'

Another deafening crack of thunder made the girl jump and reach for his hand. 'Don't go, will you? I really am scared. Always hated storms, since I was a baby.'

Clasping her hand, he moved his chair nearer to hers. 'Didn't your parents tell you it's only clouds bumping together? Mine did, and I remember thinking how silly they were to talk such rubbish.'

It brought a faint smile. 'I believed mine, but I still hated the noise.'

'Funny how sounds can induce fear,' he said. 'Remember that bit in *Jaws* when you started to feel afraid as soon as the creepy music began, although you hadn't even seen the shark yet?'

She nodded vigorously, still clutching his hand tightly. 'I later watched it on TV and pressed the mute button when the music started. You won't believe how *un*frightening that scene was when there was silence.'

As the storm intensified, Piercey drew even closer and their heads were soon almost touching as they discussed scary films they had seen. After a while, Piercey fetched them both a cake and a cappuccino, which they consumed during a lull in the violence outside. It was then that he asked her the reason for her earlier sadness.

'Am I right about the boyfriend leaving you in the lurch?'

She shook her head. 'I wasn't expecting him. It's just . . . he went away and didn't tell me he was going. I've no idea where he is.'

'That's a bit cruel.'

'He wasn't my boyfriend. Just a . . . someone I knew.'

'But you liked him a lot?'

She frowned. 'Not the way you mean. He . . . well, he made life exciting.'

'Someone else could do that,' Piercey pointed out persuasively. 'There's more than one exciting guy around looking for a girl like you.'

Zoe looked at him guardedly. 'What do you do?'

'How d'you mean?'

'Where do you work?'

Piercey was experienced. And sharp. No way did he ever give personal details to a potential one-night stand. 'I'm a rep. Always on the move.'

'Oh.' The flatness of her tone and the release of his hand told him she was unimpressed and cooling off.

'How about you?' He put as much smarmy flattery in his voice as he could muster. 'I'd guess you're either a model or an actress.'

That brought a resumption of interest, which coincided with a thunderclap and a flash of vivid lightning that lit up the cafe. She seized his hand again. 'I'm *going* to be. My dad's getting a home posting after Christmas, and I'm going to enrol at RADA, if they'll have me. Mum says it's a fore-gone conclusion.'

Just his luck! A soldier's daughter still at school. Time to back off. 'She's right. You play scared so real it'll bring tears to people's eyes. And that sad and lonely act, it's just as good.' He glanced very obviously at his watch, then stood. 'Got to go, Zoe. Things to do, people to see. Maybe we'll run up against each other again some time. If not, I'll watch you on the screen and recall a stormy day in Germany.' That last was said in extravagant enough vein to impress her. 'And remember, girl, it's only clouds banging together. Ciao!'

As he walked away, he noticed her canvas bag on the floor was chock-full of CDs. There was one obvious reason for so many. For actress read pop-singer. With that cerise hair and those thrusting boobs she would be caterwauling on the X Factor, not studying drama at RADA.


Clare Goodey spent that night on the camp bed in the Medical Centre, which was used when doctors wanted to maintain regular observation on a patient. On that night it was a wise decision, for it had grown wilder than ever outside. Around two in the morning, when the gale was banging against the side of the room she was in and keeping her awake, Clare made herself tea and went to look at Max. He was so deep in sedated sleep that he was unaware when his mobile began to ring. Thinking it must surely be urgent because of the hour, she picked it up to check on who was calling. The screen showed just the name LIVYA.

Having heard that Max was a widower, Clare knew it was not a desperate wife on the line. A sister? Family friend with bad news? She connected with the caller, saying quietly, 'This is Doctor Clare Goodey. Max is unable to take calls right now, I'm afraid. Would you care to give me a message for him? Or, if it's urgent or very personal, I can ask him to call you at his earliest opportunity.'

'What's wrong? Is he ill? Badly hurt?' The woman sounded young and very concerned.

'Nothing serious, I assure you,' she said soothingly. 'He should be up and about tomorrow. I mean, of course, later today. Shall I tell him to call you then?'

'No, you can tell me exactly what's wrong, how bad he is.'

Taking exception to the woman's peremptory tone, Clare asked coolly if she was a relative.

'I thought that restriction only applied when a patient was dying.'

'Please don't be frivolous, Ms . . . ?'

'*Captain* Cordwell. I'm here with Max's father, Brigadier Rydal. *He's* a relative, so perhaps you'll stop being so single-mindedly professional and answer my question so that I can tell him what's happened to his son.'

Tempted to request this equally determinedly professional woman to bring the father to the telephone to hear it for himself, Clare gave the details of Max's accident in clipped, strictly clinical terms. Then she added, even more coolly, 'He's suffering from concussion, so no visitors just yet.'

'No problem. Andrew and I are in Washington.'

Putting two and two together, Clare said, 'I see. Are you Max's stepmother?'

'No. I'm his lover.'

The line went dead.

# FIVE

The great storm rolled around, returning in force when it was thought to have moved on. Hurricane force winds damaged buildings and flattened stands of trees. Lightning burned others in exposed areas. Three people were killed, and many others injured by flying masonry or limbs from trees.

A month's rainfall descended in the first twelve hours, then continued with barely a break for the entire weekend. Water poured from the hills causing the river to breach its banks, thus putting several villages under siege by floodwater. The cooler temperatures were welcomed, but electric power was now lost altogether for long periods due to lightning strikes.

By Sunday morning, eleven military men had not returned from their previous day's excursions from the base, and personnel, if any were crazy enough to want to, were forbidden to leave until further notice. Among the missing was Dan Farley.

Max awoke with a monumental headache, wondering where he was. Then he remembered, and was glad not to be obliged to prepare for a day's work. The faint smell of bacon and sausages cooking made him feel surprisingly nauseous. If they offered him some he would refuse. A cup of tea would be very welcome, however. Trying not to move his head on the pillow, he put out his hand for the watch on the locker beside the bed. Seven forty-five. His knowledge of any kind of medical establishment told him patients were invariably woken at around five and told to swallow pills. He could do with a couple of paracetemol to dull the throbbing in his head. Why was he being ignored?

Without needing to glance at the window, he knew the wild weather was continuing. Rain lashed at the glass panes;

wind buffeted the walls and whistled eerily in the quad-
rangle of empty space enclosed by the building. He
wondered if they had yet moved the tree pinning down his
car. All the time it was there the road was impassable. The
car was a write-off. He would have to sign out a vehicle
from the pool until he could replace it.

The half-closed door was opened by Clare Goodey, who
was bearing a cup and saucer. She looked fresh and neat
in a starched white shirt and slim-fitting grey trousers, and
brought in with her the pleasant smell of apples. Susan had
sometimes used a shampoo with that kind of perfume.
Clare's hair looked fluffy and shiny.

'Good morning. I allowed you to sleep until you woke
naturally.' Putting the tea on the locker, she held out a plastic
cup. 'I don't need to ask if you want these. I'd guess you've
quite a headache. Would you like help to sit up?'

'I can cope,' he said, deciding to wait until she left before
attempting to raise himself.

She smiled. 'I knew you'd say that. It's no reflection on
your manhood to accept assistance. The strapping around
your chest is going to restrict movement. But tough it out
if that's what you'd prefer.'

He took a deep breath, but it hurt so much he shot her a
rueful glance. 'Point taken. I hope those pills are painkillers.'

'They are. Very effective, too.'

She slipped an arm behind his shoulders, adding impetus
to his own efforts to sit. Holding him steady at forty-five
degrees, she adjusted the angled support beneath his pillows
and eased him back on them. Then she poured water from
the jug into a glass and held it out.

'Swallow the pills before you drink the tea. You look
pretty groggy now. They work fast. By the time an orderly
brings your breakfast you'll be feeling much happier.'

She turned to go, but he stopped her. 'Tell me what's
going on outside. It sounds horrendous.'

'It is. Three men came in overnight with injuries caused
by storm damage. There's no sign of a let-up yet. The Met
boys are predicting another twenty-four hours before the
wind drops and flood water begins to recede.'

'No hope of finding Smith alive now,' said Max, then wondered where that thought had sprung from.

'Take the pills,' Clare advised dryly. 'They'll put you in a better frame of mind.' Hesitating in the doorway, she said, 'There was a call for you at two a.m. Thinking it must be urgent, I answered and offered to take a message. The caller was a woman named Livya. She was immediately concerned that I was a doctor and demanded the facts of your condition to relay to Brigadier Rydal. I wouldn't normally give out details about a patient, but I had heard that your father is with the Joint Intelligence Committee and his ADC is Captain Cordwell, so I assured her you merely had concussion following a freak accident. It appeared to satisfy her, although she declined my offer to give you a message.'

Almost out of sight, Clare turned to look over her shoulder. 'She said she's your lover, so perhaps you should call her as soon as that headache eases.'

She walked away leaving Max with much to ponder on.

At some time during Sunday night the elements finally calmed and the morning dawned blue and gold, the way summer days should look. Begging a lift to Headquarters, Max saw where his car had been pushed to the side of the road by the crane that had lifted the tree from it. It was a sorry sight. The car had been merely his means of transport, not his pride and joy, so Max's reaction to the sight was only deep thankfulness that the tree had not fallen directly on him. It was a monster.

He had been allowed back to his room late on Sunday afternoon on condition that he rested quietly. His first intention had been to e-mail Livya, but a vicious lightning session had cut off the power again and it remained off until midevening. He had then keyed in a full account of what had happened, ending with the assurance of his ability to work on the case of a missing man. He had thanked her for the call he had been too doped up to take, and said Dr Goodey, the new MO, had given him full details of their conversation. He had underscored *full* with his tongue in his cheek. Had there been an element of female verbal sparring between them, he wondered. The e-mail had ended with a request for a return one giving all her news. It had not arrived by the time he'd left his room for Headquarters that morning, more than usually upright due to the strapping around his ribs.

Arriving in his office Max encountered Tom who, because he lived outside the base, was the only member of the team who did not know about the narrow escape Max had had. His friend eyed the plaster high on his temple and the small bald patch where his hair had been cut away to stitch up the more major wound.

'Hallo, trying to match up to me?' Tom joked, fingering the scar on his own cheek, inflicted by a crazed woman shortly before Christmas. 'How did you come by that?'

In the telling, Max then heard about the tree blocking the driveway at Tom's rented house.

'I'm waiting for a crane to move it. Until it's gone we have only one vehicle in use. Nora drove me in this morning, but I'll hire a car if the pool can't come up with one for each of us.' He then noticed how stiffly Max walked. 'You sure you're up to it today? I'm surprised the reputed harridan allowed you out of her clutches so soon.'

Max smiled. 'If I were a fighting soldier she wouldn't have, but as I'm "merely a detective" she saw no harm in letting me sit at my desk.'

'Doesn't rate us too highly, eh?'

'Compared with combat troops she considers us low risk personnel.' Still smiling, he added, 'Her bark's worse than her bite, and she knows what's what in medical matters.'

Tom asked casually, 'A looker?'

'A *married* looker. End of subject.' Max knew Tom was ever hopeful he would marry again, having been with him when the news of Susan's death had come. He knew about Livya, but he presumably saw the difficulties of that relationship and had his doubts.

They went through to where the team were waiting in the welcome freshness provided by air conditioning that was working. Piercey's close friend, Sergeant Derek Beeny, should have returned from UK leave at the weekend. Aircraft had been grounded for two days, so he was attempting, along with hundreds of others, to board a flight at some time during that day. Unable to get through on the official circuit, he had surprisingly been more successful calling Piercey's mobile phone last night.

After giving this information, Piercey then offered the result of his tour of DVD stores on Saturday, before he had scuttled back to base with admirable foresight of what was to come.

'These lists Smith made each weekend must have been offered to potential buyers, who marked those items they wanted. Then he went to whoever supplied him and got them at reduced price, to which he added his commission. None of the store managers had caught him stealing. However nifty he was, someone would surely have seen him. He was watched closely during each visit, yet there's no evidence that he was there for any reason other than to list what was for sale.'

'Your reasoning is probably right,' agreed Tom. 'In which case we'll have to bring in the local police to spotlight the dealer most likely to be supplying Smith. They'll have the dodgy ones listed on their computer.'

Connie Bush then reported that she and Heather had failed to find evidence that Smith had tried to sell his rifle or other military kit to dealers in that line.

'We'll put that on hold for the moment,' said Max. 'Smith could have traded it for cash, or even for a lift in a truck heading for the Dutch border, and the recipient is lying low until he feels safe enough to approach them. Of course, if Smith is actually out on the exercise ground everything will still be with the body. If he's dead elsewhere, whoever comes across him will hopefully call us and leave everything where it is.'

'If some enterprising Jerry bumped him off and took his gear, we'll get Smith back wearing nothing but an identity tab,' Piercey said in his usual throwaway style.

Tom was again irritated by the man's semi-humorous contributions. 'In that instance, you can take on the job of finding where the kit ended up. That should keep you out

of our hair while we get on with apprehending the killer.'
He then changed the subject with deliberation. 'Just before
we convened I made a call to the manager of Smith's bank
in town and arranged a meeting with him later this morning.
He wouldn't give details of his account over the phone, but
he did consent to tell me that Mr John Smith did not have
a deposit box at their branch. So that small key in Smith's
locker has another use. I'd like to know what it unlocks.'

'And where it is,' added Heather. 'Could be in his room
at home.'

'But would he keep the key here?' put in Connie.

'Yes, if his mother is the type to poke her nose into his
drawers and cupboards when he's out of the house. You
know how some women are with only sons.'

Max leaned back, then straightened again as the strapping made lounging uncomfortable. 'Apart from being
assaulted by a tree, I had quite a profitable Saturday
morning.'

He put the two women and Piercey in the picture about
Miller's daughter's serious fall from the bridge. 'Captain
Fanshawe gave me the details when I said that one of his
NCOs was less than the high standard he assured me they
were. Gave stress over the girl as the root of Miller's vindictive opinion of Smith. He could be right, but the accident
was very recent, and we've received the impression that the
campaign of hatred against Smith is of much longer
standing. Fanshawe denied being aware of it; seemed certain
the platoon's NCOs would have reported the problem, which
he would have sorted pronto. His very words. I'm sure he
would have. Gave me the impression he's entirely on the
ball. In which case, why was the treatment of Smith so
*un*obvious to a man of his worth?'

Connie put down the pen she had been tapping her teeth
with. 'Sir, is it possible the men of 3 Platoon are all lying
to support Miller?'

'Why would they do that?' demanded Piercey at once.

'Miller's a favourite with them, so they're vilifying the man
who's not here to put his side of the business, in order to take
the heat off Miller, who's going through a personal crisis.'

'You're suggesting they believe we're targeting the sergeant as Smith's killer?' asked Max.

Connie shrugged. 'Just a thought. As you said, how could so much universal disgust of Smith go unnoticed by the Company Commander? We only have the platoon members' words on the situation, and we know how they tend to close ranks when we're around. I'm not saying there was *no* animosity against Smith, but now he's let them down big time, so they have no hang-ups about painting him even blacker than he is.'

'You might have something,' mused Heather. 'Each man we spoke to expressed the same depth of dislike in their own way. They could easily have got together and decided on how they'd play it when questioned.' Warming to the theme, she added, 'If Smith *had* been subjected to such treatment, why hadn't he asked to see his Platoon Commander to request a move? Could these men be lying their heads off to cover the fact that they've been aiding Smith's lucrative sideline in stolen goods?'

Tom frowned. 'You're all losing fact in fiction. Smith wasn't interested in moving squads. Soldiering was merely something that provided him with living quarters, food and clothing, plus a large potential market for what he regarded as his prime occupation. And his Platoon Commander certainly noticed Smith's isolation from the rest and mentioned it to Miller. Lieutenant Farley's been with the West Wilts for two months, so the campaign against Smith has been going on for that time at least.'

Staff Sergeant Melly now entered the debate having, as usual, allowed views to be aired before contributing his comments. 'The notion of mass support for Miller, who we appear to be leaning on, is feasible, but someone put the idea of murder forward with that phone call. Like George Maddox said, it was too bloody hot for any guy to ease his boredom by baiting the Redcaps. What's more, the battalion had just returned from a gruelling exercise and would be in no mood for larking about for the hell of it. So, if we take that call seriously, someone has focussed the spotlight on Purbeck Company and, most particularly, 3 Platoon.

Without that call this case would be treated as simple AWOL and we wouldn't now be involved.'

Connie looked very interested. 'You think the call was meant to instigate an in-depth investigation of Smith?'

'Isn't it obvious?' said Melly.

'Someone who's aware of the wheeler-dealing and wants to stop it without sticking his neck out as the one who ratted on a fellow squaddie?' mused Heather thoughtfully.

'So we're ruling out murder now?' demanded Piercey.

Tom called them to order. 'Until we discover who made that call . . .'

'Bloody unlikely,' murmured Piercey.

'*And* until we trace Smith, dead or alive,' Tom continued forcefully, 'we can't progress this case.'

'What we haven't delved into yet,' said Max, 'is who was buying the goods Smith was selling. Judging by the stuff in his locker, he was shifting large amounts and was confident of customers. Find some of them and we might come across one who feels he was cheated, swindled, well and truly conned. Maybe he put an end to Smith during that mock assault, when he was hyped up and aggressive and there was a time when he and his victim were temporarily out of sight of the rest. As Mr Black says, until Smith is traced we can't focus on a case of murder or simple AWOL. All we can do now is to investigate Smith's side-line. Get out and find who bought things from him, and who had an axe to grind.'

At that moment George Maddox walked in, smiling. Max turned to him. 'I hope that daft grin indicates good news. Has Smith been seen somewhere?'

The big, burly Redcap sergeant shook his head. 'My grin would have been even dafter. But we do have a lead, sir.'

'Shoot, as they say in the good ole US of A,' drawled Piercey, earning a dark look from Tom.

Settling his large backside on the edge of a desk, Maddox said, 'Lieutenant Farley, Smith's Platoon Commander, decided to join the RMP over the weekend and go in search of his missing man. Hired a quad bike, took a tent and rations for a couple of days, and hied out to the exercise ground.'

'Shades of Ben Steele,' murmured Max, recalling another lieutenant who had decided to become a gumshoe and put himself in danger during a complex case last year. 'What is it about subalterns that they feel they can do better than us?'

'In this case, he did,' confessed Maddox. 'But only by luck or the hand of God. Caught up in the heart of the storm and threatened by flash floods, he managed to take cover in that wooded stretch well away from the area used during the exercise. Tangled in undergrowth, half-submerged by swirling water, he spotted an SA80 and a helmet bearing the badge of the West Wilts. It's Smith's.

'He came in around 04.00 after being marooned for thirty hours and reported his find to us. He looked a real sorry sight,' Maddox revealed with obvious delight. 'Plastered with mud and shivering in the vastly lower temperature, but he produced the equipment like a cat proudly produces a mouse to its owners.'

Tom asked sharply, 'Just the rifle and helmet?'

'Said it was too deep under water there to spot anything else, and lightning had brought down a number of trees that were blocking the easier ways through. He seemed confident that he'd have seen a body if it was lying near the equipment. Claimed he carried out as comprehensive a search as he could manage, under those circumstances.'

'That wood is too far from the action that day for someone to have killed him during the exercise,' ruled Max. 'I think this points towards voluntary desertion. Smith scarpered and dumped his kit in the wood.' He smiled at Maddox. 'Buck passed back to you, George.'

Over the next three days Maddox, his team (including dog handlers), and twenty men from Purbeck Company, searched the wood for further evidence of Smith's presence. It was exhausting work. Fallen trees had to be sawn up and cleared away, undergrowth thinned, and paths minutely examined. One by one small items were discovered, showing that he had discarded anything marking him as a soldier. In the absence of his body, there was only one conclusion to be drawn.

Private John Smith had deserted; gone, with no intention of returning.

Fanshawe held an inquest with the three Platoon Commanders and their NCOs, asking how the hell one of their men could have slipped away during a daylight action without anyone noticing his absence until it was over. The question was met with silence. They all knew it was possible. During simulated battle each man concentrated on the task in hand, keeping his eyes on the relevant NCO who, in turn, was watching the Officer.

What was hard to believe was that Smith had survived the heat and got clean away. The general consensus was that he had had a civilian contact waiting in the wood with transport, and he was hiding out with him, or her, until he could be smuggled out of Germany. Although Fanshawe conducted the meeting in a serious vein, each person present privately thought the loss of John Smith was no bad thing. He would eventually be caught, given a custodial sentence and officially discharged from the West Wiltshire Regiment. Meanwhile, they were better off without a rat who might scuttle away on the eve of departure to a war zone.

When the rest dispersed, Dan Farley remained. 'Could I have a word?'

Fanshawe grinned in more relaxed manner. 'If you want further thanks for your sterling work in pinpointing the wood, you're out of luck. That comprehensive search has disrupted Purbeck's schedule for three days, and it's useless trying to make up the time. It's Friday tomorrow. By noon, everyone's mind will be on what they're doing at the weekend now the weather's behaving itself, and *you* are to blame.'

Taking those words as lightly as they were spoken, Dan said, 'Instead of a pat on the head and a lollipop for aforesaid sterling work, I'd really like tomorrow off. I need to go home for a couple of days, Will. I could catch a flight tonight and be back on Sunday evening.'

'Grandmother's funeral?' quipped Fanshawe, leaning back and clasping his hands behind his head. 'That girl's got you by the short and curlies, lad. It's never going to work. You're a soldier; she hates the fact. Face the truth. A weekend of lust and laughter won't change anything.'

'I think it will,' Dan argued eagerly. '*She* called *me*, begging me to take her back. She's ripe for persuasion right now. If I have to wait until we get leave before the off to Afghanistan, I'll have lost the chance. This way I can cash in on her present mood, then consolidate my advantage during the October leave.'

'We'll be away for six months,' Fanshawe reminded him. 'It had better be some consolidation for it to keep her sweet until we get back.' He nodded. 'OK, piss off tonight, but make sure you're on parade Monday morning early, even if she needs further persuasion.'

As Dan mumbled his thanks and headed for the door, Fanshawe added, 'If you spot Smith at the airport, grab him and haul him back here.'

Max was deeply frustrated. The curious case of Private John Smith had gone off the boil as far as SIB was concerned. George Maddox had regained command of the business of tracing the whereabouts of a soldier who had absented himself without official permission, and Klaus Krenkel's men were looking into the activities of known pirate traders who might have supplied Smith.

Max guessed the *Polizei* would not expend much effort on the case. Their time was heavily occupied with crime amongst German citizens, so a vague suggestion of British military involvement in a backstreet trade impossible to stamp out would be put on a back burner.

With very little on the go for 26 Section at present, Max had sent his team out, with the task of tracking down the men and women on the base who had bought items from Smith. All this would do was indicate how long he had been engaged in his sideline, and the amount of goods that had passed through his hands. So far, no single person had admitted buying from Smith. Almost everyone on the base had DVDs and CDs and iPods, but there was no way of proving these had not been bought from the legitimate stores, or from the itinerant street vendors.

The discovery of Smith's rifle and kit removed any question of a charge of theft of MoD property. SIB would hardly mount a case against him for stolen trousers and a shirt. Tom's interview with the bank manager had revealed that only Smith's normal payments passed through the account, which meant that the proceeds of his undercover business must be going to an account in the UK. Or anywhere else. Was Smith enough of an entrepreneur to stash funds in any European country with euro currency?

With his usual penchant for pointing out the annoyingly obvious, Piercey had suggested that the stuff in Smith's locker might be the results of his first adventure into subtrading, and the universal denial of buying anything from him, the truth. They had no evidence to the contrary and, since it was all still there in his locker, Smith could not even be accused of making away with it. In short, were they not chasing a *dead* wild goose? The Sergeant's last words were a dig at Max, who made a habit of chasing wild geese, usually successfully. The whole team saw the sense in Piercey's reasoning, and the last dregs of interest in the John Smith drama drained away.

Adding to Max's frustration was his inability to take part in energetic exercise. The strapping around his chest limited movement, and Clare Goodey had instructed him to take life easy until she looked him over at the end of this week. He had an appointment on the following day, but was determined to break out for the weekend. Surely he could get on the river, even if he merely paddled a canoe very slowly. The river was his escape from military claustrophobia; his venue for putting thoughts and ideas in cohesive order.

On this Thursday evening he was in his room trying to relax with the biography of Sir Edmund Hillary. His mind was only half on what he was reading because he was waiting for a call from Livya. She had sent an e-mail from Washington on Tuesday outlining the overloaded schedule of meetings she and his father had attended, careful not to elaborate on the work they were doing for the Joint Intelligence Committee. Computerized messages could be retrieved and used as damning evidence, as had been so devastatingly demonstrated in the past few years.

She had made plain her relief that the tree had fallen when it had, and not a split second later, and sent loving commiserations for his injuries. The second e-mail yesterday had been a brief comment that they would be flying home overnight, and she would telephone as soon as she had caught up on what had come in while they had been away. It was now nine thirty. Surely she was not still in the office?

Max was not an advocate of e-mails when it came to communicating with the woman he loved. Words on a screen were so *cold*, no matter what they implied. Inflections in a voice, subtle tones, made those same words infinitely more meaningful. Livya's voice was low-pitched and very attractive. On occasion, it had even made his toes curl with excitement. Over the years he had learned a lot from voices; how to judge the truth or value of what people told him. When Livya spoke words of love, he knew they came from the heart. He waited impatiently to hear some tonight.

He heard the phone ringing while he was showering and carefully washing his hair around the row of stitches. Swearing softly he walked, dripping water, to pick up the receiver.

'In the shower, honey. Call you back in five.'

'It's not honey,' said Clare. 'Saw your light on and thought I'd remind you I need to look at that head wound tomorrow. Get some sleep. She won't ring until two a.m.' The line went dead.

Max was, indeed, drifting off when Livya called at eleven thirty.

'Hallo, darling. Sorry it's so late. Such a load to catch up with after a week's absence. Andrew's still at it. No way could I persuade him to go home.'

Holding back from asking which methods of persuasion she had used, Max struggled to a sitting position and mumbled that it was great to hear from her. 'Missed you like crazy.'

'I'd love to be able to say the same but, by God, the Yanks don't let a minute go by unchallenged if business can be done during it. I'm bushed, Max. Good thing we're not on a webcam. Hair wants washing, nails need a decent manicure, eyes are puffy from lack of sleep and each yawn's as wide as a chasm. Not a pretty sight, believe me.'

Max smiled. In his eyes she was always a pretty sight. 'I'll refrain from describing what *you'd* see on a webcam. A bushed woman can do without further shocks. How did it really go over there, honey? Did you both sock it to the CIA?'

'At times I felt like literally socking them. They're so bloody aggressive and superior. They come dangerously close to regarding the UK as another US state. Andrew's wonderful. He handles them with just the right mixture of deference, resolution and British sangfroid; cuts through their frenzy of superlatives and dire predictions to create calm from the storm.'

Knowing she needed to share the frustrations and successes of the visit, Max let her talk without interruption. If her account put too much emphasis on Andrew Rydal's many splendid qualities, he tried to accept it as hyperbole after a difficult and taxing week spent with men trained to browbeat any dissidents into accepting what they considered to be the correct action.

Eventually, Livya asked about the missing soldier. After the high-powered account of her week, Max felt the burst balloon of his own was hardly worth recounting. He swiftly dispensed with the subject and returned to more intimate considerations.

'Any chance of you coming over? After that punishing session with the CIA, you're surely entitled to a break. Andrew can't expect you to be on call twenty-four seven.'

'Oh Max, there's not a chance of getting away for several weeks, at least. It'll be up to you to come here, as usual.'

Swallowing back her unconscious implication that his work was less demanding than hers, he said, 'I'm seeing the Doc tomorrow to remove the stitches from the head wound, and for a general check on everything else. If she gives the go-ahead I could get a late afternoon flight and come this weekend.'

'Sorry, darling, I'll have to be in the office for most of Saturday. Anyway, should you be considering taking a flight with that wound in your head?'

'I'd consider taking a flight with a wound *anywhere* if it meant we could get together,' he said in his disappointment. 'I really miss you when we're apart.'

'And I miss you, Steve,' she said, using the name in her usual teasing fashion as her voice grew softer. 'But the Channel and half a continent separate us, as things stand.'

'We could do something about that,' he said urgently. 'Why don't I come tomorrow and we can talk about it?'

'Wrong moment, darling,' she said gently. 'I really do have to work this weekend. Andrew needs my help, and I care too much about you to let you charge over here after that narrow escape with a tree. Give yourself time to fully recover, then we can make plans.'

He waited for her to elaborate.

'Are you still there?' she asked.

'Yes.'

'I'm sure that MO will rule that a further period of rest is necessary. She sounded a real martinet. Had the nerve to ask if I was a relative before she'd give a report on your condition.'

'Legally, you have no claim to be told confidential details about me,' Max pointed out stiffly.

Apparently missing the inference in that remark, Livya said, 'Andrew's your father. *He* had every right to know, as I informed her.'

'Once he knew, he didn't bother to discover how his son was progressing.'

'He's been extremely busy.'

'He always has been. That's why we hardly know each other.'

The tone of his comment finally got through to her then. 'You're tired, darling. I shouldn't have called at this hour. It's gone midnight, and you should be resting that poor head of yours. I'll call tomorrow at a more reasonable hour and we'll make plans, depending on what the martinet dictates.'

'She's a very nice woman, actually.'

A short silence. 'Then get her to kiss you better so that we can get together as soon as poss. Goodnight, Steve.'

She disconnected before he could respond.

Friday morning, and the tree had finally been lifted from across the driveway. It had been low on the list of priorities, being situated outside the base, and, although they had taken the bulk of it away, the entire front garden was covered in small twigs and leaves. Tom's first concern as the crane drove away was to open the garage and bring out Nora's car, so he went indoors for the keys, feeling that something had been achieved this week – if only the solution to his domestic problem.

Nora put her head around the kitchen door. 'Need another coffee after the heavy responsibility of telling them how to do it?'

'Cheeky wench! If I'd not supervised them they'd have left half of it behind. As it is, there's a mess of small stuff still to be cleared.' He joined her in the kitchen, where two mugs of coffee were already on the table. 'I'll get the girls down here in a minute. With their help we can clear it by lunchtime.'

'By *we* you mean you and me, I take it. So, who's going to cook the lunch?'

'We'll have something easy.'

'Like?'

'Egg and chips.'

Nora gave him a level look across the table. 'So you don't want lamb chops, carrots and bubble and squeak, followed by apricot crumble?'

He grinned. 'Get behind me, temptation.'

'Is that a yes?'

'OK, you're excused clearing duty. Just confirms my belief that a woman's place is in the kitchen.'

Her eyes widened. 'And there was I thinking it was in the marital bed.'

'After the cooking,' he replied provocatively. 'Talking of which, isn't the brood at a disco this evening?'

'Yes, but you'll be too tired after supervising their clearance of twigs, etcetera.'

'Test that theory and you'll get a nice surprise.'

'You're admitting I'm right about the marital bed?'

He leaned across to grasp her hand. 'You're too clever for your boots, but I still manage to love you.'

'For making apricot crumble?' she teased.

'Oh, mostly for that, of course.'

The moment was broken by the familiar sound of a wildebeest stampede, heralding three flushed girls demanding drinks.

'Aha!' exclaimed Tom. 'The three people I most wanted to see.'

They turned, with suspicion clear in their expressions. 'We're busy, Dad,' they claimed almost in unison.

'Sitting in bedrooms listening to tribal sounds mistakenly called music isn't being busy. I have something far more exciting for you to do. It's called clearing up the garden.'

They groaned and protested. 'Can't you get some squaddies to do it?' asked Gina. 'It's men's work.'

'I've just done my nails,' wailed Maggie.

'The garden's full of creepy-crawlies after all that rain. I *hate* them,' declared Beth.

Tom leaned back in his chair and surveyed them. 'To answer you in turn: No, Gina, squaddies are trained to be soldiers, not gardeners. Maggie, you can wear gloves and, if you manage to look helpless enough, maybe Hans will see you and come across to take your place. As for you, Beth, correct me if I'm wrong, but haven't I heard you boasting to your sisters that slugs and snails and puppy-dogs' tails don't frighten you one bit?'

'Oh, *Dad*,' came the familiar triple cry.

'Dad will be doing it with you. It'll be fun.'

'Can't we do it tomorrow?' demanded Maggie.

'No.'

'But we've got these new CDs and we're dying to hear them before the disco tonight.'

'Listen to them while you get ready for it. You usually

take long enough to hear an entire symphony concert,' Tom said.

Nora turned from the sink. 'New CDs? I thought you all spent most of your pocket money on Tuesday.'

Maggie explained. 'Some of the sixth-formers have started a club. It's only two euros to join, then you can buy CDs at reduced price. They're all the latest ones. It's great! Members take in ones they don't want any more and you can get them at half price.'

'And you can pay so much a week if you don't get *lots* of pocket money,' added Beth. 'We've had to do that.'

'There are three of you,' Nora reminded her.

'We know, Mum,' she replied with a sigh. 'You keep telling us.'

'Because each of you is inclined to forget.'

Tom was frowning. 'When you say half price you mean the price when new? But these are second-hand, aren't they?'

'Lots of them are, but you can get CDs people have been given for presents and don't like,' Gina said. 'Those are still sealed, so you know they're real bargains. The used ones can be swapped. It's a great club. Except for the tinies, almost everyone at school has joined.'

Still enthusiastic, Maggie said, 'The committee are talking about extending it to DVDs, which would be fab.'

'So you'll be taking the *Pirates of the Caribbean* DVD?' Tom teased. 'Trouble is, you've played it six times every week for three months, so you can't expect to get more than peanuts for it.'

'Oh, *Dad*,' groaned the three soprano voices again, and they began pelting him with various kitchen cloths and oven gloves.

Through the din he heard the phone ring, then Nora calling him. Fending off the soft missiles, Tom took the receiver into the dining room and shut the door.

'George Maddox, sir. They told me you're at home sorting the storm damage.'

'Something they couldn't deal with?' he asked in surprise.

'There's nothing to deal with. I thought you'd like to know we've had a message from Hampshire police. John

Smith's details have just got through the system to reach them. They're very interested in the guy. His description closely matches several given by witnesses of a man wanted for questioning by them about a series of robberies in and around Southampton. They grew even more interested when I told them how long he'd been with us, because those robberies ceased at the time Smith enlisted.'

'That fits,' mused Tom. 'Smith's home is in Bournemouth. Very handy for Southampton. So the lad joined a regiment stationed out here when the heat was on at home.'

'And walked away when the same happened here.'

'Possibly, but my guess is that something more threatening was behind his desertion, that held a large element of risk. Something that made it too dangerous for him to stay a moment longer.'

# SIX

I t hurt more having the stitches removed than when they had been put in. After Max said 'Ouch!' the third time, Clare apologized and explained that he had been strongly sedated when she had sewn him up, but now he was fully aware of what she was doing.

'Almost finished,' she added consolingly, still busily picking at his scalp. 'If you were a child I'd give you a toffee for being brave.'

Max countered that on a sudden impulse. 'My honey suggested you should kiss me better.'

'There you are; all done,' she said, as if he had not spoken. 'The wounds have knitted together well.' Putting aside the surgical tweezers and sterile pad she turned back, still very much the impersonal medic. 'I think that strapping could be replaced while you're here. Then it should last for another three weeks, so long as temperatures keep well below the high-sweat levels they were before.'

Max removed his shirt in defiant mood, determined not to let her treat him like a small boy who deserved a toffee. As she stood close to remove the strapping, he was once again aware of the faint scent of apples in her hair.

'My wife also used a shampoo that smelled of apples. It's nice.'

Continuing what she was doing, she said, 'Max, you're a patient in my surgery. Stop behaving like a frustrated guy trying to chat up a handy blonde.'

His eyes narrowed. 'Has *he* made you frosty?'

'He?'

'Your husband.'

She removed the last of the strapping and turned away to fetch a fresh roll of binding.

'Where is he, Clare? Will he be joining you here?'

Over her shoulder she asked, 'Will *honey* be joining *you*?'

'We're not married.'

A slight pause as she gathered together the thick roll and some scissors. 'I soon won't be.' Returning to where he sat on the edge of the couch, she avoided his eyes. 'You're not entitled to know everything about me after just one evening in a beer garden.'

'So let's have another one on the strength of that snippet you've just told me.'

Her formal manner suddenly relaxed. There was a smile hovering in her eyes as she faced him. 'You really are a frustrated guy chatting up a handy blonde.'

'Am I succeeding?'

She hesitated. 'I've arranged to view some apartments tomorrow. Can't stand living in-Mess. If you're interested in a spare seat in my car, you can come along.'

He smiled with satisfaction. 'I'd welcome a lift to town. While you're looking for somewhere to live, I'll have a shot at fixing myself up with a car. Nothing as sporty as yours, of course. I'll get one that'll make me as disappointing as the Floridan sheriff who ordered quiche and salad.'

She gave a small laugh. 'But you're not hung around with handcuffs, revolver and truncheon. There!' she exclaimed, stepping back as she finished binding his chest. 'That looks better.'

He slipped on his shirt, pulled his looped tie over his head and tightened the knot beneath his collar, then prepared to leave. 'Give me a call when you're set to leave tomorrow. After we've completed the business side, I'll buy you dinner at a different riverside restaurant I know well.'

'I'll bring a swimsuit, just in case.'

At the door he said, 'And the apple shampoo. I like it.'

In the waiting room was a soldier he recognized. Private Joe Ryan, one of the men admitted a week ago after the exercise.

'Hallo, still suffering?' asked Max in surprise.

Ryan got to his feet. 'Something different, sir. Septic toe.'

Max nodded. 'Best to get that sorted. Can be bloody painful.'

As he made to pass the young squaddie, he was halted

by the man's request to have a private word. Intrigued, because when he had interviewed him here in his bed, Ryan had been totally uncommunicative, Max nodded.

'Come along to Section Headquarters after Captain Goodey's seen to that toe.'

'No need for that, sir. Just wanted to say . . .' He glanced around to make sure he was not being overheard. 'Just wanted to say, you should talk to White and Corkhill. Those two had something going on with Smith. Always having a go at him, giving him leery looks, winding him up. He was scared of them. Don't ask me why, but they knew something and held it over Smith. They're like that, those two. Work it together.'

The orderly appeared to tell Ryan the MO was ready for him, and he darted away in something approaching relief. '*I* didn't tell you that, sir.'

'Of course you didn't,' Max said reassuringly, then walked out to the pool car he was presently using, telling himself the case of Private John Smith might be dead but it would not lie down.

At Headquarters there was an air of restlessness, although the entire team was present save Tom, who was supervising the removal of a tree from his garden. Max understood the general mood. They had all been handling a possible murder enquiry; an intriguing set of circumstances. Now it had become a simple case of a runaway soldier. Nothing more to investigate. Each of them was certainly planning a lively weekend, which they hoped would start at noon. Max had no argument with that, they deserved a decent break.

Telling them he would see them on Monday morning, he asked Connie and Heather to wait for a few minutes. He smiled at their apprehensive expressions.

'No problem. Just fill me in on Privates White and Corkhill. In your report you rated them a couple of likely lads. Anything in particular that they said to emphasize that opinion?'

Connie answered. 'They said much the same of Smith as the rest. Disliked everything about him, but mostly his persistence in butting in where he wasn't wanted.'

'Especially Smith's attempt to chum up with Lance Corporal Mason, who's still mourning his close friend killed in Iraq,' added Heather.

'Mmm, by Mason's own evidence, Smith was an insensitive bastard,' Max said thoughtfully. 'From your conversation with White and Corkhill, would you go along with a guess that Smith might have elbowed his way into a profitable sideline that pair were running exclusively?'

Connie frowned. 'The DVD and CD trade?'

'Yes.'

'You think that's what happened?'

'I don't know, but I've just been given a furtive hint by young Ryan that Smith was scared of that duo, who made it obvious they had some kind of hold over him.'

'That wouldn't surprise me,' said Heather. 'They were too cocky by half. You think Smith ran from *them*, sir?'

Max perched on the edge of a desk and gave a sigh. 'Something drove Smith to leave without delay, and those two could have been responsible. Before you start your weekend break I'd like you to bring them in for questioning. Maybe the more intimidating venue will loosen their tongues.'

'You want one of us to stay?'

'No, Connie, just bring them in, if you please.'

Heather studied him expectantly. 'Are you still considering something more complex than simple AWOL?'

He laughed. 'I'm considering one of my famous wild geese. Put it down to that knock on my head.'

While Max waited for them to return, his mobile rang. 'Hi, Tom. How's it going in the Blacks' garden?'

'Tree's gone. I've bribed the coolie workforce to help clear the remaining mess with the promise of a boat trip complete with coffee and cakes tomorrow.' A sigh came across the connection. 'I have a horrible suspicion Hans will be included in the treat, in which case several others will be added to the roll call. Pity we're not still investigating Smith. I could plead work and leave Nora to—'

'Arrange a divorce,' Max finished pointedly. 'Are you coming in this afternoon?'

'I've been promised a tasty lunch. I could drive over afterwards. Is there something on?'

'Not really. I've sent everyone off for the weekend. I'll leave after I've interviewed a couple of Smith's platoon members.'

'I thought George had taken that over now.'

'He has, but I've a hunch I might find the cause of Smith's precipitate abscondment by following up a suggestion that these two know more than they've let on.'

Tom chuckled. 'One of your WGs?'

'If I catch it, I'll call you in.'

'Called to tell you George rang me half an hour ago. Our circulated description of Smith has reached the Hants police headquarters. Some bright lad there matched the description with one of someone wanted by them for a series of robberies in and around Southampton last year. They want to be informed when we find him.'

'Ha, so Smith was nicking stuff before he joined the West Wilts. It fits, Tom.'

'Except that we have no firm evidence he's been doing it out here. All he's been up to is making lists, if the store managers are to be believed.'

'So how did he come by the pile you found in his locker?'

'We'll ask him when we get him.'

Spotting Connie and Heather arriving with two very aggressive-looking men, Max said, 'Have a good time with your clutch of kids. I'll give you the news on Monday.'

Max saw at once why his two sergeants had described them as likely lads. Both had blunt features and complexions indicating the consumption of too much junk food and not enough fresh water. White suited his name. Ash blond with pale blue-grey eyes, he was of medium height and sinewy, with tattoos on both arms.

Corkhill was black-haired with eyes so dark that Max guessed foreign blood must have been introduced among his ancestors at some time. He was short and stocky, again with tattooed arms. He made no secret of his anger at being brought in by the two women.

'What's this about? We've done nothing. We're being victimized.'

'Yeah, we've done nothing,' echoed White.

Max nodded his thanks to his sergeants, then turned to the men. 'So many people think that until we manage to refresh their memories. That's what we're going to do now. You wait here while I discover what Corkhill now remembers,' he told Charles White sternly. 'While you're waiting, you can dredge your own memory for facts buried beneath the silt.'

In an interview room, with Corkhill in a chair facing him and the door shut, Max stared in silence at the brash soldier.

'What?' Corkhill asked when he could evidently stand the situation no longer.

'I'm giving you time to think about what you failed to tell my sergeants when they questioned you about your relationship with John Smith.'

'Nothing. I had no *relationship* with that little creep, sir.'

'Ah, but you did have. You've just expressed a strong disgust of him.'

'That's not a relationship. We were never mates.'

Max maintained his intense gaze, saying, 'The word relationship means how one person *relates* to another. It doesn't necessarily mean friendship or liking. In your case, you felt exactly the opposite where Smith was concerned. In legal terms that means a *hostile* relationship.'

'Legal terms?' cried Corkhill, alarmed. 'I'm not giving no evidence. I don't know nothing about where he is, or why he scarpered.'

'I think you do,' Max contradicted firmly. 'What did Smith do to earn your opinion of him as a little creep?'

Len Corkhill gazed left and right as if seeking an answer to that written on the walls like a cue-board. Enlightenment then came. 'Yeah, he was always creeping about. You'd look up and there he was. You'd never asked him to join in. He'd just tag on like he was with you.' Further enlightenment. 'Yeah, and he'd listen to what was going off, like, then go and tell others like it was *his* idea. Caused trouble, he did.'

'In what way?'

Wary, wondering if he had given too much away, Corkhill improvised. 'Passed on bits of what he'd heard.'

'Such as?'

He shrugged. 'You know how it is. The lads shoot off their mouths over something that happened that day, or at a disco on a Saturdee. It's just talk to get it out of their systems. Don't mean half of it. Forget it next day. But Smith, he ran round passing the dirt and the lads all got uptight about it.' By now more confident that he had all the right answers, Corkhill leaned back and folded his arms. 'Three Platoon was the best in Purbeck until that little snot joined us, and none of us is surprised he scarpered.' A sneer crossed his coarse features. 'Got so piss-scared by that exercise, he couldn't face the thought of the real thing. Used to shoot men what done that in the old days.'

'So you think someone shot Smith?'

'What?' Corkhill was once more alarmed at the way the interview was going.

'You all believe Smith was afraid of going to Afghanistan. Did one of you decide to deal with the coward like they did in the old days?'

'I didn't say that! No way did I say that, sir,' he cried, completely rattled.

'So what *did* you threaten Smith with?'

The near-black eyes looked everywhere but at the questioner.

'Come on, Corkhill,' Max pressed. 'It's common knowledge you and White had Smith over a barrel.'

The soldier kept his silence while Max waited. After several minutes passed, Max got up and walked to open the door. 'White, you're next.'

Corkhill turned in his chair. 'I can go?' he asked with relief.

'Wait outside. I might need to question you again.'

'I don't know nothing,' Corkhill protested again.

'Which means you know something. Think back to your English lessons at school. It'll give you something to occupy your mind while you wait.'

Standing so that the pair had no opportunity for eyeball contact as they passed, Max was soon facing the pale soldier across the table.

'I won't keep you long,' he said. 'Corkhill has given me the background details of what hold you had over John Smith. All I need from you is how you discovered what he'd done.'

White looked bewildered. 'Corky *told* you?'

'Said Smith spoiled what used to be the best platoon in Purbeck company; that he set guys against each other by repeating wild talk he'd overheard and suggesting it was for real. Also reckons Smith tried to muscle in on whatever you and your mate had going down at weekends. That right?'

'Yeah. Yeah.' White spoke softly, weighing up what Max had said.

'As I told Corkhill, we have a witness who says you two had a hold over Smith; knew something he'd want kept quiet. Were you blackmailing him? Demanding some return for your silence?'

Apprehension flared in those pale eyes. 'No way! Corky never told you that.'

'No, he didn't. So what did you do with this knowledge you had?'

'Made him shit-scared of what we *might* do. That's all,' White declared forcefully. 'Look, sir, Smith asked for it. We – me and Corky – thought up a way to sort him for good.'

'Go on.'

'But Corky already told you.'

'I'd like to hear your version.'

White was still cagey. 'Who's this witness?'

'What was it that Smith was afraid you'd use against him?'

Gazing round the small room and realizing there was no way of bluffing his way out of his predicament, White apparently decided the game was up. 'Smith was always trying to get in on what any of us was doing. So, when he listens to what Corky and me planned for a Saturdee night with a couple of tar . . . girls, and wants to tag along, we says to get lost. Then he comes up on that morning with a couple of DVDs. Says they're ours, no strings. Thinks it buys him a place in our plan. When we don't play ball, he says he can get us a player, latest model, for free.'

White's face gained some colour as he related this. 'Me and Corky went along with it, spiking him, like. Said when he'd got the player we'd think about it. He bloody turns up with it the next weekend. New, still in the packing. Wouldn't say where he'd got it.'

White then smiled and put a hand to his throat. 'Corky, he's had it up to here with Smith trying to buy himself into our plans. So he shakes his head and says we could go in to town and lift one of them players any time we liked. He gives me the wink, then tells Smith what might work the magic would be a rifle and ammo. Says we've got a buyer and could split the dosh three ways, but we didn't know how to get hold of the stuff.'

Max's interest in this evidence suddenly doubled. This goose was wild enough to appeal to him. 'So you'd stymied Smith?'

'Had we, hell! The stupid bastard does the business. Don't ask me how. Comes and offers us a weapon and ammo next weekend.'

'You took it?'

'No way, sir. It's a serious offence, that.'

'So Smith kept it?'

He shook his head. 'We dunno what happened to it. We just told him to put it back where he got it from. Said we wanted nothing to do with it.' It seemed White saw, for the first time, what he and Corkhill had instigated, and that they were beginning to look culpable.

'So you admit to conning Smith into committing a serious offence as a means of winning your friendship, having no intention of honouring the deal?' Max demanded.

'We never thought he'd do it.' Obviously not liking the expression on Max's face, he blustered some more. 'He was a leech, sir, clinging on where he wasn't wanted. He wouldn't get the message. We had to shake him off somehow.'

'And, having coerced him into this criminal act, you then kept him in line with the threat of reporting what he'd done.'

Again, White tried to bluster. 'It was a joke, a put-down, saying we could do a deal with the rifle and ammo. We never set him up to nicking one. Any normal guy would know we was having him on. Smith, he was like a dog. Wanted a pat for bringing us a bone.'

Max stood abruptly, walked to open the door, and called Corkhill back. Once the pair were seated side by side, he outlined the result of the interviews with them. 'A rifle and ammunition were stolen from the Armoury three weeks ago. You both admit to tricking Private Smith into acquiring such items by saying you had a buyer for them. You further admit he produced these items, when you then told him you had been joking and wanted nothing to do with them. You state that you have no idea what Smith did with the items he stole, but you have been tormenting him by threatening to report him for theft. Is that correct?'

They looked at each other, then cautiously nodded.

'Then I must warn you that you will be regarded as suspects for the theft of MoD property, as listed. When Private Smith is apprehended, and able to give his evidence regarding this criminal act, a report will be sent to the Garrison Commander, who will take the appropriate action against you.'

Monday morning brought renewed focus on John Smith at 26 Section Headquarters. The result of Max's interviews with Corkhill and White had provided a probable solution to the theft from the Armoury. The team was unanimous in believing the rifle and ammunition to have been sold locally by Smith, unless he had stashed it somewhere, awaiting the chance to put it back as his tormentors had instructed. Max gave it as his firm belief that Corkhill and White had not taken it from him. Likely lads they certainly were, but each had a strong sense of loyalty to 3 Platoon, Purbeck Company, and, ultimately, to the West Wiltshire Regiment.

George Maddox arrived to reveal that, over the weekend,

messages had come in from both the Dorset and Wiltshire police in response to the information on Smith sent out by him. It seemed that Smith's description matched that of a man wanted by them for thefts ranging through DVDs, mobile phones, beer and spirits, top-of-the-range trainers, car accessories and women's sexy underwear. There was even a suspicion that he could be behind the disappearance of a silver golfing trophy from an exclusive club.

'Sexy knickers!' cooed Piercey in falsetto tones. 'Was Smith gay?'

'For his *girlfriend*,' Heather said heavily.

'A prancing Sloane Ranger from the exclusive *goff* club, of course,' Piercey retaliated.

Tom intervened. 'There's no evidence to tie these crimes to Smith. His description matches one on their records, that's all. It doubtless fits a number of men.'

George said, 'They've asked for fingerprints. We're getting underway with that. Interesting point is that these thefts ceased around the time Smith joined the West Wilts, although it still doesn't prove he committed them.' He turned to Max. 'There's a more serious query from Somerset police. Attempted rape of two girls on the same night, after a Hallowe'en party last year. The Somerset guys are trying to trace the girls to get a definite ID with Smith's picture.'

Connie, who had been uncharacteristically silent, said, 'That's not Smith's style. Theft, perhaps, because we have evidence of a collection of CDs and DVDs in his locker. But he could have been simply selling on for a local dealer. Store keepers never caught him shoplifting, did they? OK, so Corkhill and White conned him into getting hold of stuff from the Armoury . . .'

'*If* it was from the Armoury,' inserted Melly quietly. 'We've no proof of that, because we don't have the items to check on.'

'No, we haven't,' Connie agreed. 'Nor have we had any hint or suggestion from women in Purbeck Company, or *any* women on the base, that Smith had been sexually active with any of them. Aren't these guys in the UK leaping in the dark?'

Tom shook his head. 'We won't get the answer to that until they come up with proof positive.'

'By which time we'll have found Smith's body in a shallow grave on the exercise area,' said the irrepressible Piercey with an outsized grin.

Heather rounded on him. 'One of these days *your* body will be found in a shallow grave.'

'And guess who'll have put it there,' added Tom darkly.

Beeny, who had been on leave in the UK at the time of Smith's disappearance, now offered his thoughts.

'Isn't it a strong possibility that Smith is hiding out with a local contact? *If* he's the man everyone wants, no way will he return to the UK. More likely he'll stay in Germany.'

Tom nodded. 'Klaus Krenkel's team have promised to send over a list of all their known pirate dealers of CDs and DVDs. They're in no hurry. They naturally have their own cases as priorities. We can't progress that possibility without their cooperation because it concerns German nationals. Frustrating, but we need to maintain good relations with them.'

The telephone in Max's office rang. He left the discussion to go and take the call, thinking it must be personal or it would have gone to the duty desk.

'Captain Rydal.'

'Morning, Max. Will Fanshawe.' A curious pause. 'Look . . . I could be a little premature on this, but I'm somewhat concerned.'

'About what?'

Again a slight pause before Fanshawe spoke. 'Dan Farley took a seventy-two to the UK late on Thursday. Woman trouble. He hasn't come back, or called in.' A sigh came over the line. 'I stretched a point to let him go because of the impending off to Afghanistan. He knew that and promised he'd return yesterday evening. He's a good, reliable guy, Max.'

'So he's had an accident, or fallen ill.'

'Sure, but . . . well, after Smith vanishing in such questionable circs it seems strangely coincidental that his platoon commander fails to arrive back when he should.'

'You think Dan was responsible for Smith's disappearance?'

'*Christ, no*! I wasn't suggesting . . . Forget I called. Bad
move.'

'I'll come over,' said Max before any more could be said.

Knowing he had put Fanshawe's back up with that
comment, Max half expected the man not to be in his office.
The cricket-playing captain was there, however, and definitely not friendly.

'I said forget it,' he snapped. 'No way was I making it
official. Dan went out looking for Smith off his own bat.
It was he who found the SA80 and kit. He exceeded the
call of duty. I won't have you labelling him a suspect.'

Ignoring that false accusation, Max asked crisply, 'Why,
precisely, did you call me?'

Fanshawe regarded him silently for some moments before
replying. 'Dan's the last person to play monkey tricks. That
he didn't get here last night, and hasn't made contact, means
something happened that he had no control over. It's made
me uneasy, that's all. The fact that he found evidence of
Smith's desertion, after intensive searches by your people
had drawn blanks, could have put him in danger.'

He sighed heavily. 'Yeah, it sounds melodramatic, but so
was Smith's vanishing trick. Basic AWOL I'm accustomed
to, but the timing of Smith's bid for freedom, and the adverse
conditions, make the affair somewhat dodgy. You initially
mentioned the hint of murder, and Dan's uncharacteristic
behaviour . . .' He waved his hands in a dismissive gesture.
'A crazy moment, that's all.'

'I've had crazier ones. Ask my team.' Max sat without
being invited to, and smiled. 'I spoke to Dan Farley, don't
forget, and I'd endorse your assessment of his reliability.
But you mentioned woman trouble. That can make the most
reliable and level-headed of us turn into heedless idiots. He
had a framed picture of a good-looking blonde hugging a
dog. When I asked if she was his girlfriend, he coloured
and said, "Not just at the moment". Is it she who's causing
the trouble?' Seeing the other man's hesitation, he added,
'This is completely off the record.'

Fanshawe leaned back and linked his hands behind his head. 'She's playing fast and loose, but he's really gone on her. She called wanting to kiss and make up, with everything that follows kisses. He deserved a favour from me after spending a weekend out in a storm looking for one of his men. So I let him go, although I knew he would make a fool of himself again. His six months' absence in Afghanistan will bring down the final curtain, but I'd prefer him to go out there on a high. The experience will change him; toughen him up. Then he'll see the affair for what it is.'

'I assume you've called his mobile.'

'Voicemail.'

'Been in touch with the girl?'

'All I know is her family owns kennels somewhere in Sussex. Her name is Trish. Patricia, I suppose. Can't get far with that. There's no guarantee they were meeting there. From the flashpoint signs emanating from Dan I'm sure they'd need a hotel room with thick walls and well-oiled bed springs for the reconciliation.'

'Poor devil,' commented Max with a wry smile. 'He's not so far gone he'd let her persuade him to stay longer?'

'No! I'm certain of that.'

'Right. I've an interest in this inasmuch as Dan *is* linked with John Smith. Off the record, I'll see what I can find out and pass it on to you.'

They both got to their feet and Fanshawe walked to the door with Max. 'If I've no info on what's occurred by the morning I'll have to report him to Colonel Dyne as being AWOL.'

'I'll be in touch before then,' Max assured him, then had a final word. 'Of course, if Dan should be involved in anything illegal it will become official.'

Max drove to the Mess in the car he had bought on Saturday, and made coffee in his room. He needed to think without risk of distraction. Farley's failure to report back was curious. Commissioned just two months ago, he would be keen to make his mark. Hence his search for Smith? So, however deeply in thrall to the doggy blonde he might be, he was surely highly unlikely to endanger his infant career now by overstaying his leave. And, melodramatic though it might seem, his link with Smith could not be overlooked. Had someone got rid of them both?

The flood of interest from forces in the UK made the need to trace Smith more urgent, in Max's view. It seemed likely that he had successfully stolen a rifle and ammo a month ago from a well-secured building. Was he planning to revert to dealing in arms; far more serious than music and films? No, he would not have left his SA80 in the wood if that were the case.

Was he the man who had committed theft over a large area of the South of England? Music, films, alcohol, up-market clothes; even a silver golf trophy. A highly successful thief. One with a wide variety of outlets for his haul. Was it possible Smith had enlisted to escape the clutches of the law? Had he hoped to embark on a new, worthwhile life with an army regiment? No, he had taken up his criminal activities again. And had run away again. A leopard and its spots came to mind.

Max stood drinking coffee and gazing blindly from his window. His guts told him there was much more behind the facts they had. He wanted to get to the bottom of why Smith had run, and to where. Then there was the mystery of Dan Farley. What had happened to that love-struck young officer?

On returning to Headquarters he found that Klaus Krenkel's men had sent the list of suspect dealers in CDs and DVDs, along with the venues used by street sellers of mobile phones and iPods, who invariably had moved on by the time the *Polizei* arrived on the scene. Tom was engaged in allotting tasks, so Max slipped into his office and closed the door. An hour later he had traced the Brighteye Kennels in Sussex, whose owners had a daughter named Trish, and he had reserved for himself a seat on the early afternoon flight to Heathrow.

# SEVEN

Heading to Sussex in a hired car, Max felt an almost childish glee in ignoring the satnav. Having been stationed for a number of years within the military parameters of southern England, he knew the area well enough to avoid the lengthy detours these gadgets tended to select, and took the swiftest route to Brighteye Kennels on the outskirts of Lewes.

He had elected to start by investigating the outcome of Dan Farley's romantic weekend, because the young officer risked a charge of absence without official leave on the morrow. If he had been fool enough to put infatuation for the girl before his career he deserved all he would get, but Max hoped to uncover mitigating circumstances. He had been impressed by Farley's brief service record. To throw away such potential for an uncertain sexual relationship would be insane. Now twenty-three, Farley would surely encounter several more women who set him alight before he found one who would stay the course and make a good army wife.

Lost in these thoughts, Max recalled how Susan had set him alight, blinding him to the obvious. She had not taken well to army life; resented his many absences and hated living on Salisbury Plain in winter. After almost four years he still blamed himself for failing to recognize her gradual disenchantment that led her to turn to a corporal with bold eyes and roving hands, who gave her the excitement she had not found in their marriage. Oh yes, he knew well how passion could cloud a man's judgement.

Dining with Clare Goodey on Saturday had made him acutely conscious of how much he missed the company of an attractive woman to share life's pleasures. They had laughed a lot over anecdotes of their respective childhood antics, had discovered mutual interests and had relaxed in the undemanding rapport of professional colleagues.

Max had not attempted to probe Clare's apparent marital split, and she had made no mention of Livya, but that enjoyable evening had made Max even more aware that he needed to be with his lover in a closer, more permanent relationship. Back in his lonely room he had called her but, as she had warned, she was tackling the backlog of work that had accumulated during her absence in Washington and half her mind had clearly been elsewhere. Her warm apology on Sunday had simply exacerbated his frustration.

The possibility of that tree falling a split second later and crushing him had dogged Max over the past week. Not exactly a near-death experience, but pretty damn close enough to one to cause him to review the status quo. So, although he had officially flown to the UK in pursuit of the John Smith case, he fully intended to see Livya and force a resolution to their unsatisfactory situation. First, however, he would visit Brighteye Kennels.

It did not require an automated voice to tell him he had reached his destination; a canine chorus did that. Dogs' dinnertime? He parked by a notice advising visitors to leave their cars in the marked bays, and walked towards the sound of frantic barking. He had always liked dogs. His grandparents had once given him a puppy for Christmas, but they had been obliged to take it back because his father had been posted to Malaysia shortly afterwards. He had tried to persuade Susan that a dog would be good company for her, but she had preferred cats. He had found new homes for the two tabbies after she was killed.

There were a large number of pens in which dogs yelped and bounced with excitement as bowls of dry pellets were distributed by a girl in dungarees. She was too young and dark-haired to be Trish, but she gave a friendly smile and asked if he was expected.

'No, but I'd like a word with Trish, if possible,' he said with a return smile.

'Right. Go back to where you left your car, then follow the hedged path straight ahead. It'll take you up to the house,' she told him above the many-toned barks.

It was some house. Max estimated at least seven bedrooms,

plus a grannie annexe, triple garage and a tennis court. He could not imagine a girl brought up here taking to the prospect of living in a junior officer's married quarters on a military base. Unless, of course, she was deeply in love. Will Fanshawe had had severe doubts about that.

The woman who came at his knock was in her forties, but liable to remain highly attractive through to old age. Good bone structure, as the knowledgeable said. Elegant in linen trousers and a pink spotted shirt, she smiled politely and asked how she could help.

'Mrs Stannard?' Max asked.

'Yes.'

'Captain Rydal.' He showed her his military identification. 'I flew over from Germany this afternoon, and I've made a detour from Heathrow in the hope of speaking to Trish.'

The woman studied him thoughtfully. 'From Germany? You're a friend of Dan Farley?'

'I am, yes. Is he here?'

'No.' There was a moment's hesitation. 'You know my daughter?'

He smiled. 'I feel I do from Dan's enthusiastic descriptions, but Trish and I have never met.'

'Yet it's she you've come to see.'

'Yes.'

Her brow puckered as she clearly fought an inner battle. 'If Dan sent you to mediate, you won't succeed. My daughter tried to revive the relationship, but there are irreconcilable differences. Trish is very upset.'

Honesty was now called for. 'We had a strong suspicion that the meeting had not gone well. I'm not here as a mediator, Mrs Stannard. Dan failed to return to his unit yesterday. His Company Commander is very concerned. It's not like Dan to risk damaging his career in that manner. I had to come over on other business, so I offered to attempt to discover what had occurred to prevent his return. We contacted Lufthansa. Dan did not check in for any of their flights to Germany.'

'Oh dear, he surely hasn't done something foolish. A very *intense* young man.'

'But a highly-trained military officer,' Max returned. 'As such, he would handle most situations calmly and competently.' Feeling he had been kept on the doorstep long enough, he said, 'If I could have a brief chat with Trish?'

Mrs Stannard remembered her manners and stepped back, inviting him in. Max followed her along a wide hallway leading to the rear of the house, across a large sitting room, to a lofty Victorian-style conservatory housing period leisure furniture. There must be money in dogs, thought Max, then was diverted by his hostess's next words.

'My husband is in his study chairing a meeting with his associates in Hong Kong and Shanghai, and can't be disturbed. Please have a seat while I tell Trish you're here.' Making no move, she said, 'I'm certain she has no idea where Dan went from here. They quarrelled, you see. Very bitterly, as I understand it. My husband and I attended church, then went on to lunch with friends. When we came home we found Trish had locked herself in her room and was too emotional to tell us what had upset her.'

It sounded like the behaviour of a young adolescent, to Max, yet the photograph in Farley's room showed her to be around twenty.

Mrs Stannard made to leave the conservatory, then hesitated. 'Dan is a perfectly pleasant young man, but . . . Trish is just nineteen, Captain Rydal. A beautician. Her father set her up in a salon in Lewes, which is doing very well. She now employs three girls. It's ridiculous to talk of marriage. She's far too young, and he's a *soldier*! What sort of life would she have?'

Max was getting a good idea of what Farley had been up against in this family. The girl had surely echoed her parents' views.

'Then there's this terrible business of Afghanistan,' she said in protest. 'How could he expect a girl like Trish to accept that? This family has strong views on our involvement there. Stirring up hatred in the Middle East has serious repercussions on global financial markets.' She apparently remembered who she was lecturing. 'Of course, you're also a soldier, and wouldn't know—'

Breaking off, unsure how to finish that sentence, she said quickly, 'I'll fetch Trish.'

Staying on his feet, Max contemplated the immaculate lawn and borders giving out early evening fragrance. Dan Farley must have been wearing rose-tinted contact lenses during his dealings with Trish Stannard. This entire set-up was at odds with a military life. Had he been besotted enough to actually offer marriage to the girl?

When Trish appeared, Max initially understood the sub-altern's infatuation. Long legs, tantalising figure, long blonde hair and arresting blue-green eyes. At a second glance, Max was aware of her petulant mouth and disdainful expression; they marred the near perfection.

There was no greeting, merely a haughty 'I don't know why he sent you here.'

'He didn't.'

His cool tone apparently threw her slightly. 'Mummy said you're from Dan's unit in Germany.'

Max decided she needed to know the serious business behind his visit. 'I'm with the Special Investigation Branch of the Royal Military Police, Miss Stannard. Lieutenant Farley failed to return to Germany after his visit to you. I'm here to ask you about what occurred before he left you yesterday.'

Alarm, affront, defensiveness were all apparent in her mien as she sank on a chair with studied grace. 'Military Police? What Dan did after storming out has nothing to do with me.'

'Or her family,' added Mrs Stannard, entering at that moment.

Max's eyes narrowed as he studied this pair. 'Something concerning you certainly led to him "storming out". What was that?'

'I don't have to answer questions from you,' she said. 'I'm not a soldier. You can't order *me* about.'

'Perhaps you're not aware that if Dan fails to report back by tomorrow morning, he will be classified as absent without leave. His picture and details will be posted on HOLMES, the worldwide police network. The case will then be taken

up by the Sussex police. Two of their uniformed officers
will come here in a marked car, possibly with blue lights
flashing, to question you. On the other hand, you could
give me a lead on where he might have headed from here.
I'd follow it up and maybe switch interest from Brighteye
Kennels elsewhere. I'm not ordering you about, Trish, I'm
advising you on your options.'

The girl looked up at her mother. 'We need Daddy here.'

'He can't be disturbed, darling.' She appealed to Max.
'Must you harass her like this?'

Max counted to ten. 'A man your daughter has been in
a close relationship with is missing. He has not called in
and his mobile is switched to voicemail. His last known
contact was with this family. Whatever the situation between
Dan and Trish when he "stormed out", you surely wouldn't
wish harm to have come to him. He was a guest in your
house, Mrs Stannard. Don't you care what might have
befallen him when he left it?'

Trish burst into tears. 'He shouldn't have been so beastly.'

Max waited silently, guessing it would all come out now.
She was spoilt and pampered; quite immature. Farley was
better off without her and, if he had behaved irresponsibly
enough to land himself with a serious charge on his record,
he was equally immature. Yet he had seemed well in control
of himself, and dedicated enough to make that unofficial
search for Smith. His guts told Max Dan Farley was in
trouble somewhere.

'Everything was so lovely; he was so *sweet*,' Trish wailed.
'He's always known I'm not happy about him being in the
Army. I said I'd accept that if he changed to an office job.'
She peered at Max through a curtain of wet hair. 'They can
do that in the Army, can't they? He wasn't happy about it,
but he said he'd think about it when he got back from
Afghanistan.'

A further tearful outburst. 'He knew how we feel about
what's happening out there. Daddy put him in the picture.'

'The *wider* picture,' said her mother.

'He's so blind to what happens outside his precious regiment,' the girl complained. 'Wouldn't listen to my side of it.

That's when he got really nasty and said things I couldn't believe I was hearing. I told him it wasn't being a coward to refuse to go out there. There are plenty of other things he can do as a soldier without killing innocent people.'

Max was not prepared to listen any longer to this diatribe. 'Was that when Dan left?'

The girl nodded. 'I don't know where he went, and I don't—'

Max cut her off. 'Was he driving a hire car?'

'No, I met him at Heathrow in mine.'

'So he was on foot. What's the nearest bus route?'

Mrs Stannard answered that. 'They leave the village centre every hour, on the hour, to Brighton.'

'Passing Lewes railway station?'

'Near enough.'

Max turned back to Trish. 'Did he have his overnight bag with him?'

'Yes, it was ready by the door.'

'What time did he leave this house?'

'Around two thirty.'

'So he could have reached the village in time to catch the three o'clock bus.'

She put her hand to her mouth. 'No, it would be the Sunday service, every *two* hours.'

'There's a taxi firm in the village?'

'On Sunday you have to call from the phone on the wall outside the office. Jem Hawkins comes out from the farm to pick you up.'

'Unless he's already booked,' said Mrs Stannard. 'He often is on Sundays.'

Max left Brighteye Kennels sloughing off a sensation of claustrophobia. He had come upon that kind of set-up before, and had felt the same way. The husband was usually a mini-mogul living for the fast buck, the mega-deal, the element of power the world of international commerce gave him. The women hung on his coat tails, filling their days with shopping, visits to beauty salons, lunches with friends and participation on committees of local charities. Max thought one comment from Mrs Stannard had said it all. 'Dan is a perfectly pleasant young man but . . . he's a *soldier*!' Whatever had led Farley to believe he could ever enter the Stannards' world?

Jem Hawkins was heading for the black and yellow car that was the local taxi when Max drew up outside his office. Max wound his window down and leaned out.

'Mr Hawkins?'

'That's me,' he replied genially, stepping across to Max's hired vehicle. 'You don't need my services, I can see, so how can I help?'

Max smiled. 'I've no wish to keep you from picking up a fare.'

'Don't you worry. I'm just off for my supper before the late evening calls start coming in.'

'I drove down from London on the off chance of catching up with a friend I've not seen in a while, but he left yesterday afternoon around fourteen . . .' He pulled himself up. 'Around two thirty. Did someone call you to take him to the airport?'

'Oh, aye,' he said with a nod. 'My boy, Phil, radioed through to me when he received the call on his mobile. He was parked waiting to pick up a party of old dears at the Nag's Head in Dunderton, so he couldn't accept the fare.'

The silver-haired man, thin as a greyhound and suffering from halitosis, was apparently in no hurry for his supper. He leaned on the roof of Max's hired car and bent to puff rancid breath over him. 'I says to Phil to tell the caller what the boy should've done right off, that we don't do the airports. He does this, then the fare says how about Brighton rail station? Well, we don't do long trips on Sundays, d'you see? Sundays is always busy with regulars, but it turned out I was collecting a couple from the Golden Hynde way over to Meerston Ford. So I says to Phil I could take the fare to *Lewes* rail station, if he cared to start walking towards Meerston. Soon as I'd dropped Mr and Mrs Flint home, I'd drive down to meet the fella and take him on to the railway.'

'So you dropped him there?' asked Max, breaking into the long-winded answer.

'Well, I woulda done, you see. My Phil said as how the fare had told him he were desperate to get to a rail station, which I were prepared to do, but I never saw hair nor hide of him.'

'You missed him?'

Hawkins shifted his feet and leaned on his other arm. The movement did not lessen the stench of his breath. 'No, that weren't it. See, Meerston is out on the Lewes Road. Phil tells me the caller described himself as a young, dark-haired man carrying a blue holdall, but I drove all the road back to the village without a sign of him. There's only one way straight up to Lewes, so it couldn't have been that he took another route.'

'But it's possible someone stopped to give him a lift all the way to Brighton.'

'Oh, aye. Guess that's what it must of been.'

Leaving Hawkins to head for his supper, Max drove first to Lewes and then on to Brighton, knowing the chances of finding anyone who recalled seeing the young officer at rail stations were slim. If Farley had hired a car from one of the towns, there would more likely be some recognition by office staff. There might also be a clue to Dan's destination if the vehicle had been registered as returned.

Max drew a blank at both locations, by which time he guessed his suspicion could be right. Somewhere between the village taxi office where Farley had definitely used the telephone on the wall, and Meerston Ford from where Jem Hawkins was driving to meet him, something happened to the missing lieutenant. In Max's opinion this had now become an official case for SIB, and he was on the spot to investigate.

Sitting in the car in a Brighton car park, he rang Farley's mobile. Still switched to voicemail. Then he called the parents' home and casually asked to speak to Dan. The woman expressed regret, saying her son was presently in Germany. She sounded genuine, although she could be covering for him with great skill. Next, Max called Tom, who answered against a background of TV and girls' laughter.

'I'm in Brighton. Has Farley turned up, by any chance?'

'Captain Fanshawe said he'd notify me if he did. Hold, and I'll check.' Several minutes later, he said, 'Not a sign, and his mobile's still on voicemail.'

'I know. His mother claims he's in Germany. I just called her.'

'Could be lying.'

'If necessary we'll get the local boys to check. Tom, there's something about this I don't like. The girlfriend told me he stormed out with his overnight bag at fourteen thirty yesterday. He booked a taxi in the village, then failed to be in the pickup area. I've had no luck at rail stations or car hire firms so, unless someone gave him a lift right through to Heathrow, he's probably still somewhere between the south coast and London.'

'Face it, he could be anywhere by now. So we're mounting a case?'

'Yes. I seriously doubt this guy has gone AWOL. I'd guess what he felt for the girl was well and truly cancelled out yesterday. Rather than run away, he'd return to the life he loves with increased determination. Something happened down here to prevent him taking that flight on Sunday night. Get the team checking UK hospitals right away. If there's no joy there, first thing tomorrow enter Farley's details on HOLMES as missing under curious circumstances.'

'Got it,' said Tom. 'Are we linking this with Smith?'

'Let's leave that in the air for the moment.'

'You don't think Farley could be hiding out at the kennels?'

'No way. That girl and her mother rate soldiers so low I'm amazed Farley was ever allowed to darken their doorstep. Let's move fast on this. I've a bad feeling about it.'

Ending the call, Max sat for a few moments considering his next move. It was now almost nine p.m. and the August sun was setting. By the time he reached Bournemouth it would be too late to visit Smith's parents. That would have to wait until morning. He was hungry and needed a bed for the night. Pointless trying to find an available room in a beach resort during school holidays; better to drive west and stop at a small wayside pub before it ceased providing meals.

Before moving off he called Livya's landline. Answer machine. He punched in her mobile number. Voicemail. He left a brief message giving no indication of his whereabouts. If she returned his call later, he still would not tell her he was in the UK. As things were, he could not gauge when he would be free to see her and have that vital discussion on their future.

Finding a meal and a small but comfortable room at an inn near Sompting, Max enjoyed the convivial atmosphere until he began to yawn. As often happened, his mind remained busy when his body told him to rest. Although his mission tomorrow was to gain information about John Smith, it was Dan Farley who occupied his thoughts as he lay in the double bed facing a small window.

Driving from the village to Lewes he had studied the route with a policeman's eye. Long stretches with no signs of habitation between small clusters of cottages and muddy tracks leading to farms. Little possibility of witnesses to a car or lorry taking up a young man carrying a blue holdall, unless other vehicles had passed at that precise time. A general call for drivers of those vehicles would have to go out if Farley was not soon traced. Although not wearing uniform, he would have his service identity on him and, in these days of terrorist activity, the taking of a military hostage was an ever-present risk.

Tom presided over the morning briefing, glad the ball was back in SIB's court. Last night four members of the team had called every hospital within a semi-circular area surrounding Brighteye Kennels. They judged this by calculating how far a vehicle could conceivably travel between fourteen thirty on Sunday and the time of the last flight to Germany that same night. That only dealt with the supposition that Farley had been offered a lift to a point where he could easily reach Heathrow; that a car he was travelling in as a passenger, or one he had hired and was driving, had been involved in an accident so serious he was unable to call the base. The two women sergeants and Derek Beeny, and Olly Simpson, who had both returned from UK leave, all offered negative results in this task.

'Heather and I took the western sector, although he was unlikely to be heading in that direction if he intended to take that evening flight,' said Connie.

'According to the taxi driver he was in a panic to reach Lewes station,' added Heather. 'Surely that indicates his determination to return?'

'Not necessarily,' put in Phil Piercey. 'It's possible to travel to the ends of the earth from Lewes. A guy on the run would be in a panic to reach a rail station.'

'Why would he be on the run? It was just a row with the girlfriend,' jeered Heather.

Piercey adopted the superior expression he used during spats with her. 'Isn't the obvious staring us in the face? Farley put an end to Smith during the exercise, then went out there solo to move the body to a more permanent resting place and plant Smith's rifle and kit in the wood to divert searchers to that area. He gets Brownie points for his brave effort to trace one of his men, which earns him a semi-official seventy-two in the UK, ostensibly to mend a break with his girl but in reality to make his getaway.'

'He did see his girl. The mother confirmed that he was there, and the pair terminated the relationship, after which he stormed out,' Connie reminded him.

'And we accept that as gospel?' he countered. 'They're all lying.'

'Including the taxi driver?' snapped Heather.

'No, not the taxi driver,' Piercey said with mocking patience. 'His son gets a call from a male wanting to be taken to Heathrow. A compromise shortens the journey to Lewes rail station, and he agrees to walk along to where the father would pick him up. The unknown male tells the son – still on the phone, mark you – to tell the father to look out for a young, dark-haired man carrying a blue holdall. That description would fit any number of men. What proof is there that the caller was Farley? Come to that, what proof have we that the caller *was* young, dark-haired and carrying a blue holdall? Neither father nor son ever saw him. It could have been a local yobbo baiting the taxi family.'

As usual, Piercey had propounded a dramatic theory that was on the wild side, but actually just within the bounds of possibility. Tom recognized the reasoning behind it and hesitated before commenting, as did the rest of the team.

'OK, let's consider that,' he said eventually. 'As far as the first part of the theory is concerned, it should be easy enough to check whether Lieutenant Farley was operating closely enough to Smith to be in isolation with him at some time during the assault, so he could kill him and hide the body to retrieve later.'

Even as he outlined this, Tom sensed he was dealing with pulp fiction, but he pursued the theme further. 'The second development in this scenario is perfectly possible. Farley was out on that exercise ground alone for an entire weekend. The storm extended the time, of course, but he could have interred a body and planted equipment well away from the burial site in a reasonably short time.'

Piercey was nodding agreement, much to the evident annoyance of Heather Johnson. Tom continued with his summary:

'The girlfriend and the mother could have been lying about Farley's visit and the row that sent him from the house with no means of transport, and that would make them accessories to a killer's escape from justice.'

As Heather opened her mouth to protest, Tom frowned her into silence. 'The last premise is something I have to accept as sound. The taxi-driving father and son received a phone booking around the time Farley is said to have left Brighteye Kennels. Neither of them ever saw the caller, and that description certainly could fit numerous men. Therefore it has to be discounted as evidence related to the disappearance of Dan Farley.'

Heather opened her mouth once more, but Tom pushed on before she could make her point. 'Now we have to consider the negatives. Lieutenant Farley only joined the West Wilts two months ago. In that brief period would he have found cause enough to kill one of his platoon – not an NCO with whom he'd have considerable contact, but a private soldier he had had no personal dealings with? No disciplinary charge to handle; no request from Smith for an interview. In addition, even supposing there to be cause to kill, why do it when the risk of being seen was so high?'

'Temporary insanity,' put in Piercey as Tom paused for breath.

Ignoring that, Tom rounded off his case for dismissing the entire premise. 'Having committed murder and success-fully disposed of the corpse, why immediately make a run for it and advertise himself as the killer? We had never hinted that we had him marked as a suspect; and he had put himself firmly on the side of right by recovering the rifle and kit. Why ask for extra leave to visit the girlfriend, knowing we could easily check that? Why not casually drive from the base on Friday evening and not return?

'And before you produce inventive answers to those questions, Piercey, consider the fact that our canny boss is experienced enough to know when people are lying. He believes the account of a lovers' quarrel that sent Farley from the house in a fury. He also believes something stopped him from catching that flight as he fully intended. Something serious enough to prevent him sending word of any kind to account for his absence. All in all, I go for the assumption that a military officer has come to harm. We must act on that belief.'

# EIGHT

Max took advantage of a full English breakfast before heading for Bournemouth, and was glad of the fact on encountering a police diversion sending all west-ward bound traffic through Lyndhurst. Always a bottleneck, in August the narrow main street became choked with Auto-Sleepers, caravans, cars with laden roof racks, cyclists, hikers and motorbikes. Today's diversion created chaos and a tailback stretching to the M27, where Max joined it.

After seventy-five minutes of inch-by-inch progress, Max reached an area where a number of vehicles began turning right into a restricted-width lane. He followed, guessing the drivers knew something strangers to the area did not. He guessed correctly. Although this lane eventually emerged to the west of Lyndhurst, enough people had taken it to create a mini tailback at the junction with the main road. He had avoided the worst of the congestion, however.

Once on the A35 and chugging sedately towards Bournemouth in the bumper-to-bonnet stream of traffic, Max could not help a smirk of glee at the thought of all the satnavs telling people to take roads that were closed off. All the same, he used his after stopping at the Cat and Fiddle pub for half a shandy and the use of the toilet, which large numbers of drivers who had been stuck for hours on the road were also doing.

At twelve thirty, the Smiths were likely to be at home for lunch. Max had not phoned ahead. If John Smith was hiding out with his parents it would have given him time to skedaddle. When he reached the Kinson area, the automated female voice told him he had reached his destination outside a semi in a long street of similar houses. Max said a polite 'Thank you, ma'am,' and drove on until he found a kerbside space free to park in.

Back outside number eleven he pushed the bell, noting

the clean, crisp net curtains at the bay windows and the spotless red and fawn tiles of the tiny forecourt between the door and the low front wall bordering the pavement. Mrs Smith was obviously house-proud. She was also older than Max had expected. John Smith was already twenty, so Max had put the mother at around forty-five. The woman who opened the door was nearer sixty, he guessed. Had Smith been a midlife surprise?

Max smiled and asked if she was Mrs Stella Smith.

'Yes,' she replied cautiously. 'We don't want to change to paying for our gas with the electric company.'

'It's nothing like that,' Max assured her, holding up his service identity. 'I've come to talk to you about your son. And to your husband, if he's at home.'

The woman's expression immediately softened and pale pink tinted her cheeks. 'Oh, how kind of you to keep in touch with us. Please come in. Ted'll be so bucked by your visit. Not a day passes without us talking about John. Our only child, as you know. Come in, come in,' she invited warmly, stepping aside to allow him access to a long, maroon-carpeted hallway.

Squeezing past Max after shutting the door, she led him to the end of the narrow passage smelling of furniture polish and a mouth-watering aroma from the kitchen. Stella Smith was either a remarkable actress, or the absent soldier was not here.

Edward Smith was in a wheelchair and looked even older than his wife. His thin face lit with pleasure when Stella explained why Max had come. 'Sorry,' she added, turning to him. 'I didn't catch your name. I'm awful with names. They go straight in and straight out again. Sign of old age.'

'Not at all. Many young people are the same,' Max returned, liking her lack of artifice. Concentrating on the invalid, he offered his hand. 'I'm Max Rydal, Mr Smith.'

His handshake was firm as Edward expressed his thanks. 'It's very good of you to come, Mr Rydal. People knock the police so often, but it's not always deserved.'

Stella hovered at Max's elbow. 'I'm sure you could manage a cup of tea or coffee, couldn't you?'

'Or something stronger,' said Edward.

'Ted! He's on duty.'

'No, he's not. He's come unofficial. We'll both have a beer, Stel.'

By now certain this pair had no idea their son had become the subject of an international police search, Max thought the news he would have to give them shortly would come more easily in a relaxed atmosphere.

'He's been a wonderful son,' Edward said as his wife went to the kitchen. 'No parents could ask for better. Since he went we've spoken about him every day. His room's just as he left it. His mother keeps it immaculate.' He gave a wry grin. 'Not the way it was when he was here, mind you. But all lads are untidy and thoughtless, aren't they? No! John was *never* thoughtless. I shouldn't have said that.'

The man seemed excessively upset over a casual slip of the tongue. Maybe his medical condition made him emotional. 'Half the time it's not thoughtlessness in its most frequently used sense,' Max said. 'I've a friend with three girls who could be dubbed thoughtless, but it's more a case of children packing so much into their lives that their minds flit from subject to subject without giving them time to delve deeper.'

'Do you have children, Mr Rydal?' asked Stella, catching the end of that comment as she handed Max a small glass tankard of beer. The Smiths were of the generation that did not dream of drinking from cans or bottles.

'I hope to be a father one day,' he replied, with the slight twinge of grief he still felt whenever he was asked that question.

'They're the Lord's greatest blessing,' she said, giving another tankard to her husband. 'But whoever said our children are only loaned to us was right.'

'But they're never forgotten,' murmured Edward gazing into his beer.

'*Never!*'

'Tell me about John,' invited Max, thinking it time to get to the business he must broach.

He was then treated to a flood of parental memories from

run-up to the funeral, which must have been when he stole Smith's identity. Edward Smith has just told me Jack began thieving at a very young age. The poor guy was paralyzed in the hit and run, and neither of them has yet been able to accept the loss of their boy. They've been further devastated by what I told them.' A sigh preceeded Max's next words. 'The real downside of our job, eh?'

'All the more reason to catch the bastard.'

'In old-fashioned terms that's what Carr is. Edward Smith's brother impregnated Ms Carr and vanished on hearing the news.'

'Sounds familiar.'

'I'm now en route to Acton where the mother lives. With luck, I'll find Carr hiding out there.'

'Pity we can't copy the Yanks and put people like him in chains on apprehending them.'

'He won't get an easy ride from us, or from the police of several coastal counties over here. Tom, any info on Dan Farley?'

'Nothing. All we can be reasonably sure of is that he's still in the UK. We've posted details on HOLMES so it's out of our hands.'

'Pity.'

'You don't think there's a link between him and Jack Carr?'

'No. Farley's disappearance is involuntary.'

'I agree.'

'Keep in touch. I should be back some time tomorrow.'

Tom sat for a long moment, deep in thought. The discovery of Smith's real identity would mean an investigation into how he was processed during enlistment. It would not be the first time a man had joined one of the services under false colours to escape a scandal or arrest, but this one appeared to have left his chosen safe haven to escape once more from discovery and arrest. Once a thief, always a thief.

Deciding tomorrow morning was soon enough to reveal Carr's duplicity to the team, Tom drove home relishing the thought of a long, relaxing evening with his family. He was

a father and mother of a son they loved and were immensely proud of. Max began mentally to question such blind devotion of a boy whose unpleasant personality had set all his fellow squaddies disliking him intensely, until Edward outlined his son's scholastic achievements. John Smith's service record showed he had very mediocre GCSE results. These parents claimed he had gained As and Bs in his A levels. A deep suspicion began to form in Max's mind, and it was very soon borne out.

'When he was offered a place at Bath University it was the proudest day of our lives,' Edward confessed with a break in his voice. 'Our boy would have gone far and made us even prouder.'

Max knew he would have to hurt these good people further, for it was now certain they were talking about a son who had died. Certainly not the detested individual who had disappeared during a military exercise. Quietly, and as tactfully as he could, he explained that he was there because they had been named as next of kin by Private John Smith of the West Wiltshire Regiment, who had gone missing in Germany.

Stella stared at him accusingly. 'I thought you were a policeman. I thought you'd come to follow up after the hit and run. See how we were coping.'

'I am a policeman. A military one,' he corrected gently. 'Believe me, I'm as upset as you over this misunderstanding. When I asked you to tell me about John, I had no idea your son had been killed in a road accident.'

It was too much for Stella. Pulling her apron up to her eyes she left the room and the two men who were facing up to the difficult situation.

Although visibly upset, Edward was eager to get to the bottom of the unpleasant facts. 'You say there's a person in the German Army who claims to be my son?'

'Not in the *German* army, Mr Smith; in our army out in Germany. He enlisted as John Smith and gave your name and this address when asked for details of his next of kin. I'm afraid it looks like a case of stolen identity.'

Pain shadowed the invalid's face. 'Took our John's good

name and dragged it through the mud? I'll never forgive him, whoever he is.'

'He could have taken the details from some item your son lost, and applied for a replacement birth certificate to support his alias, or he could be someone who knows your family.' He took from his pocket the picture of John Smith and showed the man in the wheelchair. 'Do you recognize this person?'

'That's Jack!' he cried. 'My bloody stepbrother's bastard. He's been taking our John's name in vain? I'll kill him!'

Max watched the older man's grief spill over, and waited until Edward Smith had gained sufficient composure to continue. He then heard a fairly familiar story about a womanizing drifter who thought the world owed him an easy living, and about the woman who became pregnant with his son and never saw him again after breaking that news.

'I tried to help them out whenever I had a bit to spare,' he told Max thickly. 'She's all right, just a bit too trusting. Believed everything Charlie told her. We felt sorry for her. But that brat of hers! A right chip off the old block. Creepy little bastard. Tried getting round Stella whenever we visited.' His eyes glazed again. 'She's soft, is Stella. Felt kind of guilty because she had a husband and loving son, whereas Min . . . Stella tried to be fond of Jack, but even a motherly woman like her couldn't take his slyness. Several times after visiting them we suspected he had taken money from Stella's purse. Yes, and once it was a powder compact,' he added, remembering. 'Mother of pearl lid. A birthday present from her sister. It was missing after our visit, and my wife swore she'd not lost it somewhere.'

'When did you last see Jack, Mr Smith?'

'At John's funeral, a year ago today.' He gave a heavy sigh. 'That's why we thought you were from the police. Checking on how we were coping. Stupid! As if they have time for things like that.' There was silence while he mulled that over, then he pulled his thoughts back to the subject under discussion. 'After the accident, Min came to stay with Stella. If I'd been here I'd have sent them both packing,

good intentions or not. As I told you, Stella's soft[...] wasn't up to making decisions with our wonderful boy[...] and me in hospital.'

Max frowned. 'You were ill?'

'I was hit by the car that took John from us. We[...] walking together when it mounted the pavement. I[...] was drunk. He'll be out and driving again by Christ[...] he said with venom. 'I'll never drive again, and [...] never learned. I suppose Min was very kind at that te[...] time. Ran Stella around to make all the arrangemen[...] that left Jack alone in this house. God knows what [...] up to.'

Overcome once more, he turned away to gaze fr[...] window in silence. At that point, Stella came back[...] red around the eyes, and began to apologize. Max s[...] her as he got to his feet.

'Your husband has told me details of the traged[...] Smith. I'm extremely sorry to have revived painful n[...] ies for you both. If you could give me the address of[...] mother, I'll leave you in peace.'

Tom had spent the afternoon following up Corkhil[...] White's confessions of their incitement of Smith,[...] had resulted in his act of theft from the Armoury. T[...] all repeated what they had said at the first SIB inte[...] but one of them must have been careless. Howeve[...] John Smith was at stealing, security should have [...] tight it was impossible for arms or ammunition to b[...]

After his fruitless questioning Tom was back in hi[...] locking confidential papers away in the safe prepar[...] heading for home, when his mobile rang. It was Max[...]

'John Smith's disappearance is definitely a case[...] Tom. His real name is Jack Carr, and I'm prett[...] certain he is the man wanted for those thefts along t[...] coast of the UK.'

Tom's interest was immediate. 'So we'll get [...] enlisting under a false identity too.'

'John Smith was his cousin, killed by a hit and r[...] a year ago. Carr was in the Smiths' house alone d[...]

surprised to hear Nora's sewing machine racing in an otherwise silent house. He walked through to the dining room,
where she usually did her dressmaking.

She glanced up at his entry and smiled. 'Hallo, love.
Coming home at a reasonable hour is getting to be a habit
with you.'

'Where are the brats?'

'On their way.' She tilted her face up for his kiss and
grinned wickedly. 'So no time for what you probably have
in mind.'

'When is there ever? I swear they have antennae that
twang whenever we're here together, telling them to rush
back before we can get started.'

Nora laughed. 'That crack on the head at Easter not only
gave you concussion, it also turned you into the male equivalent of a nympho.'

'I've always been one. You've just been too busy to
notice,' he chaffed in return. 'What's that you're making?'

'D'you like the colour?'

He ran his eye over the cascade of pale green silky material on the table, and the small piece she was stitching.
'Not a bride's dress, is it? Someone wants a swish outfit
to wear at a wedding or a christening?'

'*I* want a swish outfit to wear to the Sergeants' Mess
Christmas do.' She got to her feet and showed him the
image on the paper pattern. 'The summer wedding panic
is over and the Christmas and New Year orders will soon
flood in. I never have time to make anything for myself to
wear, on the off chance that you'll be free to take me to
parties, so I'm taking advantage of this quiet period.' She
dug him in the ribs. 'Well, *say* something.'

'Put a long zip up the back. I found the last one you
made, with rows of fancy buttons, a hell of a job for a male
nympho to take off you in a hurry.'

Her eyes sparkled. 'You're pushing your luck, chum.
There's plenty of beefcake on this base to choose from.'

A sound like a gunshot, followed by excited young
voices, sent Tom swiftly to the front door with a racing
heartbeat. Outside was a brightly-painted jalopy, which had

just backfired. It was disgorging the three Black sisters, leaving two boys and the driver in the vehicle. All six were in laughing high spirits until they spotted Tom approaching.

Maggie anticipated his wrath. 'Jake's got a licence, Dad. He's been driving for six months,' she said, standing in Tom's path. 'He gave us a lift from the base.'

Tom circled his daughter to reach the car. 'D'you realize what would have happened if the *Polizei* had seen you carrying five passengers in this old banger?' he demanded grimly.

Jake, a knowing-looking lad in his late teens, said defiantly, 'They never patrol this area.'

'You've had that info from their headquarters, have you, sonny?'

Bristling at the 'sonny', as Tom knew he would, Jake continued to argue. 'It's a well-known fact.'

'One not apparently known by squaddies caught by them as they return to base on Saturday nights.'

'I'm not pissed,' he retaliated.

'You're breaking the law by overloading a vehicle.'

'*Dad!*' cried his daughters in unified protest.

He turned to them, saying quietly, 'Go indoors. Mum's preparing supper.'

They knew him well enough to recognize when he was in no mood to listen, so they went sullenly to the house as Tom demanded to see Jake's driving licence. He could not produce it, saying he never bothered to carry it when he was just driving locally.

'You'd better carry it from now on, because I'll stop you whenever I see you and ask to check it. Tomorrow morning you'll bring it to 26 Section Headquarters, along with all the documents pertaining to the purchase of that apology for a passenger vehicle, and the certificates of road-worthiness you're required by law to obtain. In the base, you're not immune to the laws governing the owning and driving of any motorized vehicle,' Tom continued in his most seriously professional tone. 'The base isn't a military playground: it's British territory where the laws apply as fully as they do in the UK. Only the fact that a father and mother of a son they loved and were immensely proud of. Max began mentally to question such blind devotion of a boy whose unpleasant personality had set all his fellow squaddies disliking him intensely, until Edward outlined his son's scholastic achievements. John Smith's service record showed he had very mediocre GCSE results. These parents claimed he had gained As and Bs in his A levels. A deep suspicion began to form in Max's mind, and it was very soon borne out.

'When he was offered a place at Bath University it was the proudest day of our lives,' Edward confessed with a break in his voice. 'Our boy would have gone far and made us even prouder.'

Max knew he would have to hurt these good people further, for it was now certain they were talking about a son who had died. Certainly not the detested individual who had disappeared during a military exercise. Quietly, and as tactfully as he could, he explained that he was there because they had been named as next of kin by Private John Smith of the West Wiltshire Regiment, who had gone missing in Germany.

Stella stared at him accusingly. 'I thought you were a policeman. I thought you'd come to follow up after the hit and run. See how we were coping.'

'I am a policeman. A military one,' he corrected gently. 'Believe me, I'm as upset as you over this misunderstanding. When I asked you to tell me about John, I had no idea your son had been killed in a road accident.'

It was too much for Stella. Pulling her apron up to her eyes she left the room and the two men who were facing up to the difficult situation.

Although visibly upset, Edward was eager to get to the bottom of the unpleasant facts. 'You say there's a person in the German Army who claims to be my son?'

'Not in the *German* army, Mr Smith; in our army out in Germany. He enlisted as John Smith and gave your name and this address when asked for details of his next of kin. I'm afraid it looks like a case of stolen identity.'

Pain shadowed the invalid's face. 'Took our John's good

name and dragged it through the mud? I'll never forgive
him, whoever he is.'

'He could have taken the details from some item your
son lost, and applied for a replacement birth certificate to
support his alias, or he could be someone who knows your
family.' He took from his pocket the picture of John Smith
and showed the man in the wheelchair. 'Do you recognize
this person?'

'That's Jack!' he cried. 'My bloody stepbrother's bastard.
He's been taking our John's name in vain? I'll kill him!'

Max watched the older man's grief spill over, and waited
until Edward Smith had gained sufficient composure to
continue. He then heard a fairly familiar story about a
womanizing drifter who thought the world owed him an
easy living, and about the woman who became pregnant
with his son and never saw him again after breaking that
news.

'I tried to help them out whenever I had a bit to spare,'
he told Max thickly. 'She's all right, just a bit too trusting.
Believed everything Charlie told her. We felt sorry for her.
But that brat of hers! A right chip off the old block. Creepy
little bastard. Tried getting round Stella whenever we
visited.' His eyes glazed again. 'She's soft, is Stella. Felt
kind of guilty because she had a husband and loving son,
whereas Min . . . Stella tried to be fond of Jack, but even a
motherly woman like her couldn't take his slyness. Several
times after visiting them we suspected he had taken money
from Stella's purse. Yes, and once it was a powder compact,'
he added, remembering. 'Mother of pearl lid. A birthday
present from her sister. It was missing after our visit, and
my wife swore she'd not lost it somewhere.'

'When did you last see Jack, Mr Smith?'

'At John's funeral, a year ago today.' He gave a heavy
sigh. 'That's why we thought you were from the police.
Checking on how we were coping. Stupid! As if they have
time for things like that.' There was silence while he mulled
that over, then he pulled his thoughts back to the subject
under discussion. 'After the accident, Min came to stay with
Stella. If I'd been here I'd have sent them both packing,

good intentions or not. As I told you, Stella's soft. She wasn't up to making decisions with our wonderful boy dead and me in hospital.'

Max frowned. 'You were ill?'

'I was hit by the car that took John from us. We were walking together when it mounted the pavement. Driver was drunk. He'll be out and driving again by Christmas,' he said with venom. 'I'll never drive again, and Stella never learned. I suppose Min was very kind at that terrible time. Ran Stella around to make all the arrangements, but that left Jack alone in this house. God knows what he got up to.'

Overcome once more, he turned away to gaze from the window in silence. At that point, Stella came back rather red around the eyes, and began to apologize. Max stopped her as he got to his feet.

'Your husband has told me details of the tragedy, Mrs Smith. I'm extremely sorry to have revived painful memories for you both. If you could give me the address of Jack's mother, I'll leave you in peace.'

Tom had spent the afternoon following up Corkhill's and White's confessions of their incitement of Smith, which had resulted in his act of theft from the Armoury. The staff all repeated what they had said at the first SIB interviews, but one of them must have been careless. However adept John Smith was at stealing, security should have been so tight it was impossible for arms or ammunition to be taken.

After his fruitless questioning Tom was back in his office, locking confidential papers away in the safe preparatory to heading for home, when his mobile rang. It was Max calling.

'John Smith's disappearance is definitely a case for SIB, Tom. His real name is Jack Carr, and I'm pretty damn certain he is the man wanted for those thefts along the south coast of the UK.'

Tom's interest was immediate. 'So we'll get him for enlisting under a false identity too.'

'John Smith was his cousin, killed by a hit and run driver a year ago. Carr was in the Smiths' house alone during the

run-up to the funeral, which must have been when he stole
Smith's identity. Edward Smith has just told me Jack began
thieving at a very young age. The poor guy was paralyzed
in the hit and run, and neither of them has yet been able
to accept the loss of their boy. They've been further devastated by what I told them.' A sigh preceeded Max's next
words. 'The real downside of our job, eh?'

'All the more reason to catch the bastard.'

'In old-fashioned terms that's what Carr is. Edward
Smith's brother impregnated Ms Carr and vanished on
hearing the news.'

'Sounds familiar.'

'I'm now en route to Acton where the mother lives. With
luck, I'll find Carr hiding out there.'

'Pity we can't copy the Yanks and put people like him
in chains on apprehending them.'

'He won't get an easy ride from us, or from the police
of several coastal counties over here. Tom, any info on Dan
Farley?'

'Nothing. All we can be reasonably sure of is that he's
still in the UK. We've posted details on HOLMES so it's
out of our hands.'

'Pity.'

'You don't think there's a link between him and Jack
Carr?'

'No. Farley's disappearance is involuntary.'

'I agree.'

'Keep in touch. I should be back some time tomorrow.'

Tom sat for a long moment, deep in thought. The
discovery of Smith's real identity would mean an investigation into how he was processed during enlistment. It would
not be the first time a man had joined one of the services
under false colours to escape a scandal or arrest, but this
one appeared to have left his chosen safe haven to escape
once more from discovery and arrest. Once a thief, always
a thief.

Deciding tomorrow morning was soon enough to reveal
Carr's duplicity to the team, Tom drove home relishing the
thought of a long, relaxing evening with his family. He was

surprised to hear Nora's sewing machine racing in an otherwise silent house. He walked through to the dining room, where she usually did her dressmaking.

She glanced up at his entry and smiled. 'Hallo, love. Coming home at a reasonable hour is getting to be a habit with you.'

'Where are the brats?'

'On their way.' She tilted her face up for his kiss and grinned wickedly. 'So no time for what you probably have in mind.'

'When is there ever? I swear they have antennae that twang whenever we're here together, telling them to rush back before we can get started.'

Nora laughed. 'That crack on the head at Easter not only gave you concussion, it also turned you into the male equivalent of a nympho.'

'I've always been one. You've just been too busy to notice,' he chaffed in return. 'What's that you're making?'

'D'you like the colour?'

He ran his eye over the cascade of pale green silky material on the table, and the small piece she was stitching. 'Not a bride's dress, is it? Someone wants a swish outfit to wear at a wedding or a christening?'

'*I* want a swish outfit to wear to the Sergeants' Mess Christmas do.' She got to her feet and showed him the image on the paper pattern. 'The summer wedding panic is over and the Christmas and New Year orders will soon flood in. I never have time to make anything for myself to wear, on the off chance that you'll be free to take me to parties, so I'm taking advantage of this quiet period.' She dug him in the ribs. 'Well, *say* something.'

'Put a long zip up the back. I found the last one you made, with rows of fancy buttons, a hell of a job for a male nympho to take off you in a hurry.'

Her eyes sparkled. 'You're pushing your luck, chum. There's plenty of beefcake on this base to choose from.'

A sound like a gunshot, followed by excited young voices, sent Tom swiftly to the front door with a racing heartbeat. Outside was a brightly-painted jalopy, which had just backfired. It was disgorging the three Black sisters, leaving two boys and the driver in the vehicle. All six were in laughing high spirits until they spotted Tom approaching.

Maggie anticipated his wrath. 'Jake's got a licence, Dad. He's been driving for six months,' she said, standing in Tom's path. 'He gave us a lift from the base.'

Tom circled his daughter to reach the car. 'D'you realize what would have happened if the *Polizei* had seen you carrying five passengers in this old banger?' he demanded grimly.

Jake, a knowing-looking lad in his late teens, said defiantly, 'They never patrol this area.'

'You've had that info from their headquarters, have you, sonny?'

Bristling at the 'sonny', as Tom knew he would, Jake continued to argue. 'It's a well-known fact.'

'One not apparently known by squaddies caught by them as they return to base on Saturday nights.'

'I'm not pissed,' he retaliated.

'You're breaking the law by overloading a vehicle.'

'*Dad!*' cried his daughters in unified protest.

He turned to them, saying quietly, 'Go indoors. Mum's preparing supper.'

They knew him well enough to recognize when he was in no mood to listen, so they went sullenly to the house as Tom demanded to see Jake's driving licence. He could not produce it, saying he never bothered to carry it when he was just driving locally.

'You'd better carry it from now on, because I'll stop you whenever I see you and ask to check it. Tomorrow morning you'll bring it to 26 Section Headquarters, along with all the documents pertaining to the purchase of that apology for a passenger vehicle, and the certificates of road-worthiness you're required by law to obtain. In the base, you're not immune to the laws governing the owning and driving of any motorized vehicle,' Tom continued in his most seriously professional tone. 'The base isn't a military playground: it's British territory where the laws apply as fully as they do in the UK. Only the fact that

you're now on German territory stops me from reporting
you to the Garrison Commander.'

'Oh, *come on*!' Jake said in incredulous tones. 'You're
not serious.'

'Try me, sonny. If you're not in my office by midday
tomorrow, you'll discover how serious I am.' He began
turning away. 'If you're planning on driving into town now,
don't have more than three passengers in that tub.'

When he was halfway up the path, Tom heard a jeering,
'Is that all, *sir*?'

He spun round. 'No. Never take my daughters for a ride
in that again.'

The pleasant atmosphere indoors had gone. Three girls
sat at the breakfast bar with cold drinks they had not touched;
not a biscuit had been taken from the plate. Nora raised her
brows at Tom as she peeled and sliced apples, but she made
no comment.

Gina, now eleven and growing rebellious, broke the tense
silence. 'Why do you always *spoil* things?'

Tom sat down facing them, and spoke gently. 'You've
been given a ride from the base by a very cocksure boy
and arrived safely home clutching what looks to me like
several brand-new DVDs. You've got glasses of milk and
a plateful of biscuits in front of you, and Mum's preparing
your favourite apple and honey crumble for pudding. If
anything's spoiled, it's you three.'

'You made us look stupid,' Gina countered.

'You do the same when Hans comes,' added Maggie,
almost as angry as her sister.

Tom looked at Beth. 'Aren't you going to join in?'

His youngest daughter shook her lowered head. She was
still very much Daddy's girl, in spite of occasional bursts
of defiance.

'The only stupid person was Jake,' Tom said, still gently.
'He's old enough to drive which, by law, rates him old
enough to be responsible for his actions. He wasn't today.
It wasn't you I was cross with, but him, for involving you
in his carelessness. *Dangerous* carelessness, Blackies!
Anything could suddenly give out in that wreck he's driving,

and it was overloaded. I don't want any of you to be hurt. *Ever*. You're all too precious to Mum and me.' He allowed a suitable silence to hang in the air, then asked what the DVDs were.

Suddenly reanimated, his daughters resumed their normal cross-chatter to enthuse about the films they had bought. Tom looked at them, checking that they were not too horrific or sexually explicit. He had already played the heavy father. Time to restore family calm.

'We bought them on the weekly payment scheme,' Maggie told him anxiously. 'It's legal, Dad.'

He smiled. 'I don't doubt it, sweetheart.'

'Some of the officers' kids can buy them outright. They get *obscene* pocket money,' said Gina, in the language of youth.

'They take the best ones,' Beth complained. 'We have to make do with the leftovers.'

Nora was leaning over Tom's shoulder to see the films. 'You haven't done bad for leftovers. They're all still in their original packaging.'

'They're unwanted presents. Stuff people wouldn't be seen dead watching,' Gina explained, unaware of the ambiguity of what she said.

'Or something they already have,' added Maggie. 'It's a magic idea to get rid of them. Everybody benefits.'

Nora turned back to her cooking. 'There's an awful lot of unwanted presents there. Don't other kids make wish lists like you do?'

Some vague idea entered Tom's mind as the girls raided the biscuits and guzzled milk. They had bought 'unwanted presents' a few days ago.

'Are Jake and his mates taking part in this scheme?'

'It's a *club*, Dad. We told you before,' said Maggie with daughterly forbearance.

'So are they part of it?'

'They run it,' said Gina through a mouthful of biscuit. 'They're sixth-formers.'

'Those three handle all the sales?'

She nodded. 'With Zoe Rogers. She's Jake's girl.'

'She's also good at maths, so she takes the money and keeps records of weekly payments.'

A germ of suspicion was fast growing in Tom's mind. 'So you've been taking in your unwanted DVDs or CDs and got whatever someone's prepared to pay for them?'

'No, Dad,' said Beth. 'Because we always make wish lists we're not given presents we don't want. If you take used ones to the club they can only be exchanged for other used ones. It's only the new ones you can buy.'

'You can *hire* used ones,' Gina reminded Beth.

'At what rate?' asked Tom

'Depends on the condition of the goods,' Maggie told him with authority.

'And Zoe Rogers records the hire payments?'

The girls looked at each other, then Gina said, 'Dad, we just go to the club and get what we want. We don't have anything to do with running it.'

'OK, but you must have earned a bit on the stuff you've taken in.'

'They've been straight swaps. I *told* you we can't sell used stuff,' said Beth with heavy patience.

'So you did.' Tom then asked casually, 'Where is this club?'

'Jake's got a den in his garden,' said Maggie with the kind of eagerness she used when speaking of Hans Graumann, her German boyfriend. 'It's an old summer-house his parents don't use. He's done it up. Made it really groovy. Put all the electrics in it himself. He's into that. In September he's going home to study lighting and effects at the Youth Theatre. Zoe says he's sure to make it big time.'

Nora began setting plates out for supper. 'Isn't Zoe upset that he's leaving next month?'

'No. She's going home too. She's going to audition for RADA. She's going to be an actress.'

'I'm thinking of being an actress,' mused Gina.

'You'll have to lose five stone. Actresses have to be skinny,' Beth told her matter-of-factly.

'I want to be a beautician,' Maggie said dreamily. 'Imagine having all that expensive make-up at special low prices.'

'I still want to work in a zoo,' Beth announced. 'While you two are prancing around trying to be glamorous, I'll be helping endangered species to survive.'

During this familiar girly talk, Tom was putting facts together. All his daughters had just told him made him determined to find out more about Jake's summerhouse enterprise. The lad behind the steering wheel had the look and manner of a budding entrepreneur . . . and entrepreneurs invariably looked after number one. If kids were being conned by Jake and his girl, Zoe, Tom would speedily close that club down.

Somewhere along that train of thought, recollection of Jake's Brummie accent registered. An anonymous telephone call and brand-new DVDs and CDs: both linked with Jack Carr, alias John Smith, whose locker had been full of them.

The moment he saw Minnie Carr, Max knew she was on the game. Hair dyed orangey-blonde, blotchy complexion, brown-painted fingernails, bags beneath eyes whose whites were yellow. In the late afternoon she looked haggard and every one of her forty-something years. Standing on her doorstep in Acton, Max took in the overall picture of a defeated woman in an old mauve wrapper, and pitied her.

Based on what he had been told in Bournemouth, he had no problem imagining her life after being deserted by Charlie Smith. Forever trying to make ends meet while caring for her baby; demeaned by Edward and Stella Smith's occasional offers of financial help; dominated by a growing son with his father's feckless personality. That same son had, for certain, treated his home as a convenient B. and B. without contributing to its upkeep, or helping the mother who had probably pandered to his demands until he joined the West Wilts and disappeared from her life until he needed her again.

Was that moment now? This sad woman would allow him to hide here, Max was certain, and would doubtless give him as much as he wanted from her nocturnal earnings. They could not be large. Alongside teenage prostitutes, this middle-aged woman would be left with the callous and desperate who wanted rough sex on the cheap.

'I'm sorry to disturb you,' he said gently as Minnie Carr stared at him, clutching the wrapper close to her throat. 'Is Jack at home?'

'*Him*?' Her voice was unpleasantly coarse and loud. 'Haven't seen hide nor hair of that rascal for more than a year. Took off with all the cash in the house and my credit card. No word of goodbye, of where he was going. Don't tell me you're a friend of his, because I won't believe you. You're police. I can tell straight off by now. Well, I don't know no more where he is than I did when your pals came just before Christmas.'

Max believed her. 'I know where Jack has been since he left home, Ms Carr.' He showed his service identification. 'My name is Max Rydal. I'm with the Royal Military Police.'

She goggled. '*Military*?'

'Jack joined the West Wiltshire Regiment last year.'

'He must've been bloody crazy. Jack wouldn't let himself be ordered around by nobody.'

'Can we go inside? I'm sure you won't want passing people growing curious about your nightwear.'

Max followed her to a small old-fashioned kitchen where she immediately filled a kettle and set out mugs bearing SAN FRANCISCO and BIG APPLE in red lettering. Places she dreamed of visiting? The room smelled of takeaway meals, probably eaten at breakfast time before she went to bed.

In the silence while the tea was made, Max wondered if there was a chicken and egg situation here. Had Minnie taken to prostitution and driven her son away, or had Jack's desertion forced her to take to the streets? As he always reasoned, surely this woman could have found another way of earning a living without resorting to the world's oldest profession?

Over mugs of tea that had a curious curry flavour, Minnie told her tale of woe that began when Jack became an infant thief.

'At first, he took things to give to me,' she explained in wheedling tones. 'He loved me so much, you see, because he didn't have a dad. That's why he did it. Course, I gave the things back to them he took them from, and he got upset.' She stirred more sugar into her tea and gazed at the swirling liquid. 'I shouldn't of done that. He thought I didn't love him, see. It was a long time after that when I found out he was still taking things, and giving them to school friends. Their mothers came round and asked me to stop Jack from bribing their kids to do things with him.'

She glanced at Max with a much softer expression. 'It was having no dad, see. He wanted everyone else to love him, poor little beggar.'

'What did you tell him about his father?' Max asked, starting to understand Jack Carr a little better.

There was a glow on Minnie's face now. This deluded woman was still in love with the youthful Charlie Smith, Max realized. How did that infatuated image meld with her sordid life?

'When Jack was little I told him his dad was an explorer at the other side of the world. On an expedition to find a secret buried city.' When she smiled, it was as if she was a starstruck girl again. 'I'd read a story about that, so I pretended Charlie was that hero. He was so handsome, you know, and full of life. He *could* have been a heroic explorer.'

It then dawned on Max why this woman was selling herself on the streets. She was a user; had probably had a shot just before he arrived. Her son was not here and she was roaming in fairyland.

'Jack believed it, of course. Boasted about it when kids teased him about having only a mum.' She gazed into a faraway place and appeared to be talking to herself from then on. 'It broke his little heart when that smug John told him about Charlie going off before he was born. He always hated that John. The boy had everything little Jack wanted. So superior, he was. Jack tried to be his friend right from the start, but John told him to get lost. So he hated him from then on, because he had got an expensive camera from somewhere and offered it to his cousin. Know what he did?

The little sod threw it back at my Jack; said he had enough friends already and didn't want one who stole from people and pretended to give presents.' Tears began rolling down her pasty cheeks. Drug-induced misery. 'My precious boy only wanted to *belong*.'

Max got to his feet and put one of his cards on the table beside the BIG APPLE mug. 'My mobile number is on this. If you'd like to call me to talk about your son, at any time, please don't hesitate. I'll let myself out.'

Walking back to where he had left his car, Max reflected on a story he had come across many times in his career. Some man had a night's enjoyment and walked away leaving a trail of unhappiness behind him. Driving through the streets of London that woman's last words stayed with him. He only wanted to *belong*.

# NINE

Dan Farley had gone through a range of negative emotions: disbelief, rage, self-disgust, panic, fear, despair, misery. He had now reached the nadir of his twenty-three years. His own weakness and stupidity had led to this.

He had allowed Trish to make a prize idiot of him. He had weakly surrendered to basic lust; abandoned self-respect to respond to her mating call. He had scattered common sense to the wind by believing she would listen and be persuaded to accept his profession. Instead, he had subjected himself to further lectures on the subject from the whole family, ending with Trish suggesting he should use some ploy to avoid going to Afghanistan.

'It wouldn't make you a coward, darling. You'd be taking a stand against oppression.'

That had finally removed the blinkers; that had delivered the coup de grâce to hormonal madness. He had snatched up his bag and left the house in a fury, eager to distance himself from her as fast as possible. The taxi proprietors were a dead loss. All he could get from them was a vague agreement to take him to Lewes rail station if he was prepared to walk to meet the man along the Lewes Road. But even walking would get him away from Trish, so he had set out still burning with anger.

At Lewes he could catch a train that would eventually get him to the vicinity of Heathrow. Better still he could hire a car, which he should have done on arrival, instead of letting Trish pick him up. Another blinkered decision. He had tramped that country road, counting each step as one more towards the regiment and sanity. He could not get there quick enough.

When the motorbike had pulled up beside him and the rider had asked if he wanted a lift, it had seemed providential.

It had seemed even more so when their short exchange had led to Sean revealing that he was heading for Brighton, and would be glad to take Dan on the pillion. So, like a trusting fool, he had eagerly climbed aboard.

They had not travelled far before several other bikes pulled out from farm tracks to form a small convoy. Even then Dan had not grown suspicious. It was common for several mates to go out in convoy on Sundays. Sean told him they were planning to chat up the talent in Brighton. It sounded about right.

Dan's first slight concern had come when Sean and his three mates turned off the road down a rough track. On asking what was going on, he was told they were just stopping for a coke. It had all happened very quickly after that.

Beside a delapidated barn he had been grabbed and held by the three, while Sean tipped out the contents of the blue bag on the ground and selected two smart shirts and an expensive leather jacket from the pile of clothes. He had then pulled off the gold watch given by Dan's parents on his twenty-first birthday and tossed it in the pannier with the mobile phone.

At that point Dan believed they would ride off, but Sean had by then studied the contents of Dan's wallet, and a simple mugging turned into something much more serious. Discovery of the service identity card turned the four into full-blooded thugs, ranting about squaddies beating them up at the New Year pop concert in Brighton. Throwing insults, they poked him in the chest and slapped him around the head to augment their feelings about military bullies.

He had then been dragged to an upright beam in the disused barn and secured to it by a thick rusty chain, wound several times around his chest beneath his arms and tightly padlocked. After a few more punches and kicks to show their contempt for soldiers, they had walked away, jeeringly telling him that he and his kind were supposed to be tough enough to handle anything, so handle *this*.

Dan had now been a prisoner for two nights and days. After his initial period of self-blame and depression he had rallied, determined to show those louts that soldiers *could* handle anything. He had surveyed the interior of the barn to assess what was available to aid his escape. A disintegrating tractor at the far end of the huge building; a low spread of mouldy hay; a few rusty tools; a wheelbarrow without a wheel. All these were at least twenty yards away.

Much nearer, but still beyond his reach, was a length of rope, loosely coiled. Close to it on a broken plank was a small drum of lubricant. If he could just get hold of that rope! During these days he had wriggled and twisted his upper body in constant endeavours to draw the rope nearer with his feet, but had only succeeded in bruising and tearing his skin as the tightly-wound chain bit into him.

He had then resigned himself to waiting to lose enough body weight to enable him to slip through the chain. Hunger was a problem, of course. His last meal had been a light lunch before Trish had outlined her preposterous terms for an ongoing relationship. It was now late Tuesday evening. Dehydration was not a worry, luckily. It had rained heavily on Sunday night and yesterday, so the rusty container on the cross-beam within arm's length had filled with water from the open section of the rotting roof. Unfortunately, he had also been drenched to the skin and had shivered convulsively until the sunshine had warmed him.

During the period between mid-morning and early afternoon, the sun shone directly on him through the open side of the barn. It was a mixed blessing. Although it dried his clothes, it sapped his strength and made him drowsy. Each time he slept, or when spasms in legs bearing his weight night and day caused him to droop, the pain in his chest increased as the chain bit into now raw and festering flesh.

Throughout his captivity he had regularly moved his limbs to keep the circulation flowing and to retain flexibility. He had kept his brain active by reciting poems and passages of prose that had been compulsory learning for school exams, by quoting the names of classmates and fellow sportsmen, and by vocally itemizing the salient points of lectures on tactics and warfare weaponry learned at Sandhurst. Even so, he was starting to feel unwell and slightly confused.

Throughout the past weary days he had prayed for someone to come down that lane and notice the blue holdall, his clothes in a heap beside it, and the sodden paperback. Someone walking a dog; a pair of lovers; a farmer who owned the land and the broken down barn. His only visitors had been a colony of rats, fat pigeons who dropped through the gaping roof to seek grains on the dusty floor, and a dog fox, whose interest in the scent of human blood was growing worrying.

Leaving Minnie Carr, Max sat behind the wheel with his mobile phone. He first sent Tom a long text outlining his interview with 'Smith's' real parent. Then he called Livya's landline. Answer machine. He tried her mobile and she answered.

'Hi, honey. I'm a weary traveller seeking a bed for the night, and wanting you to be in it with me.'

'Max! Where are you?'

'Acton. Where are *you*?'

'With Andrew. He's giving a small cocktail party. Friends, not VIPs who have to be entertained. What are you doing over here?'

Disappointed by her news, Max said, 'Investigating a case . . . and wanting a serious discussion with you.'

Muted voices in the background told him she had not fully listened. Her next words confirmed that. 'Andrew says join us.'

The last thing he wanted to do. 'I'm not dressed for it.'

More muted voices. 'He says come anyway. It's not a formal affair. Assuming you've a hired car it should take you only forty or so minutes, and you can drive me back to my place later. What a lovely surprise. See you soon.'

That appeared to be that, because she disconnected. For around five minutes he fought the impulse to drive to her apartment and sit outside until she arrived, but he surrendered to the wiser course of action. It was not that he did not wish to see his father – over the past few months they had slowly come to know each other after years of no more than a dutiful relationship – but he was geared up to consolidate future plans, and socializing before he got Livya alone would take up his precious time in the UK.

Deciding that however informal this get-together might be he could not appear dressed as he had been since leaving

Sompting after breakfast, Max freshened up and put on a clean shirt in the toilet of a large department store. When he reached his father's elegant apartment he donned the smart jacket he had packed in his flight bag.

Livya opened the door to him and her kiss set his hopes soaring. They would surely agree on plans for their future. Wearing a cream swirling skirt and the magenta silk shirt he liked so much, she looked as lovely as ever. He silently cursed this delay before they could head for her flat.

The spacious room furnished with pale leather settees and armchairs had assorted glass-topped tables conveniently placed for seated guests and, despite Livya's description of a small cocktail party, Max had expected to see upwards of twenty people standing on the pale-green carpet. Instead, he found just four couples seated comfortably in close proximity, with drinks and small dishes of cocktail savouries on tables beside them. Somewhat disconcertingly, conversation ceased and all eyes turned to study the new arrival.

Andrew rose with a smile and outstretched hand. 'What a lucky chance you could join us, Max.'

Completing the handshake, Max registered his father's immense vitality, which seemed to make nonsense of the exhausting itinerary in Washington Livya had described. A man of impressive physique with well-defined features, green eyes and dark, wavy hair not yet streaked with grey, Andrew Rydal's usual distinguished air was today heightened by additional verve. Max had always felt slightly lacklustre beside his parent, and the feeling was stronger now as he stood before the assessing eyes of these friends.

'How are things after being attacked by a tree?' Andrew asked with apparent concern.

'Fine.' Max had no intention of talking about it before these elegant strangers.

'He's still strapped around the chest. Likely to remain that way for some weeks,' Livya confided. Then she turned to explain to the guests. 'Fractured ribs.'

They all murmured sympathetically as Andrew began the introductions. Max's impression of four couples was erroneous. Two were actually married to each other; the rest were single friends or army colleagues. Livya appeared to know them all well and was at ease in their company.

More so than the host's son, who had spent two significant days following a double investigation and wanted just to relax with her. He was not a lover of cocktail parties and only attended those duty obliged him to. Right now he was having to share the woman he loved and needed with nine others. Small wonder his response to the light conversation was minimal.

One guest was determined to draw him out on the subject of police work, however. Surprisingly, it was a rather glamorous woman his father had introduced as a French cultural envoy. The title conveyed little to Max, save that Helene Dupres must be concerned with the arts. He could not imagine the slender brunette in a beige silk suit to be promoting architecture or the historic development of French civilization. She had the poise of an actress, the eye of an artist in her choice of clothes and accessories, and music in her beguiling voice. Why should she be so interested in the work of a military detective?

After he had given rather stilted answers to her questions, she glanced at Andrew with a warm smile. 'I think your so clever son is very much like you. He obeys orders not to speak of his military activities . . . especially to a *frog*.' Her laughter robbed the comment of any resentment, and everyone also laughed. Then she turned her attention back to Max. 'So we must speak of other things. What do you choose to do when you are not chasing criminals?'

Feeling this was turning into an interrogation before the assembled company, Max offered a prompt and very uncharacteristic reply. 'I chase Livya.'

Unperturbed, Helene asked, 'And do you catch her?'

'Stop tormenting him, my dear,' said Andrew with a laugh. 'Haven't you yet caught on to the fact that we don't discuss affaires de coeur with the openness your countrymen do?'

Unabashed, Helene said, 'Ah, the very cool Englishman! Then I shall ask Livya for the information when we are alone. In French, of course! That will make it allowable in this country.'

Everyone laughed, and Andrew topped up glasses with perfect timing. The minutes passed. Several times Max tried to give Livya an optical message that he wanted to leave, but she did not act on it. Eventually, he decided enough was enough and got to his feet.

'Thank you for asking me to join you,' he said to his father. 'It's been very pleasant, but I must take Livya home now. Our last meeting was cancelled because of your sudden call to Washington, and I have to fly back to Germany tomorrow. My professional demands,' he added, emphasizing that he also did significant work for the Crown. 'I'm sure you'll understand that we have things to discuss before my early flight in the morning.'

'Of course,' Andrew agreed. 'Pity your time in the UK is so limited, but it's good to see you in fine fettle after that brush with storm damage.'

Max said the conventional farewells to cocktail guests one hardly knew, then took Livya's hand to walk from the room. Andrew accompanied them to the door saying, 'When you've wound up your present case, take long leave and come over for a real break. We'd both like that.'

'Let me know when *you're* taking long leave and won't be whisking Livya off to a conference at a moment's notice, and I'll fix it.'

Andrew seemed surprisingly nonplussed for a moment, then he nodded. 'Sorry about last weekend, but you know how it is.'

Livya had collected her light coat during this short exchange, so they said goodbye and left. She was quiet in the lift and while they crossed the hushed foyer where the night porter had just come on duty. Max had left his car at a meter a short walk away through back streets that were empty at that hour; people had already set out for evening entertainment, and were not yet coming home. Livya's high heels clicked rhythmically on the pavement, which was growing damp from fine rain.

By the time they settled in the car it had become a down-pour. Livya dabbed her face dry with a tissue, and pushed back her wet hair. She still had not spoken and Max finally recognized that she was annoyed. Not a good start to what he had planned.

'Sorry to drag you away when you were enjoying your-self,' he said turning to her. 'But we only have tonight together and we need to talk.'

'I agree,' she responded coldly. 'The first thing is to make you aware of my strong objection to being treated as "the little woman". Especially in front of my boss and a group of intelligent people. "It's been very pleasant, but I must take Livya home now",' she mimicked. 'I make my own decisions; you do not make them for me. Because I've allowed you to become my lover, it doesn't give you ownership, Max.'

Stung, he retaliated. 'That applies in reverse. I told you on the phone I wanted to have a serious discussion, but you deliberately obliged me to join a group of strangers for cocktails instead. If it had been an official do to entertain VIPs Andrew has to keep sweet, I would have understood that you couldn't get away, but you weren't there as his ADC tonight and could have left at any time. You cancelled our planned long weekend because duty called. You put me off coming at the weekend just gone because you had to catch up on the backlog of work. I also have a heavy workload; that's why I'm over here now. And I have to return in the morning. Surely Andrew's little drinks party wasn't so important you couldn't have left it to spend this one evening with *someone you have allowed to become your lover*?' He emphasized those words that had hurt him quite deeply.

Starting the engine, he put the car in gear with unneces-sary force and pulled out, the windscreen wipers oscillating madly. At the junction he eased out into the flow of buses and taxis heading for the bright lights of Knightsbridge. Her comment about ownership had really got to him. So much for his bid to strengthen their present relationship. She had more or less told him she valued her independence too much to consider becoming one of a couple.

When he pulled into the parking space allotted to Livya's flat he was half-inclined to let her out, then drive to a hotel for the night, but he knew that would be immature and solve nothing. They sat staring at the wall beyond the bonnet until she turned to him.

'Sorry. I wasn't expecting your call; wasn't expecting you to be in London. Made a hash of it, didn't I? Andrew was so pleased when I told him you were here that I simply passed on his wishes without really taking in what you said.' She put her hand on his, which was still gripping the wheel. 'I didn't know you were having to fly back in the morning.' After a few moments of silence she said, 'Please come in.'

So he went in. They ate a light meal and drank chilled wine; they talked about the important and the trivial aspects of their work during the past week. They went to bed together. The tight strapping around Max's chest inhibited lovemaking, but their earlier exchange of words had dominated the mood of the evening so passion was at a low ebb anyway. After a swift breakfast they kissed goodbye and went their separate ways. Future plans had not once been mentioned.

At that midweek morning briefing Tom had plenty to get his teeth into. 'Our first breakthrough is that John Smith is an alias.'

'Didn't I say right at the start that it sounded phoney?' cried Piercey triumphantly.

'Real name is Jack Carr; son of Edward Smith's half-brother, who deserted Carr's mother on learning she was pregnant,' Tom continued, glaring at Piercey. 'His criminal tendency began not long after the toddler stage, taking anything chance offered as a means of buying affection, according to his mother. She's now on the game and into drugs small time. The Boss thinks she had just shot up before he interviewed her. There was no indication that Carr was in the house or had been there recently. Ms Carr was even unaware that her son is a soldier.

'There seems little doubt that Carr is the man who police along the south coast want for a series of minor thefts. Most probably that's why he enlisted, using his stepcousin's identity, stolen during the days leading to John Smith's funeral. The lad was killed in a hit and run last year.'

'The ultimate theft,' murmured Connie Bush.

'So, is there a possibility he did it again before going on that exercise?' Heather asked. 'Could that be why we've had no reports of him at ferry ports or airports?'

'We issued a picture,' Beeny reminded her. 'It was picked up on very fast in the UK.'

Tom followed up on that. 'It's certainly something we should consider if, as we suspect, Carr is still in this country and determined to remain here with someone who assisted his getaway.'

Connie put forward her usual thoughtful angle on the subject. 'He started trying to buy affection as a small boy. He was still doing it up until he disappeared. With no success, apparently. The men in his platoon all hated him, were disgusted by his constant attempts to muscle in where he wasn't wanted. So, the only way he would gain an accomplice to aid his desertion would be by bribing someone. With the rifle and ammo he stole from the Armoury?'

'Good point,' said Tom. 'I think we accept that both are gone beyond recall.'

'Then why leave the SA80 with ammo and the rest of his kit in the wood when he ran off?' asked Melly. 'They'd bring in a handy sum for his future plans.'

'Because he didn't abscond. He's out there in a shallow grave,' put in Piercey. 'Dug by Dan Farley.' When everyone turned to stare at him, he grinned. 'I'm going to be right one of these days . . . and he had every chance to bury Carr during that so-called search no one had ordered him to make.'

There was a vocal hiatus, because they had no proof that Carr was alive and, in theory, Dan Farley could have buried a body with ease during his solo visit to the exercise ground. Heather then recalled that she had earlier checked on who had operated near the missing man on the day of his disappearance. Farley was not one of them, and she put that fact forward.

Piercey was reluctant to abandon his theory, however. 'What if Carr had been taken ill and collapsed somewhere – a possibility Farley insisted on investigating when Carr was initially discovered to be missing. The officer comes across him during the search he made without informing anyone of what he planned, decides his platoon would be better without the creep and finishes him off.' Further inspiration dawned. 'Maybe Carr had offered Farley stolen goods in return for promotion and friendship. Being the Platoon Commander's favourite would be a real sock in the eye for all those who had spurned him. Or maybe Carr had a hold over Farley and was blackmailing him.'

This experienced team had come across most human weaknesses and complexities, so they knew everything Piercey put forward was possible. Even Tom privately admitted it, despite his reluctance to do so. Unfortunately, until Carr or Dan Farley was traced, nothing could be proved.

Connie was still pursuing her theme. 'All through his short life Carr had been thieving; not for his own benefit, note, but to buy friendship. That list of items sent by UK police should give us some clues. DVDs, mobile phones, top of the range trainers: all objects of desire for his contemporaries. Beer and spirits to please a boss or substitute father figure? Sexy underwear to gain girls' interest?'

'How about the silver golfing trophy?' jeered Piercey.

Heather was ready with a snap answer. 'Another cruel trick similar to that played by Corkhill and White. *If you had enough bottle to snatch that trophy from the snotty club that turned down my dad's membership, it'd really turn me on.*'

Connie nodded. 'There's hundreds of kids whose fathers disappear before they're born. It's down to the mothers how they handle it. Some women marry or shack up with a man who'll treat the child as his own, or at least give it a decent upbringing. Others take in a succession of "uncles" who view the kid as a nuisance: an annoying obstacle to a life of sex on demand and domestic ease with a woman desperate for any kind of partnership. A few are so besotted with the brutes who impregnated them that they live in a fantasy world that turns the absent fathers into heroes who rightly deserved someone better than they. Their kids are fed a load of romantic lies about the missing parent, and they believe them until the inevitable revelation by someone who knows the truth. Depending how old they are when this happens, they either believe everyone looks down on them and consequently withdraw into themselves, or they're so desperate to prove to the world how lovable they really are that they actually arouse the reverse emotion. Like Jack Carr.' She pursed her lips. 'I'd say he's a psychological mess who needs straightening out. Prison will only make him worse.'

'That's where he'll go when he's caught,' said Tom firmly, knowing Connie tended to look for reasons behind criminal acts. 'The list of Carr's thefts is growing longer the more we probe into his background. Now, let's move on to Lieutenant Farley. Following the posting of his details on HOLMES, police in Sussex are making enquiries of the girlfriend's family, the taxi drivers and residents bordering the road to Lewes from the village, hoping for sightings of a young man carrying a blue holdall. George says Panda patrols in Lewes have a description of Farley and are keeping a look out for him. He was last seen at fourteen thirty when he left the kennels. Someone *must* have seen him after that.'

'Are we regarding this as a possible kidnap and hostage situation?' asked Beeny.

'Not until the Sussex boys have come up with a few answers.'

'Or until his people receive a ransom demand,' put in Piercey. 'Have they been told he's missing?'

'Our lads checked that he wasn't with them. Mrs Farley is very upset. Her husband is the colonel of a tank regiment at Tidworth. He's been warned that it could be a terrorist situation and he could be next on their list. I personally have doubts on that, but it has to be considered.'

Tom moved on to something that had been bothering him since yesterday. 'I've been made aware of a newly-formed club run by some sixth-formers in the summerhouse of an officer's married quarters on the base, and I want it checked out. Quietly and unobtrusively. I can't get on it because my girls are involved.'

'What's the prob, sir?' asked Melly.

Tom outlined his concerns. 'The boss of this group is a cocky seventeen year old named Jake Morgan, whose father

is with the REME detachment. Jake's henchmen are Scott
Pinner, Tim Jackson and a girl called Zoe Rogers, who takes
the money. According to my daughters, almost every pupil
at the school participates. Now, this club might be perfectly
straight and I've no wish to spoil something the kids enjoy,
but I get the impression that there are far too many "unwanted
presents" being sold. DVDs and CDs still fully packaged
are linked in my mind with our friend Carr's locker.

'From what I've gleaned with casual questioning, used
items can only be swapped or hired. The "unwanted presents" have to be bought. The hook is the reduced price.
Fair enough, but what I've not yet discovered is who gets
the purchase money. Or the hire fees. My three are too
enthusiastic about the venture to delve into that aspect of
this club, but the amount of new stuff they're acquiring on
regular weekly payments set alarm bells ringing for me.
When I asked which members had contributed "unwanted
presents" I was told, somewhat impatiently, that they were
put on a separate table if they were for sale and were already
there when the club door opened.'

He glanced at the faces of his team and asked, 'Does that
smell rather unsavoury to you?'

'Carr was targeting kids instead of adults?' Melly suggested.

'*In addition* to the troops,' Heather added. 'He'd not earn
enough from the kids alone.'

'You think these sixth-formers were buying the stuff from
Carr and selling it on to the kids?' asked Connie. 'What's
in it for them? Unless Carr reduced the cost considerably,
Jake and Co. won't make a profit if they're also selling at
reduced prices.'

Tom gave a grin. 'Any further input if I throw in the fact
that this club was only set up two days after Carr vanished?'

'Jake's taken over the business,' several said in unison.

'Maybe,' Tom replied. 'That's why I think we should
check this enterprise out. If there's a link with Carr, we
might get lucky with evidence leading to where he is now.'

'If he's not in a shallow grave on the exercise ground,'
murmured Piercey, although it looked as if his mind was
very much elsewhere.

# TEN

'There *is* a God,' Dan breathed, offering up a vote of thanks as the fox finally caught his prey and trotted from the barn, all interest in human flesh put aside for now.

A pigeon had sought refuge in the barn soon after daybreak. Dan saw that a shotgun pellet had disabled it, so when the inquisitive fox paid his daily visit, the bird instinctively tried to fly up out of his reach. The ensuing chase was more like a cat and mouse hunt. Unable to fly, the pigeon simply flapped and hopped in its frantic bids to escape, while the fox pounced and missed so many times that the barn was soon filled with flying dust and small wisps of hay kicked up by the thrashing animals.

Reynard won, as he was certain to and, with the bird held firmly between his jaws, went out past the blue holdall and disappeared from view. It was then that Dan saw the animal activity had achieved what he had been unable to do during his three days of captivity. One end of the greatly disturbed coils of rope was now lying within his reach, and escape had become a certainty. His sense of relief was so great that his legs grew weak and he drooped in the chains, fighting the onset of tears.

Having had three days to plan the details, Dan prepared to put them into practice. It would take patience, dexterity and considerable time, but he would keep at it until he was free. Yet, now it was a possibility, he found it difficult to get his brain around the matter. Dear God, it had been a masterpiece of ingenuity; a classic example of a tactical solution to a tricky problem. Why was he having trouble remembering it?

Pushing back a rush of panic, he stared at the rope for inspiration. Ah yes, draw the end of it to him, then pick it up with his feet and raise it until he could seize it with his hands. Several minutes passed before he recalled the next step. Make a lasso to throw over the drum of lubricant. Haul the drum up to rest on the cross-beam. Open the drum. Remove his trousers and underpants, then thickly smear his lower trunk with the grease. His shoulders were too wide to make a downward slither through the triple links, so he must pull himself upward. To do this he must then throw the rope over the second cross-beam, several feet above him, and make handhold loops in both ends. With these he would pull himself up like an Olympic gymnast.

It was something he had done with ease from his teens, but it would take a deal of strength to drag his greased hips free of the tight chain, and he was presently not at peak fitness. Last night he had vomited several times, and he was burning as if with a fever. He added a swift rider to his thanks to the Almighty, asking for an injection of strength when his deliverance depended on it.

Those louts who had left him here after slapping him around, stealing the gold watch that meant a lot to him along with his only means of summoning help, would pay for what they had done. They might all have been wearing crash helmets that exposed only their eyes, but he had taken note of their number plates and had been repeating the digits constantly to ensure he did not forget them. They would think twice before tangling with a soldier again.

It was quiet in the Incident Room after the briefing. Because Heather had two teenage brothers, she had been given the task of investigating the sixth-formers' club, on the pretext of buying something for the birthday of one of them. Connie was absorbed in tracing Carr's school in the Acton area, and where he had worked on leaving it until he had enlisted. Beeny was talking to staff at Wellington College and Sandhurst about Dan Farley. Tom was going through that officer's personal effects and checking data on the computer in his room, with Will Fanshawe as a witness. Although it seemed unlikely, there could be evidence that Farley was a member of some seditious group or malicious secret society; hence his sudden disappearance.

Piercey had volunteered to compile information on Jake Morgan, Scott Pinner, Tim Jackson and Zoe Rogers, because he saw an opportunity to earn kudos if his suspicions proved correct. He soon understood why Jake was boss of this venture: he was the only one whose father was an officer. Cliff Pinner and Simon Jackson were corporals. Malcolm Rogers was a sergeant. Piercey's enthusiasm increased on discovering that Rogers's quarters were next to Miller's, which meant Zoe could well have been a bosom friend of the girl who was in hospital after falling from a bridge. Piercey had a score to settle with Eric Miller.

The moment Tom had mentioned Zoe Rogers, Piercey had recalled a girl with scarlet hair who was frightened of storms. She had said her father would soon be posted to the UK: Malcolm Rogers was listed for deployment to Lincoln in the new year. Zoe was involved with a trio selling CDs. Her bag had been chock-full of them in that restaurant. Time to renew her acquaintance.

Piercey parked where he had a clear view of the Rogerses' house, and fifty yards down the road in the direction the girl would take to walk to Jake's club. He was happy enough to sit in the sun with the windows open and music playing. Zoe was sure to appear sooner or later, and it was better than sitting in the stuffy atmosphere at Headquarters. He swore the air conditioning system had not operated fully since that storm.

Shortly after ten o'clock the girl with the bizarrely-dyed hair came from the house and began walking towards him. He immediately turned the CD player to full volume, which brought the intended reaction. Zoe's attention was first caught by the blare of music; then she stared at the man who smiled and waved to her.

'That's right, sweetie, come over to make sure your eyes aren't deceiving you,' he murmured, giving her the full optical come-on as she crossed the road to his car. When she was near enough, he went into the next phase of his tactic.

'Hi, Zoe! No storms around today. No excuse to hold your hand.'

She looked puzzled. 'Phil? What are you doing here?'

He gave his girl-pulling grin. 'Looking for Zoe with the scarlet tresses.'

'Oh yeah?' she returned caustically. 'How would you know how to find me? I didn't give you my address or mobile number.'

'You told me your dad was soon to be posted back to the UK.' He tapped his temple. 'Put two and two together and reasoned that you're an Army brat.'

'And?'

She had more fire now than ten days ago in that café. A smart cookie, he decided. 'And I wanted to see you again.'

Still visibly unimpressed by his line, Zoe bent to rest her elbow on the door frame, put her chin in her hand and gave him a provocative gaze from heavily outlined eyes, along with a generous view of her luscious cleavage.

'What about those deals you had to clinch? Places to go, people to see, you claimed as you beat a pathetically obvious retreat.'

Yes, a very smart cookie. He continued to play the game. 'Ah, Zoe, you have no idea how much it warms my heart to know you remember every word I said during that dramatic first encounter with you.'

She straightened abruptly. 'Where'd you get that corny spiel? From TV?'

He laughed. 'You were doing such a great act as a raunchy drama student, I had to reciprocate. Has RADA accepted your application yet?'

She shook her head absently. 'What are you doing here?'

'It's quite a story. Come and sit beside me while I tell it.' At her hesitation, he added, 'You can hold the ignition key if you don't trust me the same way you did during that storm.'

She held out her hand and, with a shrug, he pulled out the key and gave it to her. 'Wise girl. Never get in a car with a man you don't know much about.' He produced his identity card and held it out for her to see. 'You're perfectly safe with me, Zoe.'

'SIB!' she exclaimed. 'You liar! You said you were a rep.'

'I was on an undercover job,' he lied smoothly. 'I had to leave abruptly because the guy I was watching made a dash from that café.'

It did the trick. She was on the seat beside him in a flash, demanding to know the full story. Never short of ideas he wove a tale guaranteed to appeal to a girl of her histrionic bent, which banished any remaining wariness on her part. How easily a practiced sexual predator could con his victim, he reflected.

Taking one of his usual bags of marshmallows from the glove compartment, he offered it. 'That's enough about me, Zoe. You really are going to train as an actress?'

She nodded. 'If RADA turns me down, I'll do it the other way.'

'Oh, what's that?'

'My boyfriend Jake has already been accepted by the National Youth Theatre to study lighting and sound. He's brill. Once he gets to know who's around and who else *they* know, he'll fix me up with an interview with the guy who's a drama coach. He'll swing it, I know he will. Jake has everything sussed.'

'Smart guy!' Piercey offered the marshmallows again. 'Tell the truth, I had you clocked as a singer. Jazzy hair, gorgeous, expressive eyes, sexy pazazz. Could just picture you wowing them with a really cool backing group.' Busying himself with returning the bag of sweets to the glove compartment, he said casually, 'Saw you had a bagful of brand new CDs. Thought you were learning some tricks of the trade. Wondered if you even had a couple of your own demo tracks for auditions among them. They'll do that for you at The Jumping Bean on Rathausstrasse, you know.'

Completely won over by this opportunity to talk about herself, Zoe confessed that she had considered becoming a pop star. 'But I love acting more than singing, Phil. I might do musicals once I've tired of the dramatic roles. That'll be the time to make the switch. Like Meryl Streep.'

In your dreams, thought Piercey. 'So you'd bought all those CDs just for listening pleasure?'

'Mmm?' she queried, loath to leave the romance she was weaving. 'No, they were for J.S. A friend.'

'Not the one who went off leaving no address, I hope. You were very sad and upset over what he'd done, if you remember. I asked if he was your boyfriend, and you said he was just someone who made life more exciting.'

Zoe frowned. 'Did I? That was two weeks ago. I've forgotten him.'

'Jake makes life exciting now?'

'He's *brill*,' she said dramatically.

'So I don't stand a chance?'

The actress in her could not resist the despondency in his voice. 'I didn't say that. If you're around after Jake goes home, who knows?'

'Not free this afternoon, I suppose?'

'Uh-uh, I'm going to Jake's.'

He looked suitably dashed. 'Can I at least drive you there?'

'OK.' She held out the ignition key. 'You'd better drop me before we get to his house.' Eyelashes fluttered. 'Can't have him getting jealous, can we?'

Piercey took the long way around the perimeter road, keeping to the low speed limit. 'Of course, you must have been involved in the real-life drama next door to you. Girl who fell in the river and hit her head. Friend of yours?'

She turned to him, eyes flashing. 'Silly bitch! Ruined everything, Jake says.'

'Almost ruined her future, Zoe.'

'Yes, well . . . Sharon's always showing off, you know, and only a dimmo would try walking along a narrow wall when they're pissed. Jake says that's why J.S. jacked it in. He was totally gone on her until he saw what she was really like.'

'The friend who made life exciting?'

The fact that she was talking to a detective sergeant had clearly flitted through her butterfly mind and straight out again, because she was eagerly dramatizing once more.

'Yes, but *he* wasn't. Can't think what Sharon saw in him, but she was desperate for a man. *Any* man. He tried it on

with me, you know. But *yuk!*' She gazed into her artificial
world. 'I suppose he must also have been desperate, to want
to go with Sharon.' Turning to him with a smug smile, she
added, 'Soon saw the light, didn't he?'

'And faded out of the picture?'

'Daft twit went AWOL, just when we had something
good . . .' She broke off and her colour rose. 'You can let
me out here. I'll walk the rest.'

'Daren't make Jake jealous, eh?' he commented with a
reassuring smile. 'Great to see you again, Zoe. Maybe when
Jake leaves we could get together sometime,' he added, to
banish any suspicion she might have that he had heard
anything interesting in her gossip.

'Yeah, maybe.' She slid from the car, then poked her head
back in to add, 'If there's a storm, I'll come alookin' for
you. Cheers.'

Continuing around the perimeter, still at the correct speed,
Piercey inwardly rejoiced. She had given him just what he
wanted: the link between Carr and Jake's club. The additional link between Carr and Sharon Miller needed to be
investigated. One aspect of her guileless information puzzled
him. Why had she said the CDs in her bag were *for* J.S.
rather than *from* him, for surely Jake and Co. were selling
the stuff Jack Carr had acquired by the same method as he
had the DVDs in his locker?

Max was choosing shirts in a Knightsbridge store when
Tom called. Conscious of impatient scowls from elderly
female shoppers at this further evidence of people who
could not even buy clothes without having a mobile phone
clamped to their ear, he left the shirts and walked out to
the emergency stairs.

'Not about to board, are you?' Tom asked.

'Haven't even set out for Heathrow.'

'Good. We've just had info come in from Sussex police
at Lewes. Two sightings of a biker taking on his pillion a
young, dark-haired man with a blue holdall. Reports vary
between two and three miles from the village centre on the
Lewes Road.'

'Not a terrorist situation, then,' Max said with relief. 'So where the hell has Farley gone?'

'Not far, if witnesses are to be believed,' came Tom's clipped rejoinder. 'Several drinkers saw, from the windows of the White Ram, a group of four bikers heading for Lewes at around that time. They wore leathers decorated with a startling orange and white design. The lone biker was described as wearing similar gear, but none of the group of four carried a passenger. Seems they looked set to enter the pub for some kind of celebration, but then decided to move on, much to the relief of the landlord and customers.'

'So what are the Lewes guys saying?' Max asked urgently.

'They're saying their force is presently tied up with a missing schoolgirl and a double mugging on Worthing beach when both victims were stabbed. RMP involvement in the Farley case would be welcomed.'

Max gave a grim smile. 'You bet it would! Tom, I'll head down there now. I drove the length of that Lewes road. There are a number of narrow tracks leading to farms, and an area of woodland which borders the tarmac. If there's a guy out there mugging at knifepoint, and ready to use his weapon, Farley could have been a plum target walking that country road. Plenty of places to dump a body.'

'Make sure it isn't yours.'

'I'll call with any info. Thanks, Tom.'

Max disconnected and went quickly to where he had left the car at a vacant meter a few roads away. Still smarting from the spat with Livya, and the unexpressed suggestion that her work was of greater importance than his, he embarked eagerly on the journey south. There was no proof that the biker who had taken Farley on the pillion was one of the four seen by patrons of the White Ram, nor was there any evidence to suggest he was the violent mugger, but Max was convinced something had happened to Farley on that road to Lewes. He had sensed it when he had driven up from the kennels on Monday, but surely there was now enough information to make an investigation necessary?

Farley had been missing for three days. Max's experienced judgement of human characters told him the young officer had not stayed beyond his official leave voluntarily. That meant something or someone was preventing him from making contact. A mugging resulting in GBH would provide answers to those suppositions. If Farley had been lying hidden for three days, Max knew he could well be too late on the scene.

The clock above the bar in the White Ram was an hour slow, the landlord explained, when Max questioned only eleven chimes.

'Never bother to change it in the spring. Only have to change it back again in the autumn. My reg'lars know that. What can I get you?' he asked in a real Sussex burr.

Max ordered half a shandy. He was thirsty and wanted to ask a few questions of the landlord. His thirst was quenched, but he learned very little. The people who had seen the bikers had stopped for jacket potatoes and salad on their way home from a week at a Dorset caravan park. The police would know where they lived. John Kearns had taken their details.

Max left the pub and drove to the village where Farley had used the wall telephone to call for a taxi. Witnesses said they had seen a young man with a blue holdall getting up behind a biker two or three miles from the village, so Max decided to make it his starting point for a slow drive in the direction of the White Ram. He was convinced Farley had come to some harm somewhere between those two sites. If he found evidence to support that belief he would call up military reinforcements for a full-scale search.

For the next two hours he drove down rutted farm tracks and knocked on doors all the way along his journey back to the pub. It was August, and harvesting was in progress. Farmhouses were empty, everyone being out in the fields, turning swaying carpets of ripened crops into a number of tight, golden rolls scattered across the stubble. Watching a distant combine harvester crossing one field, Max had a terrible fear that the slicing blades might cut into a human body, lying injured where it had been left after a knife attack.

Telling himself he was letting his imagination swamp his

calm intelligence he drove to within two miles of the White Ram, where a narrow overgrown track ran off on the far side of the road. The surface was appalling, but Max drove down it with determination while reflecting that the car hire people would not be happy with the state of their vehicle when he returned it at Heathrow.

Bumping and lurching over ground a tractor would cope with more easily, Max eventually reached an overgrown field where a disused, ramshackle barn stood as evidence that whoever owned the land had not used this corner of it for some years.

But *someone* had!

Max called Tom from the hospital where Dan Farley had been taken in the ambulance.

'He's a very plucky, lucky guy,' he said, after giving his friend the welcome news that he had found the young officer. 'He's being treated for fever, induced by drinking rainwater from a vessel containing traces of insecticide, and for blood poisoning resulting from rust particles entering suppurating weals on his chest and back. He's also slightly hypothermic and traumatized.'

'But he'll recover?'

'Fully.' Watching the pathetic traffic of patients being wheeled on trolleys along the corridor, Max said, 'Tom, he won't go to Afghanistan the untried boy straight from Sandhurst that he was. I wish that bloody self-absorbed wench at Brighteye Kennels could see him now, although I doubt it would ever occur to her, or to her mealy-mouthed family, that he's a mile higher above them in human stature. Always has been.'

'Have you informed his parents?'

'First thing. They're on their way here. You'll tell his commanders?'

'Soon as you've given me the story.'

'Only as far as I know it. Farley's somewhat incoherent at present, but he's given us plenty to work on. Despite throwing up now and then, he's quoted clearly and insistently a set of four reg numbers he memorized. Said they were on the machines of the louts who assaulted him. The local guys are tracing the owners, and have put out a general "wanted for questioning" bulletin. I'd say it's highly likely they're the four who were seen from the window of the White Ram on Sunday.

'I'm not certain a charge of attempted murder would stick, but that's what they deserve. Farley was assaulted, then secured to a vertical beam by a rusty chain, wound several times very tightly around his chest and padlocked. They rode off leaving him that way in an abandoned barn at the end of an overgrown and unused track. They knew it was extremely unlikely that he would be discovered and released. They must also have known he would die a slow, unpleasant death unless the unlikely happened. I'd call that attempted murder, wouldn't you?'

'Any chance they intended to return and let him go in a day or two?'

Max pursed his lips in consideration. 'That's what they'll plead, and the prosecution won't be able to disprove it. It'll be Farley's word against the four of them.'

'How the hell did he get himself in such a situation?'

'What I was able to deduce from Farley's jumble of comments is that he accepted a lift to Brighton so he could make his way to Heathrow, then three others made up a convoy. They took him down that track and robbed him of a gold presentation watch, his mobile phone and several items of expensive clothing that were in his holdall. When they opened his wallet to take his money, they found his service identity and began beating him up. What had been a group mugging turned into something pretty nasty.

'When I found him he was half naked and lying in his vomit in a confused state. He mumbled something about chasing a fox, and grease on the end of a rope. Didn't make sense, but his lower body was thickly smeared with engine oil so I took a look in the barn. There was a drum of lubricant on a cross-beam, within reach of an upright with a rusty chain at its foot. Directly above the vertical was another cross-beam. Over it hung a rope with a handhold loop tied at both ends. It didn't take much for me to work out that

Farley had greased his body, then hauled himself free of the chain restraint with the aid of the rope loops. In his weakened, fevered state it must have taken a Herculean effort.'

'So he was free, but quite ill. What if you hadn't acted on your hunch?'

'He'd have crawled to the road and waited for a passing good Samaritan. Might have taken time and enormous effort, but he'd have done it, believe me. This lad's fighting mad beneath his exhaustion. Tom, I'm going to delay my return until tomorrow. I need to get a clearer account from Farley when he's recovered a little. I also want to square things with the local guys. They should be able to pick up the bikers without much trouble, and I'd like to see these specimens of manhood who think being tough means hijacking a solo stranger, robbing him, then leaving him to die.'

'OK. Nothing vital has developed here. I'll be in touch if it does. Farley needs a military rep on hand to fight his corner. Those yobs will concoct a story that's sure to heap the blame on him: he threatened them with a weapon, they had to restrain him for their own safety, etcetera.'

'You've got it, Tom.'

'What I've got is four likely lads seizing an opportunity to exercise power and help themselves to some unfortunate's attractive belongings. Take a victim somewhere off the beaten track, relieve him of his valuables, then ride off, leaving him to find his way back to civilization. That I understand. What I don't, is why they then turned on him with such viciousness.'

'Because he's a soldier.'

'*Because he's a soldier*?' echoed Tom in emphasis.

'That's right.'

'Jeez!'

# ELEVEN

Max drove into the base late on Thursday afternoon. His flight had been extremely bumpy, despite perfect weather. Something called 'still air turbulence', he had been told by an RAF crewman he had once encountered. An atmospheric state almost impossible for a pilot to avoid by changing altitude. The Lufthansa one had not managed it. Not overfond of being enclosed in a flying cigar for long periods, Max had disembarked thankfully and driven through the late August sunwashed countryside, enjoying the sense of freedom.

Tired after a long morning of intensive investigative sessions with Dan Farley and the CID group at Lewes, he decided to go directly to his room. Tomorrow morning would be soon enough to lay the facts of the Farley case before his team. He did not even plan to call Tom tonight. That could also wait.

Booking a room at the White Ram last evening, Max had felt disinclined to call Livya. In truth, he was unsure what they would find to say to each other. She had apparently felt the same way, because there was no call or text from her. Better to let a little time elapse.

All the same, he had flown to the UK determined to reach an agreement about their future together. Susan's death was now behind him, and Livya had revived the need for the kind of closeness found with a loving and caring woman. It was suddenly not enough to have it only spasmodically. He was young and healthy, not the type to have sex with any willing woman, but the desire for it was strong and tormenting him more frequently. He had returned to Germany no nearer to getting what he wanted. If anything, it seemed to be further from his grasp. He would sit in his lonely room and lick his wounds. Feeble, but so what?

Pushing open the door from the Mess car park, he almost

collided with Clare Goodey. He stepped aside to let her
pass, but she halted and smiled. 'Hail the returning hero!'
'What?'
'Found young Farley and got him to a hospital, didn't
you?'
'How d'you hear about that?'
'Word gets around.' Her smile widened. 'Will Fanshawe
came in for his annual check-up this morning. We haven't
been on good terms since I let fly about his men being put
through an exercise during the heatwave, so I chatted him
up a bit. Give a male patient a touch of TLC and he'll pour
out his heart, pronto. How's that strapping standing up to
heavy detecting?'
'Detecting isn't hampered by it,' he replied, thinking how
it had hampered lovemaking. Providentially, perhaps?
'Want me to take a look at it?'
He shook his head. 'It's fine.'
'Sure? You don't look too comfortable.'
'Rotten flight. Plane yo-yoed all over the sky. Don't think
I'll bother with dinner. Get an early night.'
'And have your bed yo-yoing? What you need is a large
dose of fresh air, a stiff drink, a late supper and bed much
later than midnight. I can provide the first three and steer
you to the fourth.' As he made to speak, she added, 'I'm
off to look over an apartment in a rural area just this side
of town. Come with me.' She cocked her head enquiringly.
'I'd value your opinion, Max.'
    She looked attractively fresh and glowing with health in
a lime-green linen dress with white touches on cuffs and
pockets. That scent of apples was enticing; the frank gaze
from blue eyes so different from the dark depths of Livya's.
He need not lick his wounds; Clare was offering soothing
balm for them.
    'More TLC for a male patient?' he asked quietly.
    'If you need it, yes.' She smiled again. 'I can't ever forget
I'm a doctor. How about forgetting you're a policeman for
a while?'
    He caught himself smiling back. 'Best suggestion I've
had all day. Give me ten minutes.'

After a swift wash, Max dressed in a pale checked shirt
and chinos, then ran his shaver lightly across his chin with
one hand while combing his thick hair with the other. That
took a bit of coordinating dexterity, but he looked fresher
than before. Snatching up a lightweight jacket and his wallet,
he descended the stairs and went out to where her jaunty
car was waiting.

'Bravo!' she said with a chuckle. 'I timed you. Dead on
the dot.'

'A woman couldn't have done it,' he said, settling beside
her. 'They can't simply change their clothes; it has to be
matching shoes and handbag and necklace and eyeshadow
and perfume and . . .'

'You stand in danger of being ordered out of my car,
Captain Rydal. Male chauvinism will not be tolerated.'

He grinned. 'Can I stay if I eat humble pie?'

For answer she started up and drove towards the main
gate. Once they were through and on course for the town,
Max asked for details of the apartment they were to view.

'It's above my quoted price, but you were right. There's
mainly a choice between a poky bedsitter or a place huge
enough for a large family. However, this apartment is one
of a pair with an adjoining common sitting-room. A
German woman is very interested in one, provided
someone signs the rental contract for the other. If the
landlord gets two tenants signing for a minimum term of
nine months the rent is slightly reduced. He wants to
avoid fly-by-nighters now he's spent a lot on refurbishing
the rooms. It's a great opportunity to have a place to go
to away from work. It's near enough to the base to drive
in swiftly on an emergency call, and the prospectus
mentions peaceful surroundings with open rural views
from the rear windows.'

'Ha, I bet the view from the front windows is the gas
works or a sewage farm. If they don't mention it, it's sure
to be the stumbling block to the property.'

She pulled a face at him. 'Misery!'

He laughed, already relaxing and enjoying the pleasure
of an open car driven with skill and care. If only it could

be Livya beside him. Such simple pleasure was surely not
too much to ask for.

They arrived at the small cluster of residential buildings
within half an hour to find a suave, good-looking agent waiting
beside a silver BMW. He approached, offering his hand.

'Good eeffening, Miss Goodey.'

His smile was surely the result of studying orthodontists'
brochures, Max thought sourly. He took an instant dislike
to him.

'It's *Mrs* Goodey,' Clare told him coolly.

The smile could have been painted on. It remained perfect
as he apologized and turned it on Max. 'Good eeffening,
Mr Goodey.'

'My name's Rydal. I'm Mrs Goodey's legal advisor,' he
said.

The smile slipped a little, but not much. 'Off course.
Please to come inside this most attractiff apartment. A residence so suitable for a lady as yourself, madam.'

Max could not dispute that. Airy, with large windows, it
had pale walls and ceilings with toffee-coloured carpets
throughout. The bedroom was furnished with twin beds
zipped together, which could be separated or used as a large
double, fitted wardrobe units, a folding leaf table with two
chairs, a TV and DVD player, two small armchairs and a
broad shelf with a telephone and a computer point. In all,
a bed-sitting room.

The en suite bathroom had double washbasins, a shower
cubicle and a corner jacuzzi. This was an apartment for a
working couple, Max thought, deeply impressed. They had
entered through a main door opening on to a small hall.
The agent now took them back to that hall and opened the
door that revealed a compact but fully-fitted kitchen.

'It is complete just for yourself,' he explained, 'but venn
you wish to haff the friends you can use this.'

He flung open the third door leading to a large square
room containing a walnut table with eight chairs, a side-
board stocked with china and glasses, two settees and four
armchairs with side tables. It was the crowning delight of
this offer and Max studied it enviously. He had been wrong.

The rear windows certainly had pleasant rural views, but this enormous picture window at the front overlooked the road to a distant view of a lake and manor house. Wonderful!

While Clare chatted to the man with the painted smile, Max imagined living in a place like this with Livya. Not with anyone else in the adjoining flat; he would fight shy of sharing. He had once done it at university. Never again. His neighbour had used the communal room as if it were his own, filling it with rowdy friends and girls who damn near wrecked the place.

He would advise Clare to turn this down for that reason. Anyway, could she afford this superior apartment? It then occurred to him that she might not live here alone. Would the husband be sharing it as a reconciliation? He knew nothing of Goodey, although base gossip had it that he was a captain in the Blues and Royals, with some kind of title. Max had dismissed it as exaggeration, but maybe there was some truth in it. His mouth twisted. A Guards officer of that stamp would be able to afford both apartments.

They parted from the agent, saying they would be in touch soon, and Clare drove to the riverside inn where Max had pulled the unconscious girl to safety. He felt curiously resentful when Herr Blomfeld greeted Clare by name, at a place he had only introduced her to two weeks ago.

It was much more pleasant in the garden this evening than it had been on that other sweltering occasion. It was also a Thursday, not a Saturday which was the traditional night to relax and have fun. They ordered, and Max waited for Clare to ask his opinion of the apartment. Instead, she raised her wineglass.

'Celebrate with me the discovery of my perfect new quarters. I fell in love with it the minute we walked in.'

'You're going to take it?' he asked, his stein still firmly on the table.

'When we've drunk the toast, I'm going to call our German fashion model and clinch the deal. I can't afford to lose it to someone who gets in before I do.' Her eyes were bright with excitement. 'Farewell to dreary officers' mess bedrooms, communal dining and male bravado.

I'll be a *woman* there.' She looked pointedly at the stein. 'You won't celebrate with me?'

He raised it immediately. 'Off course, madam. Here's to your happiness at Mariensplatz.'

They drank, then she said, 'You're welcome to visit.'

'In that large sitting room? I'd need to bring at least ten others or we'd be communicating with semaphore.'

She laughed, then used her mobile phone to secure the apartment. Their food arrived. Clare chatted easily as they ate: how she was getting to know the local area, how she planned to spend her leave periods exploring further afield, how she intended to update the medical regulations used by her predecessor.

Max listened, but did not heed her words. She spoke what used to be called BBC English. Livya's low voice held very slight Slavic undertones, which made it very appealing. Clare's speech was quiet, assured and soothing. As doctor to patient? Livya's was crisp, concise, authoritative. As a military ADC. Except when she teased. *Reduce the revs, Steve!*

'. . . along the towpath?'

Max came out from his reverie and registered the questioning look from the very different woman facing him. 'Sorry?'

'Let's take a walk. It's too soon to return to khaki boredom.'

The discreet lighting along the towpath came on as they strolled beside the river, which was not only back to its usual level, but swollen by the great storm following the heat-wave. Water had poured from the hills during two days and nights of excessive rainfall. They were silent for a while; then Max spoke of his pleasure in rowing this waterway.

'A solo sport,' Clare commented.

'I suppose I'm a solo kind of man these days. I used to indulge in team sports. Obligatory at school and during basic military training, of course, but I opted out as soon as I could.'

'But you're the athletic type, Max.'

He gave a short laugh. 'I do my quota of physical exercise, Doctor. Cross-country running, hill walking, swimming, press-ups.'

'On your own?'

He threw her a quizzical look in the semi-darkness. 'You get no fitter if you do it with others.'

'So, why the shunning of team sports?'

It was peaceful there with only the soft gurgle of surging water, the occasional plop of river creatures seeking food, and their own footfalls on the earthen path. It seemed natural to give her the true answer.

'My father is a brilliant sportsman. When he was younger he represented the Army so many times he couldn't fit his trophies on one single shelf. He still plays squash and tennis, fences at his club and turns out for his polo team whenever he's able to. He's pretty well known, so you can guess what happened when I grew old enough to participate.'

She glanced up at him, her face pale in the half-light. 'You were expected to be the star player in every team?'

'When they discovered I wasn't, it seemed sensible to go solo in things athletic.'

'*Very* sensible. For that same reason I stopped trying to beat my father on the racing circuit,' she admitted quietly. 'I became a doctor, which he isn't . . . and you became a policeman who finds missing officers undergoing trauma, which Andrew Rydal can't do. Makes things easier all round, doesn't it?'

'Absolutely.' He smiled. 'What canny people we are!'

Not until he lay in bed, relaxed and not yo-yoing, well after midnight, did Max realize just how canny Clare was. *Give a male patient a touch of TLC and he'll pour out his heart, pronto.* Along that shadowy towpath he had told her about Livya and his dashed hopes for a resolution to their situation. Oh yes, she had laid on the TLC quite lavishly, and he had poured out his heart. She now knew a great deal about him, but he still knew next to nothing about her.

The Incident Room was buzzing on that Friday morning. After a somewhat languid period, two cases were now producing intriguing information.

Max began by telling his team the outcome of his interviews with Dan Farley and members of Lewes CID. 'The ball is now firmly in their court. Having been given the bikers' reg numbers by Lieutenant Farley, they brought the four in very swiftly for questioning. As you'll guess, they denied everything; said Farley must have noted their reg numbers when they dropped him just short of the White Ram at his request.'

'They do admit to picking him up along that road?' asked Heather.

'The Lewes guys told them there were witnesses to that at the outset. The ringleader, called Sean, claimed they had over-heard Phil Hawkins, the son in the taxi business, tell a caller they didn't go as far as Brighton on Sundays. They heard him tell his father to look out for a young man with dark hair who'd be carrying a blue holdall and walking along the Lewes Road. Sean says as he and his mates were going to Brighton they decided to help the guy out. He thought he said as much to Phil, but he couldn't be sure. They offered Farley a lift and he got on the pillion. Soon after, he took a call on his mobile and asked to be put down as his plans had changed. They continued to Brighton and never saw him again.'

'The Sussex guys *believed* that?' asked Piercey incredulously.

Max grinned. 'Sean was wearing a very upmarket shirt exactly like the one Farley said they had stolen, and one of their women constables in another room called the number of Farley's mobile. It rang in Sean's pocket. Mobiles have their moments of glory, however much we curse them in railway carriages and restaurants.'

Intent on his doodle, Olly Simpson asked, 'What had they to say to that, sir?'

'Ah, story number two was that they diverted down a side track to drink some coke, and Farley got worked up about the delay. Said he had a flight to catch at Heathrow. Said he'd lose his job if he didn't get back that night. He tried to persuade them to take him all the way; began bribing them with designer clothes. Forced them to take them. They kept telling him no way could they go up to Heathrow, but he grew wilder and wilder and more and more agitated, pressing his gold watch on them. And his mobile. And all the cash he had on him.'

'Were Lewes CID rolling on the floor with laughter by then?' asked Connie Bush, highly amused.

'The next bit's even more inventive. They reckoned Farley then lost it and produced a gun. "'im bein' in the Army, like",' Max added in a suitable accent. 'That obliged them to restrain him with whatever was available.'

'He wasn't foaming at the mouth when they rode off, by any chance?' asked Beeny. 'Pity if they missed out on that.'

'So why didn't they go straight to the police?' asked Heather. 'Don't tell us one of their beloved grannies turned up her toes suddenly and grief put all else from their minds.'

'Our friend Sean reckoned they had rightly to tell the Army in Germany, where the "nutter" was frantic to fly to. They tried everything they could think of, but never managed to make contact. The one time they connected with a number in Farley's personal phonebook, the person spoke in a foreign language.

'That's when we get to story number three. Firstly, they intended to go back and release him when he'd had enough time to calm down. Then they reasoned that, being a soldier, he'd have no problem getting free. They'd only wanted to teach him a lesson or two; show him he couldn't order them around like other soldiers. They couldn't credit what had happened. If they'd had any idea he wasn't as tough as they're cracked up to be, they'd have checked that he'd gone off to Germany all right.'

Max surveyed the amused expressions on the faces of his team. 'It wouldn't be the least funny if Farley hadn't been resourceful and determined. Those dickheads had secured him so tightly to the upright that only a fox chasing a pigeon, and a hell of a lot of ingenuity, provided his means of escape. If witnesses hadn't seen him climbing on Sean's pillion, and similarly dressed bikers outside the White Ram further along that road, minus a passenger, my attention wouldn't have been focussed on that area. Farley could have died in that barn. Not for a gold watch and a few designer clothes, *but because he's a soldier*. That's the value those louts put on one of their country's fighting men. I'd charge them with attempted murder, but you and I know they'll get away with a lot less.'

'How is Lieutenant Farley?' asked Connie, the most compassionate member of the team.

'I called the hospital first thing this morning. He's doing well and should return to duty early next week.'

Heather gave Piercey a sly glance. 'He wasn't in a shallow grave, after all.'

The Sergeant narrowed his eyes, looked knowing. 'Jack Carr still has to be traced.'

Max glanced at Tom. 'I'll leave you to review that case. Where are we at with it?'

'Some disturbing facts have been discovered by Piercey,' Tom said heavily. 'I'm not able to follow them up because my girls are innocently caught up in the business.'

He outlined what Zoe Rogers had told Piercey about Jake Morgan and the sixth-formers' club. He also revealed what Maggie, Gina and Beth had said about what went on in the summerhouse at Captain Morgan's married quarter.

'Zoe's use of the initials J.S. suggest Carr, alias Smith, was the person who made life exciting for her, and her comment that he went AWOL would confirm that belief. Now, she's apparently a consummate actress who could make a drama out of frying an egg, so we have to tread carefully. On the surface it could be that this enterprising foursome is selling stuff that Carr acquired illegally, or at least somewhat questionably.'

'We've no solid evidence that what the kids are presently handling ever passed through Carr's hands,' Staff Melly pointed out. 'According to local storekeepers, Carr only made lists, never stole the stuff. That's always puzzled me, because he has a history of thieving.'

Tom nodded. 'That's why I said there are disturbing facets to this case. We've never sussed where Carr got his supplies.'

'We've not come upon anyone who'll admit they bought things from him, either,' Connie reminded them.

'Yet Zoe spoke several times of J.S. And surely the mention of his going AWOL clinches the fact that it's Carr,' Piercey insisted. 'When I encountered her during the storm she said her friend had gone off without leaving an address, and that was three days after Carr vanished. The link's there. Got to be.'

'I agree,' said Tom. 'There's also a probable link between Carr and Sharon Miller. Zoe claimed they were in a close relationship. I sent Carr's picture through to Klaus Krenkel; asked him to show it to the German who pulled the girl from the river. Had a message back this morning. Witness says it was too dark by that bridge to make any identification with the man who ran off.'

Heather then revealed her failure to discover anything useful from her undercover attempt to buy a present for her teenage brother.

'Jake Morgan's an arrogant misogynist in the making. Told me in no uncertain terms the club was for members only, and adults, however enterprising, were denied membership. We'll have to approach it from another angle,' she concluded. 'Jake Morgan is one very sharp character, and it's always tricky questioning minors.' She looked at Tom. 'I know the problem with your daughters, sir, and it's important that we sort this before they become too involved. Is it possible for you to keep them away from Jake's summerhouse until we know if what they're buying are stolen goods?'

'I've already told my wife we're investigating the club. She'll keep the girls otherwise occupied.' He gave a wry grin. 'I may have to claim heavy expenses if she has to take them to *Demoiselle* too often.'

Heather returned his grin. 'That store's a teen's paradise.'

'I agree it's tricky to advance the case through schoolkids,' said Max, 'but there's a vital lead we must follow. Zoe claimed Carr had a close relationship with Sharon Miller. She hinted that it was sexual?' he asked, looking at Piercey. At the Sergeant's nod, he continued. 'Sharon is sixteen. That's not underage, but she is still at school. We have to establish if her parents knew what she was up to. It seems unlikely, in view of Miller's fierce hatred of Carr. So have we found the reason for it? Could Miller have been told of his daughter's affair on the morning of the assault during which Carr disappeared? In short, is Sharon Miller the key to why Carr had to go AWOL, or be got rid of?'

'We're back to the body in a shallow grave,' murmured Piercey. Then, louder, 'Miller has a very short fuse. He'd have no problem with putting an end to someone who'd been bonking his school age daughter.'

'But he stayed with the Warrior during the assault,' Heather reminded him. 'It was geographically impossible for him to kill Carr.'

'Then he paid someone else to do it,' snapped Piercey. 'He bloody knows where Carr is.'

Tom intervened. 'I suspect Sharon Miller could give us info that would help us get on top of the case. The only response we've had from posting his details on HOLMES has come from UK forces who want to question him about year-old crimes. No recent sightings or anonymous tip-offs—'

'Apart from the call saying someone had finally done for him,' inserted Piercey doggedly.

'—so it's very likely Carr is still in Germany, hiding out somewhere.'

'In a shallow grave?' suggested Heather with a poker face.

'OK, we've had enough adolescent jibing,' Tom ruled harshly. 'Start behaving like adults with some sense of responsibility. You had bugger all to do with the Farley case, so get your thick heads around this one and do some bloody serious thinking. The I in SIB stands for *investigation*. You've forgotten the meaning of the word.'

Max got to his feet. 'I have to spend the morning writing my report on the Farley case. After lunch I'll tackle Captain Morgan; find out if he's aware of what Jake is doing in that summerhouse. Mr Black says the boy has a Brummie accent. Did he or his father make that call to George Maddox? How well did they know Carr, or Smith as he was then called?'

He turned to Connie. 'We need to speak to Sharon Miller. Find out if she's in a fit condition to be questioned. She received head injuries, and brain specialists are always hot on protecting their patients from emotional stress. We've had no reason to chart her progress, so I want you to interview her mother. Ask if the girl is allowed visitors other than next of kin. Discreet probing regarding Sharon's friendship with Carr will tell us if Zoe lied about its depth.' He smiled at the ultra-proficient girl. 'You'll manage, in your inimitable way, to coax far more from the woman than she'll be aware of giving. Get her when she's alone. Avoid an hour when Miller is likely to arrive home.'

He concentrated on Piercey. 'I want you to interview Zoe Rogers; in correct fashion this time, in her mother's presence. Get her to confirm that the J.S. she mentioned *is* John Smith, and persuade her to reveal just how he made her life more exciting. Apart from the obvious. He surely wasn't having sex with her too.'

'She made it pretty obvious not. I imagine *yuk* was a denial of anything of that nature.'

Max gave a faint smile. 'I don't know what definition the Oxford English gives the word, but the mere sound of it is probably self-explanatory. Use *tact*, Sergeant. We don't want a complaint of police brutality from the parent.'

'This suggestion of Carr making life exciting is intriguing,' put in Derek Beeny. 'Every male we've interviewed found him creepy, slimy, sly, cowardly, you name it. Doesn't sound as if he could make *anyone's* life exciting.'

'You're not a sixteen year old who imagines she'll be the next Meryl Streep,' said his friend, Piercey.

'All the same—'

Max interrupted Beeny's further observations. 'Have another go at CD and DVD suppliers. Market traders, and the foreign immigrants who sell from suitcases in the streets. You'll have to fix for one of Klaus Krenkel's guys to go with you. Carr *had* to get them from someone a bit dodgy.' He then focussed on Olly Simpson. 'Tour the pubs and clubs. Suss out if anyone's doing business there. You can go solo on that. We'll inform the *Polizei* if we uncover anything.'

He crossed to where Heather sat. 'We'll need to stay abreast of the Farley case. Contact Lewes CID. Ask how far they've got with those bikers; whether they have evidence that Phil Hawkins, the junior half of the taxi business, was in on the plan to pick up and steal from Farley. Try to wheedle from them what charge they're likely to bring against those four louts, and the possible date of it going to trial. Lieutenant Farley will have to attend, which could mean flying him home from Afghanistan. It might even prevent him from being sent out there with his platoon. I hope not. He might see it as a triumph for Trish Stannard.'

'*She* would certainly see it that way,' said Heather tartly. 'The backlog in UK criminal courts will more likely mean Farley will have done his tour in Afghanistan and been back here some weeks before he's called.'

'I'll have to give evidence of how I found him, and the state he was in. I shan't mince words, believe me.'

Once everyone had been detailed to undertake one task relevant to a case that had been revitalized by Zoe Rogers's gossip, Max and Tom went to the former's office for a less formal discussion.

'Have a nice time last night?' Tom asked casually. 'Saw you leaving with the Doc. Medical emergency?'

Max laughed. 'Cheeky bugger! She wanted my opinion on an apartment she was going to view.'

'Big enough for two?'

'She's married, Tom.'

'Not for much longer, I hear. He's too fond of the GTGs.' He saw Max's eyebrows lift. 'Good time girls.'

'Guards' officers get the pick of 'em frequenting the exclusive clubs in town. I don't envy him. Not my scene at all.'

'How about his missus?'

'She's her own woman.'

'So, he turns to one-night stands to compensate? Add the fact that she's over here and he's in London, and you've got one very dysfunctional marriage. The moment she became a military medic it didn't stand a chance.'

'It cuts both ways. He can be sent to any place on earth at any time, and at very short notice.'

'But he can only be a soldier in the Army. She could be a civilian doctor.' Tom allowed a moment or two to pass before asking, 'Manage to see Captain Cordwell this week?'

'Briefly.' He hesitated, then said somewhat reflectively, 'Your Nora is an exceptional woman.'

'She's not in the Army. Never has been. That's what you have to look for.'

'Yes, and end up the same as Farley, with a girl like Trish Stannard.' He then turned back to the job. 'In view of this new info regarding Carr and Sharon Miller, I sense that the relationship is truly behind Carr's sudden panic to run. We need to question Miller again, find out if he was contacted by his wife or someone who had discovered what was going on, on the very morning of that assault. Did he then threaten Carr with a parent's fury? Put yourself in Miller's place, Tom. How would you react if you received a call from Nora, on the brink of taking part in a simulated battle exercise, telling you your teenage daughter was having sex with a squaddie you regarded as the lowest of the low?'

Recalling how he had behaved at Easter when he had come upon Maggie kissing Hans Graumann, a perfectly innocent gesture of farewell to a thoroughly nice lad, Tom sighed.

'I guess my initial urge would be to half-kill him, but in that situation I'd be limited to telling him I'd see to it he never had sex with anyone for the rest of his life. I'd put the fear of God in him.'

'Exactly, and there we have the totally plausible answer to why Carr was impelled to leave before the end of that day.'

'And to why Miller was visibly resistant to Farley's determination to send the Warriors out again to search for the missing man.' Tom got to his feet. 'I'll go over to the West Wilts now and tackle Miller. Must remember to call the bastard *Smith*.'

Max called after him, 'Tom, douse the fire! It's not one of your girls he's been playing around with.'

Tom glanced back with a grin. 'Wait until you become a father. You'll be equally protective.'

As he left the building he realized what he had said and regretted it, although Max had surely recovered from the loss of his embryo son, along with Susan. Livya Cordwell had helped Max to put his life back on track, yet their relationship did not appear to be running smoothly.

# TWELVE

'That little slag's not my girl, she's his. Thinks the sun shines out of. Won't accept the truth,' Molly Miller told Connie aggressively. 'Craig and Pierce are mine. She even had a go at *them*. Go on, tell the sergeant what she did,' she ordered. 'Go on, *tell* her.'

Connie regarded the two flat-faced, overweight boys leering at her and had an inkling why Eric Miller and his daughter behaved as they did. This woman must be hell to live with.

'Could we talk in private, Mrs Miller? I'm sure your sons want to carry on with their computer game.'

'There's nothing you'll say that they're not entitled to hear. This is their home, even if they have to share it with Sharon. They have every right to know what she's been up to.' A satisfied grin. 'Just you wait until you hear what they've got to say about their *sister*.'

The fatter of the two boys said, 'She come in our bedroom in just knickers. Them ones that show all yer bum. Said did we know what girls look like.'

'We was watching telly, like,' the other boy added. 'Took no notice.'

'So she took 'em off. *Right* off, like, and hung 'em over the telly.'

'We tells 'er to bugger off,' the first one said with relish, but she stands there mooning at us until she 'ears 'er dad come in.'

'Ran to 'er room then, din' she, Craig?'

'Yeah. Left 'er knickers on the telly, though.'

Their mother treated Connie to a smug smile. 'See what I mean? I told my husband what she'd done. Did she get the tanning she deserved? Nah, he won't have a word against her, and she denied it, of course. Said the boys must've took the knickers from her room when she was out.'

Connie had heard enough to tell she would get nothing useful here, so she asked whether Sharon had recovered enough to answer a few questions. 'Is she allowed visitors apart from her family?'

'Eric goes to the hospital when he can. We don't, of course. Silly bitch brought it on herself, didn't she? No way do we feel sorry for her.'

'Is she allowed visitors?' Connie asked again.

Molly Miller sniffed. 'Go if you want. She'll only give you a pack of lies. That girl is bad through and through.'

'It's better 'ere without 'er and 'er knickers, in't it, Pierce?'

'Yeah.'

Connie left, unsurprised that Sharon had turned to Carr for friendship, even if Zoe Rogers's opinion of him was *yuk*. In desperation, people respond to anyone offering a hand. Had it been a case of two unhappy misfits getting together?

Tom found Eric Miller in the Warrior sheds with several mechanics, checking repairs to his vehicle. The Sergeant scowled when he saw who had approached, and muttered something that sent the other two men away pretty smartly.

'You haven't found Smith yet.' It was a clear challenge that gave Tom the perfect opening.

'We have reason to believe your daughter might be able to help us with that.'

'Sharon? She's been in hospital seriously ill. I told you that.'

Something about Miller's manner, some instinct, told Tom the man was unaware of the truth. If it *was* the truth. They only had Zoe's gossip to go on, yet Connie's call to Max regarding her very short encounter with the Miller family, which Max had passed on to him only minutes ago, gave Tom a fair idea of what Sharon might be like.

'Let's talk outside,' he said, walking from the vast shed to one of the small grassy areas dotted around the base to soften the military austerity.

Miller followed, leaden-footed. 'What's this about?'

Tom faced him, deciding there was no point in pussy-footing with this blunt man, who more than probably had to defend his daughter to his vindictive family, while privately despairing.

'We have a witness who says Sharon was in a close relationship with John Smith before her accident.'

Miller's face suffused with ruddy colour. 'Bring him here. Let him say it to my face and I'll shut his filthy mouth for good.'

'You weren't aware of the relationship?'

'*There was no relationship*! With that slimy, creepy bugger? Tell me who says there was and I'll soon put him wise.'

Tom changed direction. 'Your wife told one of my team she's not Sharon's mother. Did you divorce the woman who is?'

Miller angled his head to look back at the Warriors parked in the shed, wiping his large hand over his mouth several times. 'She died three hours after the baby was induced,' he said after a moment or two.

Tom waited silently.

'We weren't married. She wasn't quite seventeen; I was in Bosnia. Her people kicked her out when she got pregnant, so she was living with mine. They looked after the kiddy until I married Molly.' He wiped his mouth again with his oily hand. A sign of stress. 'It worked fine while her boys were small kids, although Sharon went through a jealous patch after being the centre of attention for five years.'

'The boys aren't your sons?'

Miller shook his head. 'Molly's ex set up house with another poof just after Pierce was born. Craig was at the same nursery as Sharon. That's how I met up with Molly. We both thought it would be a good arrangement, and Moll was taken with having a little girl.'

'Now she's grown into a developing woman, which brings different problems. I know, I have three daughters.'

Still gazing at the sheds, Miller said, 'The boys are getting interested in sex, *that's* the problem. Sharon's sixteen and she's not their sister. She's no blood relation, and they know it.'

'So your daughter found someone more mature than the adolescent schoolboys she lives with. John Smith was shunned by every member of his platoon, so he found friendship with another person unhappy in her environment.'

Miller's head swung round. '*No!*'

'Who was with Sharon when she attempted to walk along that wall?'

'Who knows? A group of friends?'

'The German witness saw only one man with her. A man who ran off when she fell. Mightn't he have been Smith? Isn't that the kind of cowardly act you'd expect of that "slimy, creepy bugger"?'

Miller stared at Tom for several moments as that idea took root. Then he said with quiet menace, 'I'll kill him!'

'Is that what you told him on the morning he vanished?'

'What?' He seemed bewildered. 'I was sick of his faffing around with his daysack straps while the rest went into action. I yelled at him that I'd sort him out good and proper at the end of that day.'

And Carr/Smith read something more sinister in those words, and ran. In Tom's mind facts began rapidly to click into place. The possibility of it being Carr who took fright when Sharon toppled from that bridge became a near certainty. Zoe Rogers lives next door to Sharon; she knew the girl was dating Carr. Zoe is the girlfriend of Jake, who is selling fully-packaged CDs and DVDs. Carr had a locker full of them. Jake Morgan has a Brummie accent. *Don't bother looking for Smith. Someone's finally done him in.* Had Jake taken over Carr's enterprise because he knew the young squaddie was dead?

Max was driving to the local hospital instead of seeking out Jake Morgan's father. Tom had called half an hour ago after his interview with Eric Miller, which had put a wholly different slant on the Carr case. Had they been investigating the wrong people? Did the answers lie not with 3 Platoon or, indeed, even with the West Wilts, but with a group of teens trading in a garden summerhouse? Max had been given the go-ahead to question Sharon Miller by the consultant dealing with her case. He had also agreed to Max's request for a nurse to be present throughout his visit. The appropriate adult.

Although deep in thought, Max was nevertheless aware of passing the apartment Clare was due to occupy at the end of next week. Pity. He would miss seeing her in the Mess. She provided a touch of feminine freshness amid the khaki-clad horde. It remained to be seen whether her titled Guards' officer would share it with her in a bid for reconciliation.

Sharon was in a side room, at the end of the ward in which Max had visited a corporal's son who had been attacked, prior to Christmas. A terrible tragedy had played out following that attack. One of the saddest cases Max had handled.

A nurse, busy in the ward, spotted him and came over. They went together into Sharon's room, after a swift warning in excellent English from the motherly woman that the patient had said she would not speak to any more policemen.

'She is an unhappy girl, Colonel. I think it is at home that she feels very alone. Because she does not wish to return, she is pretending headaches and pain. You must understand her manners.'

Ignoring his amazingly fast promotion, Max was again reminded of the boy, Kevin, who had also done his best to prevent being sent home. No lover of hospitals, Max had done everything in his power to leave as soon as possible on the few occasions he had been ill. Having heard the reports from both Tom and Connie, it was easy to understand why the girl would be happier here than in a home dominated by a stepmother doting on two spoiled boys.

Sharon Miller was a very plain girl: straw-coloured hair with vivid pink stripes here and there, watery blue eyes and thin lips. Her arms and shoulders were bony; her breasts almost as flat as a boy's beneath the pyjama top. Her aggressive expression did nothing to enhance her looks. Would this girl be desperate enough for a boyfriend to cultivate the detested John Smith? Possibly. And would *he* be desperate enough to encourage her? That was what he was there to find out.

'I *told* you I won't talk to any policemen,' Sharon shouted at the nurse, her face twisting in fury.

'I don't particularly want to talk to you, either,' Max said equably. 'Unfortunately, my job demands that I do.'

The scowl had been replaced by slight surprise. 'You're not with the *Polizei*?'

Max shook his head. 'Special Investigation Branch. We're trying to trace Private John Smith. We've been told he was your boyfriend.'

'By that bitch, Zoe Rogers?'

'Was he your boyfriend, Sharon?'

The girl angled her head to look through the window alongside her bed. 'Never heard of him.'

'He went missing during the exercise your dad took part in. He was in your dad's Warrior, but never came back in it. I'm sure you heard about that.'

She stared wordlessly from the window.

'You don't recall your dad mentioning it; don't remember your friends discussing his sudden disappearance?'

'I'm suffering from retrograde amnesia.' It was said with scathing pomposity.

'Dating from when?' Max asked, already sensing he would lose this present battle. The hospital authorities, and the Army staff on the Joint Response Team who protected minors, would not allow him to persist in questioning her if she kept up this resistance. There was also the girl's father, who would swiftly launch a complaint of police persecution, he had no doubt.

'From when I fell off the bridge.'

'So you do remember doing that?'

She turned back to glare at him. 'No, dimmo, they *told* me.'

'Did they also tell you the man with you ran off and made no attempt to pull you from the river?' She continued to glare. 'Did they tell you that man was John Smith?'

'He wouldn't of run away,' she cried defensively.

'Because he was fond of you?'

Recognizing her slip of the tongue, she turned back to the window. 'If that John Smith you're talking about was a soldier, he wouldn't of run away from *anything*. I want you to go. I'm seriously ill, you know, and you're making my headache worse.'

'Pity you've forgotten everything. From what I've been told, John was very fond of you, regarded you as his special girlfriend. He would want to share your suffering. If we could only discover where he is we could tell him you're seriously ill. He'd e-mail or text you.'

Suddenly and distressingly, she began to cry. 'No, he wouldn't. He wouldn't care. Nobody cares.'

Pretending not to see the nurse's warning gesture, Max sat on the chair beside the bed, saying quietly, 'Your father cares, Sharon. He told us about your mother, and how your grandparents looked after you for five years. Surely they care too.'

She swung round, face streaked with tears. 'So why'd they let that cow have me? She's got those two monsters of her own, so why didn't Gran and Pop keep me? We were all right as we were.'

'I can't answer those questions. Perhaps your dad needed someone to care for *him*.'

'She doesn't. All she thinks of is those two ugly snots.'

'So you spend as much time with your friends as you can?'

Tears flowed again. 'They all hate me now. Say I've spoiled everything. It's not my fault he went. I wouldn't of sent him away. I just wouldn't of.'

Max could not ignore the nurse this time. She gripped his arm. 'You must go. My patient is distressed. You have to leave.'

Seeing Sharon turn from a rude, aggressive girl into a desperately unhappy child, Max was again reminded of the boy in his earlier case. So often his investigations lifted the roof from a seemingly normal household to reveal unsuspected desires and resentments, which led to criminal activity. Ordinary people who had become dangerous when put together.

Lightly touching Sharon's hair in leaving, Max walked to his car thinking of Edward and Stella Smith, whose dead boy's identity had been taken by the son of a man who had abandoned him, and of a woman who was sinking to the depths of helplessness. Two houses in a row of others like them with no evidence of the tragedies within, yet he had had to uncover them. He was now on the brink of another in the Miller household.

Sharon had said her friends accused her of 'spoiling everything'. Piercey's report on his second conversation with Zoe Rogers quoted that girl as saying Jake claimed Sharon had 'spoiled everything' by falling in the river. Just how that made sense still had to be revealed. One thing was certain. Jack Carr had been involved with Jake and Co. in the sale of CDs and DVDs. The source of the goods, and the outlet for sales, had still to be discovered, but the clue to Carr's whereabouts was surely somewhere in that set-up.

Sharon would have to be questioned again. Max's instincts told him she held the key to this curious case. One of the women on his team – probably Connie Bush – would have to coax more from her, possibly in the company of a woman from the Joint Response Team. Useless for either parent to be present. They would simply agitate her beyond medical limits.

At the late afternoon briefing, Piercey was forced to admit he had been unsuccessful with Zoe Rogers. In the presence of her mother she had denied everything she had said about the Miller girl, and pretended she had no idea what he was talking about when asked if the J.S. mentioned was a private in the West Wilts named John Smith.

'Never heard of him. Must've been someone else told you about J.S. Maybe when you were acting undercover,' she had added with wide-eyed innocence.

'I don't think there's any doubt that these kids are running a scam in the Morgan summerhouse,' Piercey concluded. 'Carr was involved, hence the comments that Sharon Miller had spoiled everything. They blame her for Carr's absence, yet she was in hospital when he took off.'

Tom came in on that. 'We have a possible explanation

for his abscondment.' He outlined what Eric Miller had revealed. 'His threat to sort him out good and proper at the end of that day could have been seen by Carr as proof that Miller had discovered what he was up to with Sharon.'

'And if Carr was the guy who ran off when Sharon fell from the bridge, he'd have additional cause to disappear,' put in Max. 'From what we know of Carr he's always run rather than face the music.'

Tom then spoke of his interview with Kenneth Morgan, which had taken place while Max had driven to the hospital. 'Far from deploring his son's choice of a career in the theatrical world, as some military fathers would, he's convinced Jake's a genius. Being REME, Captain Morgan is into things electrical. He enthused ad infinitum about the way Jake has turned a run-down summerhouse into an audio studio single-handed, and at his own expense. As far as the club is concerned, it was only set up by Jake and his pals a couple of weeks ago. Just after the great storm.' Glancing at them all, he said, 'You'll realize the significance of that timescale. As soon as Carr was out of the picture, Jake stepped in.'

'So they must know where Carr got the stuff,' said Heather.

Tom nodded at Beeny. 'Any joy with your check on dodgy suppliers?'

He gave a faint smile. 'Because they're dodgy, it's not easy to check them out. Drew a blank, sir.'

'OK, understood. We may have to get what we need from the kids themselves.'

'We'll have to tread carefully,' Max cautioned. 'These kids aren't military personnel, although they come under our jurisdiction. I suggest we consider our options again on Monday. Meanwhile, I want you all to go on a pub crawl tomorrow night; check out anyone selling CDs or DVDs that fell off the back of a lorry. The weekend will give the kids the notion we've given up on them. They'll relax. More chance of catching them unprepared if we have no alternative but to solve this case through them.'

\*　　\*　　\*

Max woke on Saturday morning totally unrefreshed. Sleep had been troubled by the problems that had haunted him the previous evening. Images of people had paraded through his mind as he attempted once more to read the biography of Sir Edmund Hillary.

The Smiths, whose lives had been broken up by the loss of their only son; Minnie Carr who, paradoxically, suffered similarly; a scared, despairing child fated to become just like the very people she presently condemned; a tailor's dummy parading as an estate agent and calling him Mr Goodey; Clare, to whom he had stupidly confessed secrets; Dan Farley, naked and vomiting beside a rotting barn; the spoiled and egotistical Trish Stannard; her bigot of a mother.

It had been recollections of that pair that had stopped him from calling Livya yesterday. He would not be as weak as Farley had been over a woman. This morning, he knew he could not let the silence continue between himself and someone he cared for. Clare had not offered advice; she had simply listened. Did she see reflections of her own relationship in what he had told her in that beguiling dusk beside the river?

A sudden sense of betrayal had him reaching for the telephone. He punched in Livya's landline number and waited with quickened heartbeat.

'Livya Cordwell.' It was the voice of someone roused from sleep.

'Hi! Thought I'd call early before you shoot off on urgent business.' It was not what he had meant to say, and had it sounded rather cool?

'That was yesterday. Can you believe I have an entire weekend to myself? Talk to me nicely; tell me gentle things. I intend to stay in bed until mid-morning, so I need cosseting words and sweet promises that'll keep me in this drowsy state until you end your call. Then I'll slip back into sleep without any problems.'

Cosseting words and sweet promises? What on earth did she mean? Not an account of how he had found Dan Farley, and certainly not a description of the apartment he had viewed with Clare before having dinner with her.

A sexy chuckle came over the line. 'Lost for words, Steve? I can almost picture your expression.'

'If I was there with you you'd have no difficulty slipping back into sleep after my *physical* cosseting,' he said, back on course now she had called him Steve.

'Not with that strapping to inhibit you,' she said softly. 'Come over when she's removed it and declared you fit for anything.'

'You come here. There's less chance of my father calling you out urgently at the worst possible time.' He developed that thought. 'Why didn't you come last night, knowing you had a free weekend?'

'We were together only four days ago, and I really need to laze around and recoup my energy. I'm dog-tired, and I know I was snappy with you on Tuesday. When we meet next time I want us to have a truly relaxing time.'

'And I want to resolve this bloody long-distance relationship. It's been going on for nine months and I . . .'

'I know, darling, but now isn't the moment to make important decisions. We have to get together and review all the options; take time over something demanding dramatic changes.'

'I'll come over on the noon flight and return on the late one tomorrow night. That should give us long enough.'

'Max, you're being uncharacteristically impetuous. That's no way to make a decision that'll affect our careers.'

'Bugger our careers! I'm talking about happiness, peace of mind, enduring devotion, a home together, children . . .'

'Marriage?'

'Of course marriage.'

There was a brief silence. 'That's why I said we have to get together and review the options. We can't do that with a phone call.'

Max was heading on a course that refused to meet buffers. 'I can ask you to marry me with a phone call. And you can give me your answer with a phone call.' Into the resulting silence, he said, 'Livya Cordwell, will you do me the honour of becoming my wife?'

'You silly, romantic idiot,' she said softly.

'Is that a yes?'

There was another brief silence until she said, 'If we decide we can make it work.'

'I'll come over.'

'No, Max. Nothing's changed. I'm still dog-tired, and you're in the middle of two complex cases.'

Feeling thwarted and needing an outlet for his strong feelings, he said, 'I've solved one, and the other is close to resolution.' She failed to respond. 'As a woman who's just been proposed to you're supposed to be in transports of delight and eager to be given a diamond ring to dazzle your friends and colleagues with. I want to fly over and buy you one.'

'Oh God, one of us has to be sensible about this, and you appear to have been reading too much Barbara Cartland. We're not straight out of the egg, Max. We've been around a bit and seen the pitfalls; why marriages fail. We're both aware that our respective careers could be a stumbling block and we need to consider those problems before we go ahead with something like this.'

Deflated, disappointed by her common-sense attitude when he was hyped-up, he made his feelings apparent. 'You're right. I've mistimed it. Should have waited until I could go on one knee with low lights and champagne, and produce a velvet box containing an impressive solitaire.'

After a moment or two, Livya said, 'You can do all that once we've thrashed out the pros and cons of living as a married couple, darling. One thing, though. I have my Slavic grandmother's betrothal ring. I'd prefer that to a modern solitaire.'

'Yes, of course. But you won't start wearing it until we've thrashed out the pros and cons?'

'That's only sensible.'

'Yes.' He tried to sound sensible. 'As soon as this remaining case is wound up, I'll take a week's leave, possibly longer. I've several days due to me. If you tell my father you need a long break at the same time, we'll consolidate our plans.'

'The first weeks of October should be ideal. I know there's a good chance of a quiet period then.'

'That's five weeks away!'

'We'll talk every evening, and it'll give us time to get our minds around the issues involved.'

'The main issue is that I want to be with you all the time.'

'Exactly, darling, so we have to work out the best solution to that.'

He knew, even then, that she did not consider it to involve relinquishing her appointment as ADC to Brigadier Rydal, and he ended the call unsure whether she was engaged to him or not.

Restless, angry with himself for handling things so badly, deeply disappointed with Livya's response to his proposal – weren't women supposed to be thrilled and excited on such occasions? – Max had to ease his frustration with action. Tamping down the urge to take the noon flight anyway, he drove to the river. A skiff was out of the question and he very soon discovered the strapping round his chest also made a canoe impossible to control. Yet he longed to seek the solitary, shady stretches of green water, where he could ease his bruised spirits.

Gerhardt, who hired out the boats, suggested Max take one of the small motor-powered craft. 'There is no exercise. It is just sit and steer.' Seeing Max's frown, he added, 'It is possible to go far in this one. To the weir is such easy and you will like to go on a day with sun. Yes, I say you this will be good, Captain.'

Against his inclination, Max set off in what he thought of as a tub more suited to the elderly or a young woman with children. *We're not straight out of the egg, Max.* No, but they were young enough to be impulsive now and again. *You appear to have been reading too much Barbara Cartland.* Books the elderly read to try and recapture their youth? Is that how she saw him?

Unbidden, the old suspicions of her feelings for his father returned. Did she prefer the wisdom and steadiness of an older man; someone who would never make a proposal of marriage over the phone? Was that why she had avoided a direct acceptance? *If we decide we can make it work.*

Even his flippant comment that he should go on one knee, with low lights and champagne, she had countered with the suggestion of waiting until after they had thrashed out the pros and cons of living as a married couple. She did not even want his ring. She had her own.

At that low point he realized he was doing what he had vowed not to: emulating Dan Farley's refusal to look beyond hormonal passion. Opening the throttle, he sent the little craft faster through the water, heading to the unfamiliar stretch leading to the weir. What he should do was go out tonight and pick up a bimbo who would satisfy his hunger and match this urge to go a little wild.

The river was deeper and darker here. It also ran faster after tumbling over the dam. White foam capped the wavelets that set Max's boat rocking. Something about that boisterous water and the thunder of the cascade ahead excited him. It suited his mood. He never came here in the skiff. Too risky. But this broad-waisted little tub could ride the rushing, dancing flow with sensible handling.

The river widened slightly, the banks having been worn away over the years. They were edged with a tangle of debris, deposited by the surge that had been considerably swollen during the recent storm. Now, even two weeks later, the huge glistening wave sliding over the dam breached the banks to swamp the wooded stretch along the first fifty yards.

Max eased the throttle so that he could just hold the boat steady while he gazed in delight at the natural waterfall, enjoying the coolness of spray on his face. Gerhardt had been right. This was very good on a day with sun, and the evidence of power and certainty this gave out restored his equilibrium. The vessel was sucked in towards the right bank, but he was content with that. He was in no hurry to leave this spectacle.

Progress was halted by debris beneath an overhanging bough. Max tied the painter to it, and sat reviewing more calmly what Livya had said. She was right in saying big decisions must be made before they embarked on marriage. As he grew even calmer, the small voice he had heard before whispered that the kind of life Tom had with Nora would never be found with the woman he loved.

Time passed as he recalled the ups and downs of his years with Susan. What had been so wonderfully promising at the start had gone spectacularly wrong. Did he want to risk that happening again? The charm and vibrancy of the weir suddenly vanished and he saw only a cold, green slide of water that carried everything inexorably forward. Go with it, or cling to an anchor and be pummelled by its relentlessness. To defy it would be a long, hard struggle.

Growing cold in the shade of the trees, and chilled by his thoughts, Max reached up to untie the painter. The knot remained untouched as he saw something floating in the middle of storm debris. Something he recognized very well. The body wore combat trousers and a khaki T-shirt.

# THIRTEEN

Tom drove to work on Monday morning in a bad mood, wishing the school holiday was over. The effort of keeping their girls away from Jake's club was wearing Nora down. She had tackled him on the subject last night, declaring that it was growing too expensive. Maggie, Gina and Beth naturally wanted to be with their friends, so the outings to *Demoiselle*, or to various local attractions, frequently meant Nora escorting six or seven youngsters. Entrance fees and refreshments, to say nothing of petrol costs, were mounting up in an alarming fashion. She was also having to invent reasons why the Black sisters could not accept invitations, for fear of these culminating in a visit to Jake's summerhouse.

Tom sympathized because it meant Nora had little time to herself, a breather from the demands of motherhood, yet he was unable to see a solution while SIB interest in the sixth-former's enterprise remained. Nora had asked that he tell their offspring why they were being kept from the club, but he claimed it would be putting too great a burden on them and involving them in police activities, which was unacceptable.

At breakfast there had been a difficult scene and Nora had lost her temper. They had turned to him for support, which he could not give. Instead, he had rashly suggested they and their mother could go over for three days to a favourite Dutch holiday resort, where they could sail and waterski on the lake. He had been smothered with kisses of delight from the girls, but received mixed messages from Nora. Maggie's delight had diminished on being told Hans was not included in the scheme. Or any schoolfriends.

Advising them to spend the day packing and preparing for the trip, Tom had then been followed to his car by a

wife asking if he would get to the bottom of the suspicion
surrounding the DVD club before they were broke.

On reaching Section Headquarters, Tom found the team
all looking bright-eyed and bushy-tailed. The advent of Jack
Carr's body had started a buzz of renewed interest in the
case. The 'floater', as corpses found in water were named,
had been positively identified by Carr's dental records.
Because it had been discovered in the river, Klaus Krenkel's
men had initially dealt with the case, and a German pathologist had examined it. Once identity was established, the
*Polizei* were happy to let SIB work in conjunction with
them and gave them free rein.

Tom opened proceedings by dampening any suggestion
that the Carr case had been resolved. 'We have the answer
to where he is, but he's left us with a number of questions
on why he ended up in the river.' Unable to resist it, he
glanced across at Phil Piercey. 'Rather knocked on the head
your theory of Dan Farley killing him and putting him in
a shallow grave.'

Undeterred, Piercey grinned. 'He dumped Carr in the
river instead, during that bogus search of the exercise
ground. That's when the storm broke and the river broke
its banks. Easy peasy!'

Derek Beeny, Piercey's friend, intervened before Tom's
temper reacted to that bit of baiting. 'Doctor Mannfried's
report gives an approximate period of immersion as two
weeks, which certainly ties in with the date of the great
storm.'

'It also states that Carr had received a blow to the side
of his skull caused by contact with a smooth, round object,
although the cause of death was water in the lungs. In effect,
drowning. There could be a sinister interpretation of that
injury to his head, but it's perfectly possible it could have
been received during an accidental fall, so don't get carried
away by thoughts of murder,' Tom warned.

'So why the phone call saying someone had finally done
in Smith, as he was then known?' asked Olly Simpson,
doodling as usual.

'That was received on the day before the storm, and I've

a good idea who made it. Jake Morgan has a Brummie accent, and he's a cocky little bastard who's surely tied in with Carr's DVD enterprise.'

Max looked up from the pathologist's report and nodded. 'I agree there appears to be a significant link between the dead man and the club run by Jake and Co. So far, there's no evidence to link it with Carr's death, however, and I doubt we'll find any to support that.

'Let's review what we do know. Carr disappeared during the exercise and drowned in the river two days later. There's no indication of where he entered the water but let's say he fell, or was pushed in somewhere around the area just six Ks from the exercise ground. During and after the storm the swollen waters swept the body along until it crossed the weir and lodged in the debris, where I came upon it. One fact is surely unarguable. If Carr had been bludgeoned and shoved unconscious to his watery grave, the perpetrator could not have been a member of the West Wilts. They had returned to base.'

'It could have been the local racketeer who'd been supplying Carr with pirated goods to sell,' suggested Heather. 'His outside contact who'd promised to aid his desertion. They fell out, and the dodgy German ensured Carr would never scupper the business.'

'But all our exhaustive questioning over the past two weeks hasn't produced a single lead to that premise,' Beeny pointed out. 'We've scoured the pubs and clubs again this weekend and got zilch. All we do know is that Carr made lists in almost every store in town, but bought nothing.'

'Or stole it,' added Piercey. 'They watched him carefully, yet no one caught him shoplifting.'

'So he *must* have had a supplier,' Heather insisted.

'Must be a very, very shy one, because all our combined efforts didn't uncover even a hint of his identity,' Beeny reminded her.

Tom brought them back to the subject of Jake Morgan's club. 'Zoe Rogers told Piercey, when she was unaware of his real job, that J.S. had made life exciting. She also said he and Sharon Miller were an item.'

'And when I mentioned the name John Smith to Sharon she certainly betrayed having knowledge of him,' added Max. 'Those schoolkids are tied in with Carr's dubious activities. We have to get from *them* clues to what led to his death.'

'You think Jake Morgan killed him?' asked Connie in surprise.

'I didn't say that.'

'But he could've,' reasoned Olly Simpson. 'A kid like him could get too big for his boots and make demands that Carr wasn't able or prepared to meet. Jake wasn't home exhausted after the exercise. He had every opportunity to rendezvous with Carr by the river and, when Carr wouldn't play along, shove him in.'

Grabbing that theory, Piercey elaborated on it. 'Jake could have been the outside contact to aid Carr's desertion. That would have given him a hold over Carr and furthered his chances of getting what he wanted.'

Tom shook his head. 'No, no, that kid is more mouth than motive. He might think himself a big fish in the pond, but it's a very small pond and he has his sights on a career in a much bigger one in the theatre world. I called him a cocky bastard, and that's all he is.'

Connie Bush, who had also encountered Jake Morgan, agreed. 'Add male chauvinism and you have the complete description of him. He's certainly all for number one, but he's no killer. When he enters the tooth and claw world of theatre he'll soon be cut down to size.'

Tom studied them all, then addressed Beeny. 'Go and talk to Jake about where he was in the week preceding the West Wilts' departure on exercise. Now we know Carr *did* desert, that lad might provide a clue as to why. Don't go in heavy enough to inflate his self-importance, but make it clear we're aware that he was associated with John Smith through his girlfriend Zoe.'

He then focussed on Olly Simpson. 'You can tackle the girl. Take Heather along to satisfy regulations, but do all the talking yourself and make no secret of your authority in investigating the suspicious death of a man we know she had dealings with.'

As these three prepared to leave, Tom detailed Piercey to seek out and question the other two sixth-form lads running the club with Jake. 'I'd say they're simply basking in his shadow, but they might have something useful to contribute towards Carr's behaviour leading up to the exercise. You *can* go in heavy with them, impressing on them the seriousness of our investigation.'

Piercey left, relishing these instructions, and Tom turned to find Max talking intently, to Connie Bush. She nodded and went to collect her bag and car keys, before also going on her way. As Tom cast an interrogatory look, he was invited to Max's office for a cup of coffee.

'Where've you sent Connie?' he asked, as Max switched on the kettle.

'The hospital.' He turned. 'We need info from Sharon Miller. I swear she holds the key to all this, Tom. It's tricky. She's a minor and recovering from a dangerous fall. She's also in a volatile emotional state. That's all ranged against us, but that girl needs to pour out her troubles to someone she senses she can trust. Connie's good in such cases. She empathizes, people respond to her.'

'But you said she's hiding behind imagined amnesia,' Tom reminded him, spooning coffee into two mugs.

'Because she doesn't want to be sent home to face a blowsy stepmother and two lewd, pubescent boys. She fears her father's reaction to discovering her relationship with Carr, and she's shattered by what she sees as rejection by a man she believed had some love for her. Her so-called friends are blaming her for spoiling whatever they had going. Who can she unload her burden on?'

Stirring the coffee as Max poured boiling water, Tom gave the official answer. 'A professional woman trained to deal with such cases.'

'And I consider our Connie to be such a person. OK, she's not an accredited member of a child protection group, but she's experienced enough to approach Sharon correctly.' Max poured milk in the mugs, took one, then perched on the corner of the desk to look Tom in the eye. 'I'm not ignoring protocol. When I visited Sharon she began to respond, but I guess I haven't Connie's finesse and the girl became so distressed that her nurse sent me away. I told Connie not to conduct an interview, just to coax Sharon to talk. About anything. It might produce the evidence we want, it might not, but once Sharon finds relief in being listened to with understanding, it'll all come out.'

Tom saw the sense in that and began to drink his coffee, lost in thought. Although Nora was the mainstay of his daughters' lives, when any one of them had what they considered to be a serious problem it was to him they turned. Unless it was a 'woman's' problem. They, of course, were in a stable family group. The Miller girl was not. Where she might feel her father was there to deal with her usual difficulties, this was one instance when she was actually afraid to approach him.

'I spent yesterday collating evidence in the Carr case and these are what I believe to be the facts,' Max said, breaking into Tom's introspection. 'Carr has a psychologically-flawed personality. He has a history of stealing in order to buy acceptance and friendship. He joined the West Wilts to escape police prosecution, having stolen his cousin's identity. When he failed to find the comradeship he expected, he reverted to his habit of trying to buy friends, to the extent of being persuaded to steal from the Armoury to gain inclusion in White and Corkhill's activities. I'd rate him as big a pest as a stalker. Lance Corporal Mason told me he felt Carr was trying to climb into the skin of his dead friend. Creepy, or what?

'Then Carr meets Sharon Miller. At a disco on the base, perhaps. The unhappy, unlovely Sharon is also desperate for affection and acceptance by her peers; desperate for what's essential when you're sixteen – a boyfriend. The unbelievable happens. J.S somehow makes life exciting for Zoe Rogers, the girl next door, and for Zoe's little gang. Sharon is suddenly accepted by them; becomes the bright star in their firmament. She has sex with Carr to show her gratitude.'

Taking a couple of biscuits from the tin beside the kettle, Max bit into one as his brow furrowed. 'Then she falls from a bridge and everything changes. She's hurt and frightened. Her new friends accuse her of spoiling everything and, worst of all, her trophy lover disappears, leaving no message for her or any indication of where he's gone. She feels betrayed, senses that Carr had just used her for his own ends, and yet she clings to the dream she had been living for a short while.'

Max drained his mug and began on the second biscuit. 'Now let's get back to Carr. Prior to the exercise the situation is this. He has something going with a group of schoolkids; he's having sex with Sharon. Yet day-to-day life with 3 Platoon is as lonely and restrictive as ever. Unlike other jobs he's had, he can't walk away and find something he'd like better. Then Sharon falls from the bridge and he's deprived of the one pleasure he hasn't had to buy. In some way this adversely affects the scheme he had with Zoe Rogers and Co. In addition, Corkhill and White constantly taunt him with the threat of reporting his theft of a rifle and ammo, a crime that would earn him a really long stretch.

'He participates in the exercise, which is more arduous and demanding than previous ones because of the debilitating heatwave. He's told he'll be operating in similar temperatures in Afghanistan. 3 Platoon gang up and exceed each other with horror stories of what the Taliban will do to little creeps like him. That's when Carr decides it's time to move on. He can't go home, where he's wanted by police in several counties, but he has the whole of Europe to get lost in.

'I think it's safe to assume he planned to return to base and slip away fully prepared, but on that last morning Miller yells a threat to sort him out at the end of the day. Carr reads into it his fear of Miller discovering what he'd been up to with Sharon becoming reality. He knows Miller hates his guts, so he's terrified of being beaten up while everyone turns a blind eye. As he has run from everything unpleasant in his life, so he runs from Miller.'

While Tom considered all those points, further conversation was made impossible by a pair of Lynx helicopters flying overhead to the Army Air Corps hangars on the far side of the base. When the roar faded, it was possible to hear the tramp of boots and loud chaffing between soldiers passing on their way to the NAAFI for their mid-morning break. Military routine continuing as usual.

Putting his empty mug beside the kettle, Tom said, 'We'll never know what went through Carr's mind on the day he scarpered, but I'll go along with the probability that he'd grown shit-scared of deployment to Afghanistan, fearing he'd get no back-up from the rest of the platoon. He's friendless and his girl is in a bad way in hospital. Things aren't going right for him, and his usual reaction is to run away and begin again.

'I agree, have maintained all along, that it was something that occurred that morning that made it imperative for him to leave immediately. Everything points to sudden urgency. Whether it was Miller's threat is pure conjecture, in my opinion. Sergeants threaten squaddies as part of their daily routine. You know as well as I do that it's no more than blasphemous tongue-lashing designed to send the lads to the latrines in a hurry.'

Seeing Max's expression, he gave a faint smile. 'OK, when I suggested a sexual relationship between Carr and his daughter, Miller vowed to kill the bastard, but he hadn't heard rumours of it before that last morning. He bawled Carr out for always hanging back on leaving the Warrior, that's all.'

'Carr wasn't to know that.'

'But we have no *proof* that he'd been shagging Sharon, only Zoe Rogers's comments to Piercey. Knowing her histrionic tendency I wouldn't convict a man on anything she said. And another thing, we have no *proof* that Carr stole a rifle and ammo to buy Corkhill and White's friendship, so we can't accept that Carr was burdened by their taunts on that subject.'

'Private Ryan told me they had some hold over Carr,' Max pointed out. 'And they both admitted to coercing him into getting those items, which he later produced.'

Tom nodded. 'Fair enough. I guess those two wouldn't expose themselves to the possibility of criminal charges unless there was a basis of truth there. Carr's death has let them off the hook. He can't defend the charge, and we haven't got the items to prove they came from the Armoury. No case!'

'Any more input?' asked Max.

'We have no *proof* that the J.S. who made life exciting for Zoe was John Smith, as he was known. Could be anyone with those same initials. We're basing our premise on the fact that Carr's locker was full of DVDs etcetera, and Jake Morgan's club is selling such items.'

'That's why I said Sharon Miller holds the key to this entire case.' He grinned. 'Know why I enjoy working with you? You question my wild theories.'

Tom shook his head. 'Not so wild. I just wish we had the means of proving what is simply experienced professional guesswork. Cases like this leave me unsatisfied. I suspect we'll never discover whether Carr's death was murder or an accident.'

'One thing I'd bet a year's salary on is that it wasn't suicide. That guy runs but hasn't the nerve to jump.' Max reached for the telephone on his desk as it rang. 'Captain Rydal.' He listened for a while without making notes, then said, 'I'll come right away.'

'Problem?'

'The answers to some,' Max responded eagerly, sliding from his desk and grabbing his car keys. 'Call Connie and tell her to wait for me in the hospital car park. Sharon's had a text telling her about Carr's death. She's hysterical and demanding to speak to me, no one else.'

The girl in the hospital bed looked plainer than ever with red-rimmed eyes and tear-stained cheeks. The nurse remained in the small side room, despite Connie's presence and Sharon's rude instruction to piss off.

'Is it true?' she cried in anguished tones. '*Is* Johnny dead?'

'I'm afraid the person you knew as John Smith drowned in the river,' Connie said at Max's nod. 'Captain Rydal found the body himself, and it's been identified. We're sorry you learned about it by text, but you denied knowing a man with the initials J.S when Captain Rydal came last time, so we had no reason to give you the sad news.'

A fresh bout of sobbing halted conversation, and Max inched the nurse through the doorway to ask quietly, 'Have you called her father? He should be here.'

'She will not have him, Colonel. She is screaming when we say such. It is that she has the fear of him. The Herr Doktor says he will have talking with him before he can come in.'

Max frowned. 'I'll see that someone at the base speaks to Sergeant Miller today. He has every right to see his daughter.'

'And we have right to keep patients from harm,' she said firmly. 'Please to go back and have speech with this angry child. It cannot continue, this tears.'

'If you'd be good enough to leave us alone with Sharon?' he suggested. 'Sergeant Bush is very good with young people. They respond to her. You see, the crying has now stopped.'

The nurse was not happy, but she gave a brisk nod and folded her arms purposefully. 'I will be here outside for your meeting.'

'Thank you.' Max turned back into the room to see Connie sitting on the edge of the bed, holding the girl's hand. He turned the chair around and sat facing Sharon over the back of it. 'You asked to speak to me. About Johnny?'

'It's all my fault,' she cried, threatening to lose control again.

'That's not true, Sharon,' said Connie soothingly. 'He had a lot of problems that were nothing to do with you.'

'Why should you think his death was your fault?' Max asked.

Twisting the sheet in her hands, she spoke at the knotted material. 'I lied about the baby. I was jealous of them all. They were taking him away from me. I wanted him to myself, so I told him I was pregnant.'

'When was that?' Max saw light starting to dawn over the mystery of Carr's precipitate desertion.

'The night I fell from the bridge. We was out with Zoe,

Jake and the other two. The boys had a barney. Jake threatened to run it himself. Said he'd make a better job of it.
Said he was sick of being one of Fagin's runarounds, whatever that meant.'

Max knew very well what it meant, and his interest grew
rapidly.

'Zoe was being bitchy, as usual. Said I'd drop my knickers
for anyone just to score, so I walked away.' She glanced
up at that point. 'I thought Johnny wasn't going to come
after me, 'cos he and Jake were really going at it. I hung
around outside for a bit until the bouncer sent them all out
with a warning. I hurried off and Johnny caught up with
me, going on about how I'd got a lot of shitty friends. I
was mad and went for him.' Her gaze returned to the sheet.
'He said things, and that's when I had the idea about the
baby.'

'You thought it would make him concentrate more on
you?' prompted Connie.

Sharon nodded.

'But he was bound to find out eventually that it wasn't
true.'

'I didn't think,' she mumbled in a wobbly voice that
suggested she would cry again soon.

'What did Johnny say when you told him?' asked Max,
seeing more clearly what Carr would have read into Miller's
threat to sort him out. Small wonder he abandoned any
careful plan he had had and just ran.

It was an effort for Sharon to answer that question, but
she eventually said with quiet desperation, 'He was shocked.
Said I must get rid of it. Said my dad would kill him. It
hurt me, that. I was reely, reely upset.' She wiped her eyes
and nose with the sheet.

'Go on,' said Connie gently.

'We'd all been drinking. You know how it is, and I was
*reely* upset. We was crossing the bridge, so I got up on
the wall and told him I'd jump to get rid of it, if that was
what he wanted.' She gave a twisted, watery smile.
'Frightened the shit out of him, it did. He told me not to
be crazy. He tried to grab me, but I started to walk along

the wall to pay him back a bit for what he'd said. Then I lost my balance.'

She suddenly looked stricken. Lost and frightened. 'When I came to they told me what had happened. I tried to call Johnny and text him, but his mobile was turned off. I couldn't tell him it wasn't true about the baby; that I'd made it up because I wanted him to myself. I couldn't tell him that and that's why he . . . why he went away. It's because of me he's now dead.' She ended on a wail.

As Connie repeated her soft assurances, Max thought that, indirectly, Sharon was probably right.

# FOURTEEN

Monday afternoon, and the Incident Room was buzzing with the energy that came with the winding up of a case. The heatwave was set to return to a lesser degree, and there was a chance of some free time to fill a few heady late summer days with pleasant pastimes, for once. Tom was relieved that he would no longer have the expense of preventing his girls from visiting Jake's club. In fact, he could possibly go on the three-day break to the Dutch resort and join in the fun with his family. The prospect mellowed him enough to view a smug-looking Piercey without irritation. They were all entitled to look smug over the resolution of this curious case.

Max was buoyant. Once he had done the paperwork he would take long leave and sort out the future with his fiancée – if that was what Livya was. He was not entirely sure. He would soon persuade her, chest strapping or not.

He opened the briefing by revealing what he and Connie Bush had learned from Sharon Miller. 'She encountered Carr in a music store, appropriately enough, when she accidentally sent a stack of CDs cascading from a shelf. He helped her to pick them up, and one thing led to another. They went for a pizza and a coke. That's when she discovered a CD she thought must have dropped unnoticed in her bag. Carr then told her he had slipped it there himself. She had thought it a bit of a giggle and told him she wished it had been more than one.

'It clearly gave Carr the germ of an idea a week later, when Sharon deliberately gatecrashed an elite group at the base disco to show off her new boyfriend. These were Jake Morgan, Scott Pinner, Tim Jackson and Zoe Rogers. Jake came over big about his career in the theatre; how he couldn't wait to get started. He was out of his skull with boredom, living with military tunnel vision and immature schoolkids. He couldn't take up his place at the Youth Theatre until September, and his parents insisted on his remaining with them until that time. The school summer holiday was about to begin and there was nothing on the base to occupy someone with his talent. He was going places; he had the nous to make it big once he could get started. Why should he faff around for four stifling weeks with all his energy and ingenuity going to waste? His sycophantic pals and girlfriend agreed. They were all bored and longed for some excitement.

'That was when Carr put a proposition to them. He would take orders from squaddies for CDs, DVDs, iPods. He would then track down the stores stocking the things and give them the info. They would then go to town, spread out, and do a bit of shoplifting. Carr would give them sixty per cent of what he sold the goods for. Were they up for it?

'Sharon told us they jumped at the idea, led by Jake. She didn't want to be part of it, but Jake and Co. had no intention of including her. They were a tight little group, yet they treated her with new respect because she was John Smith's girl.' Max grinned. 'Gangster's moll, you'd phrase it, Piercey.'

Phil Piercey grinned back. 'Right on the button, Boss.'

'Well, as you've probably all deduced from your interviews this morning, the club was set up five weeks ago. The four kids went into town, split up and operated in different stores so successfully that they got hooked on it. It brought in spending money, but it was the thrill of stealing beneath the noses of German shop assistants that mostly appealed. The risk of being caught brought the frisson of excitement they had desired. As a result, when school ended they thieved every day and soon had more items than Carr had orders for.'

'Hence the stack of new stuff in his locker,' put in Tom. 'I suspect he created something that gave him not only a sense of belonging, but a respect bordering on admiration he had never before managed to inspire. Or buy. Jake got it right when he called Carr Fagin. Unfortunately, *his* gang of urchins began to run out of control.'

Max took over again at this point. 'According to Sharon,

Jake began to hustle Carr for their share of the money. When he confessed he hadn't yet sold the stuff, Jake demanded it back. He said *he* would run the operation from then on. Carr tried to act the big boss, but Jake called him a useless little creep and got nasty. They had a set-to that only stopped when the bouncer sent them from the bar. That's when Carr went after Sharon, who had left when insults began flying. It's not surprising he couldn't take it when she told him she was pregnant.'

'Ya, the oldest trick in the book,' Piercey said scathingly.

'Speaking from personal experience?' asked Heather.

'It *was* a lie,' said Connie, 'and Carr's reaction was also the oldest one in the book. His panicky instruction to get rid of it prompted her drunken walk along the bridge wall, with its drastic outcome. Carr was obviously the man seen running away by the German who went in the river to rescue Sharon.'

'Add together the facts that Carr *believed* he'd made her pregnant, and that he had made no attempt to save her from drowning, and we have a pretty good idea of how Carr interpreted Miller's threat to sort him out at the end of that last day on exercise. Add the collapse of his Faginesque scheme and the prospect of going to a war zone, and escape would have seemed imperative,' Max concluded.

'So there never was an outside supplier,' said Olly Simpson. 'No wonder we couldn't find even a sniff of one.'

'No outside supplier means no outside contact to aid Carr's desertion,' reasoned Staff Melly. 'Which then leads to little likelihood of such a person clubbing him and chucking him in the river. So we're not looking at murder?'

'*We're* not,' Tom affirmed. 'The *Polizei* will be given the task of ascertaining whether it could have been an opportunistic mugging by a passer-by who grew too violent. We can only record it as death by drowning in unknown circumstances. Klaus Krenkel will inform us if they ever find evidence of foul play.'

Max nodded agreement. 'I understand Carr's mother has been told just the bare facts. The poor woman will probably invent a heroic story to account for her son's desertion, as she did with his father.' He glanced around at his team. 'We have to decide what to do about Jake and Co. Input, please.'

Derek Beeny, who had that morning interviewed Jake Morgan, put forward the results of that meeting. 'The kid's clever and talented. He's also got a big mouth that betrays him when he puts on the "I'm an officer's son" act. He claimed he only knew J.S. as Sharon's guy; said he rated him a total waste of space. When I inspected the contents of the summerhouse, he bluffed an answer to my questioning the amount of unwanted presents. Muttered a superior comment about having contacts in the entertainment industry because he would soon be part of it.' He gave Max a frank look. 'I can't see how we could prove any of his stuff was stolen, sir, even with Sharon Miller's statement about the shoplifting. One thing I did get him to admit was that he made the call suggesting someone had killed Carr. He said it was just a bit of fun because J.S. was such a piece of shit. We could have him on that.'

Heather had an opinion on that. 'The Garrison Commander wouldn't wear it. That kid's off to the UK in a couple of weeks, which'll put him out of our remit. He shot himself in the foot, however, with that call, because it brought *us* in on Carr's disappearance, which has led to the discovery of his illegal business in Dad's garden shed. We can close the club down tonight and confiscate any goods still in shrink wrap. That'll ruin his credo with his mates and all the kids who've been using the place.'

'His father will be told the full details,' said Tom with some satisfaction. 'Maybe that'll stop him believing the sun shines from Jake's arse, although he'll probably admire the kid's enterprise. He struck me as that kind of parent.'

Beeny had one more point. 'Jake couldn't have killed Carr. At the time of the storm he, with Tim Jackson and Scott Pinner, was camping in the hills with a school party.'

Piercey nodded. 'When I questioned those two they mentioned the camping, which they'd regarded as a Boy Scouts' jamboree rather than as an SAS proving test. Ha!

I'd like to see them have a go with guys from the Regiment.
They'd eat 'em for breakfast.'

'What did they say about the stuff being sold at the club?'
asked Max.

'Played innocent, but agreed that Jake and Zoe handled
the financial side. No hint of where all the cash went. We'll
confiscate the ledger or record of takings, and quiz them
on that.'

'We had little more success with Zoe,' said Simpson,
glancing at Heather who had accompanied him. 'She
resorted to tears when things got too hot for her, and she
wasn't putting on an act.'

'I think it was the discovery of Carr's body in the river
she couldn't take,' added Heather. 'I'd guess the charming
Jake had regaled her with stories of aquatic creatures eating
eyes, tongue and other delicacies, and gases making the
body swell until it burst open. She repeated some of what
Sharon said, but claimed J.S. had made life exciting by
suggesting the idea of the club.'

'When we asked about the bagful of CDs she had when
Phil met her in the restaurant she threw a wobbly, and her
mother began laying down the law about police brutality.
We had to leave,' Simpson said heavily. 'People watch too
many TV detective dramas these days.'

There was a mixed reaction to Tom's announcement that
he would be going with them on the three-day holiday, but
it would now be delayed for a couple of days. Happy that
their father would take part in the water sports – he always
made it more fun, allowed them to do things their mother
forbade – the girls nevertheless protested over the delay.

'*Why* can't we go tomorrow?' demanded Gina.

'Because I won't be free until Wednesday.'

'Can't you work harder and leave earlier?' asked Beth
across the supper table.

'Well, I could stay in my office through tonight and
tomorrow morning, but then I'd sleep solidly when we got
to the lake. No fun with you three.'

His youngest daughter's face puckered into a familiar

disapproving expression. 'Why d'you *always* have an answer like that?'

Tom laughed. 'Because I have a daughter who *always* asks questions like that.'

'Oh, *Dad*!'

'If you're coming does it mean I can bring Hans?' asked Maggie.

'No,' Nora ruled firmly. 'For once we're going just as a family. I've had my share of carting all your friends around with us.'

She gave Tom one of those looks married couples use to signal messages only the partner can translate, and he accepted that the time had come to break the news to their children. He gave a slight nod and laid down his spoon.

'Blackies, there's been a development regarding Jake Morgan's club. I'm afraid its existence breaks military regulations on trading on the base, so we've had to close it down.'

There was a chorus of protest; three voices drowning each other out with their individual complaints. Tom let it continue for thirty seconds, then silenced them. 'The law is the law. Didn't you all agree with that a few years ago when I explained that my job is to see that everyone on this base behaves correctly, the way you do at school and here at home? You understand that without laws or rules there would be chaos? I said then that without traffic lights and road signs, cars and lorries would crash into each other all the time. Without laws *people* would be crashing into each other. Right?'

They all nodded reluctantly. 'Jake and his friends have been taking money from members illegally. Those new DVDs and CDs you bought were *not* unwanted presents, so the money wasn't passed to anyone else. Jake, Tim, Scott and Zoe kept it themselves, which meant they were officially trading. Anyone trading on the base has to have a licence to do so. There are also regulations about premises where trading takes place, and a back garden summerhouse doesn't meet them.'

'Does that matter?' asked Maggie petulantly.

He studied her. A pretty girl with long, dark hair and a fast-developing woman's body, which occasionally dismayed him with its implications of vanishing childhood. 'You saw that tree across our driveway two weeks ago. Suppose you and your friends were in Jake's summerhouse when a tree fell on it. It's so frail it would collapse and crush you all. Would you think regulations didn't matter then?'

She was adolescent enough to want the last word. 'We wouldn't be there in a storm like that one was. The club was *fun*. Why does the law always stop fun?'

'It stops people from doing some horrible things which are definitely *not* fun.' He cast a quick 'help me' glance at Nora, but she had rules of her own and gave him another of married couples' silent messages which translated as 'nothing doing'.

'Jake is going home in two weeks to take up a theatre job, so the club would have closed soon, anyway,' he reasoned. Then he offered some good news. 'Any money you spent there will be refunded.'

Another mixed reaction, and triple cries of, 'Must we give the stuff back?'

'Yes. Anything that was shrink wrapped.'

The telephone rang. Nora rolled her eyes expressively at him as she went over to take the call. Saved by the bell? She held out the receiver. 'Max!'

'Sorry to interrupt your evening, Tom. Captain Morgan has Sergeant Rogers and Corporals Pinner and Jackson with him. They want to talk about our closure of the club run by their kids, and the confiscation of stock and ledgers. I want to finish this report on Carr's death tonight. Will you handle this?'

'Only too glad to. On my way,' he replied, giving Nora a knowing grin.

Kenneth Morgan led Tom to a rear office where Malcolm Rogers, Cliff Pinner and Simon Jackson were standing in an uneasy group. Morgan was not the breezy character Tom had interviewed earlier, but he still exuded authority.

'I was expecting Captain Rydal to deal with this personally,' he said as Tom nodded to the three NCOs.

'He's dealing personally with a soldier's *death*, sir,' he replied with subtle emphasis.

'Well now, gentlemen, let's sit down. This is an unofficial meeting. No need to stand on ceremony.'

Tom put him right immediately. 'Captain Morgan, if you intend to discuss our closure of the club run by your children in your summerhouse, I must caution you that I'm here in my official capacity. Anything said in this room could be used as evidence by SIB.'

Morgan looked annoyed. 'That's why I expected Captain Rydal to handle this. On a man to man basis.'

'Let me first make you aware of what we already know about the activities of Jake, Scott, Tim and Zoe. Then you must judge how this meeting will continue,' Tom said, sticking to the rules. 'We have a witness who says a soldier known as John Smith set up a scheme whereby he took orders for CDs and DVDs, which your children would then roam around town acquiring. For this, they would receive sixty per cent of the sale price. After this had been up and running for several weeks, supply outstripped sales. At that point, Jake Morgan took over the business and ran it from a garden building on this property, selling to children on the base those items he, Zoe, Tim and Scott continued to acquire from stores in town. These items, still in shrink wrap, were sold as unwanted presents brought in by members. The youngsters who bought them were not aware that they were participating in illegal transactions.'

He glanced at the fathers in turn. 'That is why we've shut down the club and are inspecting the books.'

There was a lengthy silence while he waited for some response. The NCOs all looked towards their commissioned host, who eventually sorted his thoughts and became their spokesman.

'The instigator of this business, as you rightly quoted, was Private John Smith, who talked vulnerable youngsters into doing something they didn't fully understand. I've been told Smith subsequently deserted, which gives indisputable evidence of the kind of character he was.'

As nothing more was forthcoming, Tom gave his opinion on that. 'Sir, Jake's intelligence and ability has earned him a coveted place with the Youth Theatre.' He turned to Malcolm Rogers. 'And I'm told Zoe is expecting to enrol at RADA when you return to the UK shortly. I don't think a jury would consider them vulnerable youngsters who don't fully understand right from wrong.'

Morgan did a swift about-turn. 'Mr Black, our kids are about to embark on their careers. They're bright and talented enough to go far, make a valuable contribution to society. Taking an official attitude towards this slight transgression would cloud their overture to adult life.' He grew persuasive. 'They're going through the transition from sixth form to university. They're lively, healthy, they're full of the normal teen restlessness. Don't they all run wild at that age? Many have a gap year and travel overseas, getting up to all kinds of crazy antics. They're not *criminals*, they're just letting off steam. Our grandfathers knocked policemen's helmets off, and drank bubbly in the fountain in Trafalgar Square. Our fathers raced their MGs along Brighton's Strand or put chamber pots on church spires.' He gave a chuckle, albeit a rather forced one. 'Our kids saw this as a lark, nothing more.'

Tom knew all about youthful escapades. He had indulged in some himself. Nevertheless, he said, 'Shoplifting is *stealing*, sir. Selling stolen goods is an additional crime, especially when they're sold to genuinely vulnerable youngsters who're unaware of the felony they're compounding.'

Sergeant Rogers, who was looking very worried, put forward his case. 'I had no hint of what my girl was doing, I swear. And that goes for the rest of us. We'd have put a stop to it pronto. I've given Zoe a lecture she'll not forget in a hurry, and I'll personally recompense any child whose money she has taken. Captain Morgan's right about our kids starting off their careers with a record. They're not criminals, just high-spirited youngsters.'

Corporal Pinner nodded. 'Scott's got his mind set on the

RAF next year. I've had a real go at him, pointing out that he's likely spoilt his chances of that, and he's prepared to do anything to put things right.'

'And our Tim,' said Corporal Jackson. 'Short of walloping him, I've left him suffering and scared. He's a good lad, sir, but easily persuaded. If you take this business the whole way it'll do him and the others a real blow. Like Sar'nt Rogers, I'll make up any money kids have lost at the club.' He glanced at the other three fathers. 'We were none of us aware of what our kids were up to or we'd have come down hard on them right away. What they did was stupid and they bloody know it now, if they didn't before. But, as Captain Morgan said, it was that Private Smith who put them up to it.'

'Unfortunately, the dead are unable to mount a defence, so we have to regard that claim as open to question,' Tom told them, knowing these men were deeply concerned for their own careers. Having a son or daughter with a criminal record was not exactly a bar to promotion, but it could suggest that failure to control a child was hardly a recommendation for the ability to command men.

He got to his feet and the others hastily did the same. 'I'll report all you've said to Captain Rydal. When he's had time to consider what action to take, he'll contact you.' Knowing that there was little SIB could do to present a case against the four youngsters, he softened the atmosphere slightly. 'I'm sure the facts that your children have confessed, and that all monies taken at the club will be repaid, will influence his decision. Thank you for making all this known to us. Goodnight, gentlemen.'

Out in his car Tom wondered whether to drive now to Section Headquarters, but decided it could wait until the morning. Max was busy on his report of Carr's death, which was mostly a mixture of guesswork and unsubstantiated accounts by a series of people who heartily disliked the man. Except Sharon Miller, who had had a love-hate relationship with him.

Turning on the ignition, Tom was about to pull out from the kerb when a brightly-coloured old banger came around the corner and swung into the drive with a roar. Jake Morgan gave Tom an American-style salute as he passed.

His father's been fighting his corner for the past twenty minutes, thought Tom, but there's one cocksure young bastard who'll never regret *anything* he does.

After contacting Lewes police to check on the progress in the Dan Farley case, and inform them that he expected to be in the UK for two weeks starting on Friday, Max called Livya's landline, then her mobile. Both on voicemail, so he resorted to e-mail. After changing the wording three times, he decided to end by putting a reference to his opportunity to do the business properly, on one knee with a bottle of champagne chilling in readiness. He sent it, then settled to his unwelcome report.

When he eventually reached his room he began thinking about the decisions he and Livya must make during his leave; decisions that would set their future together on the best course. Compromises would have to be made, but he was certain they could find a workable solution. He checked his laptop. Nothing from Livya, and both her phones were still on voicemail. Somewhat wryly he reflected that, unlike his marriage to Susan, complaints about long working hours would not be just one way.

When his phone rang as he was drying himself he heard not Livya's low, slightly accented voice, but Clare's clear, crisp tones.

'Saw your light on so I knew you'd finally got in.'

'Oh, hi,' he muttered, thoughts on an entirely different woman as he waited to hear her reason for calling.

'I had a message from that prissy estate agent this afternoon. That German woman has pulled out of her agreement to rent the adjoining apartment, and the bloody landlord is holding out for a dual let. Won't let me move in until the other place is also about to be occupied. Some guff about letting my friends use the other premises illegally. I think he imagines I'll hold orgies and drunks'll camp out overnight there.'

'Doors can be locked from the inside,' Max pointed out, wondering why she was telling him all this.

'Have you ever known a locked door get the better of an inebriated soldier?'

'I guess he might have a point if you were a guy.'

'*I'm* a soldier, chum.'

'So you can't move in at the weekend after all?'

'No.' A short pause. 'You once said you were unhappy living in the Mess. I don't suppose you'd be prepared to become my neighbour?'

He laughed. 'Then he'd have *two* soldiers living it up in his posh apartments.'

'I'm serious, Max.' When he made no immediate reply, she said persuasively, 'You were impressed with the place when you viewed it with me.'

Recalling what he had confessed to her while walking alongside the river afterwards, he gave her his news. 'I've just got engaged to Livya and I'm taking fourteen days' leave to settle everything. I don't want to wait too long before we marry.'

'Oh! Well, congrats.' She sounded taken aback, then added something Max found curious. 'I hope "honey" deserves you.'

# FIFTEEN

Tom was at Section Headquarters early the next morning, putting a small pile of DVDs and CDs with those taken from the Morgan summerhouse. The girls had been surly over surrendering them, but Tom could not allow his own family to be part of an illegal scheme.

He was called by Connie from the rear area where confiscated items were stored, because Captain Will Fanshawe wanted to speak to him. The Cricketing Captain, as Max called him, was waiting in Tom's office and greeted him heartily.

'Morning, Mr Black. Great result regarding Lieutenant Farley. Heard he's being set free from the hospital today, arriving back for duty tomorrow.' He sobered somewhat. 'As for Smith, as we knew him, I fear we were all a bit careless about failing to recognize the problem and reassigning him.'

Tom shook his head. 'From all we've learned about him, I doubt reassignment would have changed anything. He was one of life's perpetual misfits.'

Fanshawe put on the desk a tin box similar to those frequently used for petty cash. 'Let me tell you about this. I was asked to speak to Eric Miller about his daughter, who was refusing to see him.' He wrinkled his brow. 'He's a good man, an excellent sergeant, but he's in a no-win situation with his second wife and her two rather loathsome sons. In consequence, he's short-tempered and intolerant. This unfortunately extends to his own daughter, who rebels. Because she apparently had a juvenile liaison with Smith, it makes her afraid of her father's reaction. Together with the Padre I discussed this with him, and the outcome is that Miller has arranged for the girl to go to his parents, who reared her until she was five.

'She'll stay with them until we return from Afghanistan

in the spring. Sharon's doctor gave her this news, and Miller went to the hospital last evening to reassure his daughter.

'The welfare of the girl is not my concern, but the efficiency of one of my sergeants is, so I'm relieved this grotty affair is over.' He put his hand on the tin. 'Miller brought this to me this morning, having found it in Sharon's room where she said she had hidden it. Smith gave it to her early in their relationship; asked her to keep it safe for him because his mates had found where he kept it, and pestered him to show them what was in it. The contents were very private and personal, he told her, and he was afraid they'd break it open. Sharon claims she never had a key for it. As the guy's dead, the responsibility for it passes to you. Mission accomplished.'

As soon as Fanshawe left, Tom opened the small drawer in his desk and took out an envelope containing the key he had found beneath the DVDs in Carr's locker. Not the key to a bank safety deposit box, nor the key to a sports locker, as they had thought. It opened this cheap tin cash box. Inside lay Jack Carr's birth certificate and National Insurance card. There was also a passport in his name, which appeared never to have been used.

Under these items was a yellowing snapshot of a good-looking young man in a blazer and white shirt, with a jauntily knotted cravat. Tom turned it over. On the back, in a schoolboy hand, Carr had written: My dad the famus esplorer.

Dan Farley put his few possessions in the blue holdall and checked the time on the small travelling clock his mother had brought in on her first visit. She was due to pick him up in ten minutes. He had said he would hire a car to drive to Tidworth, where he would stay overnight with his parents before flying back to Germany, but she had insisted on fetching him.

The clock followed two paperbacks into the holdall. Lewes police had recovered his gold watch and his mobile, but they had had to retain them as evidence. Dan did not mind too much. They were safe enough in police custody.

He would have left his watch with his parents when he went to Afghanistan, anyway.

He knew his platoon would be minus one man when he got back tomorrow. His friends had phoned to tell him Smith had been found in the river. Dan still felt a mild pang of responsibility. Not a good start to lose one of your men two months into your first command. He would have to be more diligent in future. And he would never again accept a lift from a biker.

On the point of closing the zip on his bag, the telephone beside the bed rang. His mother was running late? Not unusual.

He stiffened as Trish's voice greeted him with breathless emotion. '*Darling*, I've just heard a *terrible* story from one of my clients, who heard it from Jem Hawkins in the taxi coming here. Tell me it isn't true. Those bikers didn't *really* leave you to *die*.'

Dan silently cursed. As far as he knew, the MoD had put a press embargo on the case. If that man was relating the facts to every passenger he carried, it would soon hit the headlines.

'How did you know where I was?' he asked harshly.

'Jem Hawkins told my client you were fighting for your life there. Oh *darling*, I can't stop crying. It's *my* fault. If I hadn't been so cruel to you, you wouldn't have had to get a lift to Heathrow. Can you ever forgive me? I don't know what—'

Dan held the phone away from his ear while he picked the clock from his holdall to check the time. His mother would be waiting.

'—and they made up the most gorgeous bouquet of red roses. I've also bought you the biggest box of chocolate-covered nougat Thorntons had. I don't suppose you're able to eat things like that yet, but you'll know how much I care when you see the box. And the flowers. I'm about to leave, so I'll be with you in forty minutes. Hang on in there, my darling. It must have been terrible, sweet-heart, but at least you have the perfect excuse not to go to Afghanistan.'

She was still talking when he took up the holdall and headed for the main entrance.

Max overslept, but his only concern was that he might miss breakfast. He had worked late last night so he deserved a couple of hours to compensate. As he dressed he reflected that he ought to get Clare to change the strapping around his ribs before going on leave. That reminded him that he should reserve a seat on Thursday evening's flight, so he lingered long enough to make the booking online. Still no e-mail from Livya. He would call her mobile after a satisfying breakfast.

As he walked through the lobby he took three letters from his pigeon hole, noting that two were non-official and from the UK, which was unusual. Egg, bacon, sausage, mushrooms and the inevitable spoonful of baked beans, surely enough to rate another rung up Clare's ladder of approval. She would presently be dealing with the early morning sick parade, so could not witness his man-sized meal.

Smiling at the thought, he slit open the envelope directed in an unfamiliar hand. As he read the single page a curious burning sensation began to creep through his senses.

> My dear Max,
> A surprise, perhaps, but I hope not an unwelcome one.
> You were such a young boy when your mother died, and I have no intention of acting as such. It would be absurd when so few years separate our ages. My wish is to be a close friend who has your welfare and happiness at heart; someone you feel you can turn to in trouble.
> It was so fortunate that we became acquainted at Andrew's small party. I think you resented my many questions on that occasion, but you will now understand my interest. I look forward to seeing you again next month. Until then, I send my affection.
> Helene Dupres

Stunned, Max stared at the address at the top of the faintly scented letter, slowly accepting that it was not a joke from one of his colleagues. Pushing aside his plate he opened the other letter posted in the UK and took out a gilt-embossed invitation to attend, on October 2nd, his father's marriage to Helene Lisette Dupres, and later an evening reception at the Saint Germain Cultural Institute.

Ignoring the brief accompanying note from his father, Max sat in frozen stillness gazing at the card. His name on it, and his address on the envelope, had been written by Livya. She would have dealt with all the invitations; would have collaborated with Helene Dupres to provide a list of guests Andrew deemed it necessary to invite. This had not happened overnight. How many days ago had Livya suggested early October would be a good time for him to take leave? How many days ago had she been reluctant to see him or discuss their future? Four days. She had known then that this was being planned.

For long moments emotion battled with visual evidence, then he got to his feet and returned to his room to snatch up his mobile and punch in the number of the head-quarters of the Joint Intelligence Committee. Giving the information clerk his name and rank, he snapped out Livya's extension number. She had given it to him to be used only in serious emergency. This was one.

'Good morning, sir,' she said in her official manner, although the girl would have told her who was calling before putting him through.

'If you had told me why early October would be a good time to take leave I wouldn't have sent that e-mail yesterday. How long have you known about this? At the drinks party? Is that why you were so angry about my assertiveness? She hadn't had long enough to size me up.' There was silence on the line, so he continued. 'I can excuse him springing a surprise of this magnitude on me – it's typical – but not you.' He took a steadying breath. 'Why didn't you warn me this was on the cards?'

'It wasn't my place to give that information before the Brigadier deemed it to be the right time.'

'I can't believe you just said that. Yes, he's my father, but you're my . . . how *could* you have kept quiet? We spent a bloody night together after that drinks party.' He took another deep breath. 'Did you regard me as just another name on the guest list?'

Into another silence, he said, 'Please answer that, Livya.'

'I'm sorry, sir, I have a visitor with me and we have a meeting with the Brigadier in ten minutes. I'll call you when the meeting ends and we can discuss this situation more fully. I really am sorry, sir.'

He disconnected slowly. Livya had been professionally formal because she had a high-powered visitor in her office. Correct, of course. The JIC Headquarters was not the place for impassioned telephone calls between lovers. All the same, there was only one interpretation to put on 'It wasn't my place to give that information'. Even as Andrew's prospective daughter-in-law, did her loyalties lie with her professional boss, rather than with the man she professed to love? Apparently so, because she had lain in bed with him after that drinks party, allowed him to make love to her, yet kept this knowledge to herself.

Max walked to the window and gazed from it for a long time, observing the moving fabric of his life here in Germany; a life he found professionally fulfilling and worthwhile. Eventually, he turned back to his landline telephone and punched in an extension number.

'Captain Goodey. Good morning.'

'Call that prissy estate agent and tell him to inform the landlord he has a tenant for the second apartment.'